A
Little Girl Named
Sad

pk potts

A Little Girl Named Sad is a work of fiction based on actual events. All names, places, characters, incidents and dialogues are products of the author's imagination or are used fictitiously. Any resemblance to actual events or persons, living or dead is entirely coincidental.

For additional copies or to order other books by this author, visit:
www.pkpottsStories.com

Army the Armadillo
If The Tree Could Talk
Featured poet in "*A Poet's Word*" by Steady Moon Press

Cover illustration and graphic design by
Lauriel Webb-Sawin and **Jack Wilson**

ISBN 978-0-578-48767-0
Library of Congress Control Number: 2019903704

Introduction

When I first began writing *"A Little Girl Named Sad,"* I did not know where it would take me or what it would accomplish. I just knew that I had this overwhelming need to get a message out to the parents, relatives or anyone with knowledge of children being abused. I hoped by writing this book I might send forth a warning that the damage inflicted on children is everlasting.

It doesn't go away.

Instead it becomes ingrained, just like the fine grooves in a freshly cut, beautiful piece of wood.

Children come to us so pure and innocent, full of joy and beauty, that it amazes me that God even allows them to leave heaven.

But He does.

And so their journey begins.

Will they be broken beyond repair? Will they shine like the morning star? Will they rise like a Phoenix from the ashes of despair?

What will they choose to keep when looking back on how they were raised? Will they keep those memories like treasured charms on a bracelet or bury their past in a safe with no key and throw it out into the deepest sea?

I've come to realize that the choice remains within us. We are never alone with our past, present or future. We have a choice to shoulder our burdens and carry them alone, or share them with a trusted friend, counselor or God.

We are never alone. Unless we choose to be.

The choice is ours.

Every decision we make might be a mistake or the start of a fabulous new adventure.

pk potts

To

ricky,

cookie,

nonnie,

becky

"for I am yours and you are mine"
Oceans, Hillsong United

Sorrow is not a raven
perched persistently
above a chamber door.
Sorrow is a thing with teeth,
and while in time it retreats,
it comes back at the
whisper of its name.

Dean Koontz
"The Good Guy"

PROLOGUE

Two Moons

As I've gotten older, I find I am able to be nourished more
by sorrow
and to distinguish it from depression.
~ Robert Bly ~

The man walked slowly out into the night, the babe snug in his arms. Out in the dark, the cicada call and the warm summer night cast their nightly spell. The stars were all a' twinkle, tiny little blinking lights on a black velvet backdrop. The moon was full, peering down with her benevolent smile.

Left behind in the smoke-filled kitchen was the clackity-clack of dominoes, shuffled for another round of 42, and the soft murmur of voices. In his mind he could see them sitting around the table, his wife, daughter and son-in-law. He had left abruptly, and as he passed the babe sitting on the living room carpet, she held her pudgy, little arms up to him.

Her solemn, big chocolate eyes lassoed his heart and her words sealed a deal, "Papa, out?"

They stole out into the secret night, their own private rendezvous.

The hazy nights under barroom lights were still too vivid in his memory. The dominoes and stale cigarette smoke brought back an itch for the drink. Haunting him, like a stalking ghost; clutching him by the throat sometimes, at odd moments; when alone in his tool shed or sleeping peacefully next to his wife. He often woke in a cold sweat from the want of it: that first swallow of whiskey. He could almost smell it, taste it, even feel it, as it rolled off his tongue and to the back of his throat, burning warm inside his gut. But, it had almost destroyed the best of him. The best of all he had in life.

Out here in the dark he felt different, inhaling the sweet innocent scent of the baby in his arms. His very own blood. His precious first granddaughter. An overwhelming feeling of tenderness pushed inside him, choking back the itch, making him feel strong, clean, and alive again. Yes, this is the best of the best. *Hold on to this.*

"Papa, moon!" said the babe and pointed her tiny finger up to the great face of the pearly moon.

"Yes darlin', that's the moon."

He held her close and walked around to the other side of the house, his fingers callused from working his land. A piece of land that he could barely believe was his after all the years of drinking, barhopping and beating up on his wife. He shook his head in wonder that she had never left him. He had so much to be thankful for. He would make them all proud one day. He would show them what kind of man he could be. Tenderly carrying the babe, they went around to the back yard. She looked up. A wondrous smile lit her tiny face.

"Papa, two moons!" She lifted her arms as if to embrace the moon. He was puzzled, then realized that she thought there was a moon in the front yard and another in the back. He smiled. Her happiness was his happiness.

He turned and held her high, as if to offer her up, her arms still lifted in the glowing moonlight. He held her high until his arms grew tired and made his vow to the moon.

When he turned her back around to face him, her little face solemn again, she seemed to search his eyes.

"Papa. Want. Moon."

He looked at her, not knowing if she was asking him if he wanted the moon or asking for it herself. He knew if he had it in his power, he would give her that and more, so strong was his love for her. He knew her life would be a struggle, for the itch of the drink was in both of the ones with the responsibility of raising her.

He returned to the smoke-filled kitchen. No smile upon his face when he placed her back on the floor. Her face was a mirror, reflecting his own. The glow now gone, as if the moon had never cast its spell.

PART ONE

What comes of tightly held fiction,
fragile like a sparrow,
Is a crushing.

And what comes of crushing a sparrow is
The death of a body,
But also
The liberation of a spirit.

Now, we are all sad yet ready to fly.

~ David Flesher ~

The Early Years

Texas　　　Illinois　　　California

1. The Tree of Things

2. A Pig is a pig is a pig is a pig…

3. Nippin' Things

4. Doggie in the Window

5. not gud wif frak-shuns

Psssst, psssssst

hey, come over here
bend yer ear way down close
I wanta tell you sumpin
I know dis litl' gurl named Sad
she's litl' like me.
I'm dis many
count my fingers
one, to, free…
So dis
litl' gurl name Sad
she wans ta tel ya sum storees.
some of dem r scary
so we might hafta go n da closet
but it's okay in dar
I know cuz me and my bruders
hide in dar
wen mommy and the daddy are mad.

The Tree of Things

Sorrow is a fruit;
God does not allow it to grow
on a branch that is too weak to bear it.
~ Hugo ~

There once was a little girl named Sad. She was born into a topsy-turvy, twisty-turny, upsy-downsy kind of a world.

She did not know her name was Sad. She thought her name was Sunshine. When she sat cradled by Mother Earth, she giggled and played and grew. When surrounded by people who loved her, she didn't have a clue.

One day Grandmother came to visit. She looked at Sad sitting in the room with scattered, empty cans. She looked at the chipped bowls filled with smelly cigarette butts. She looked at Sad's long golden, tangled mass of hair. That was the day she knew Sad's name. She took the little girl by the hand and led her outside to sit in the sun.

"What is your name?" she asked.

"Tree," replied Sad.

"Tree?"

"Yes Grandmother, my name is Tree!" And Sad jumped up and stretched her arms to the sky and waved them merrily. "Look, Grandmother, birds sitting in my hair!"

Grandmother laughed. "I cannot see the birds, but I can see the nest they left. Come with me and I will show you a tree."

So, the grandmother took her by the hand and they went to Grandmother's house.

Outside was a very large tree. Sad looked up into the leafy branches. She heard the birds singing in the top. She saw the sun shining down through the tree to tickle her nose and toes.

"Grandmother, I want to sit in Tree like the birds."

"Okay, let me get Grandfather. He can lift you up to sit in Tree."

Grandfather came and lifted Sad to sit in Tree. Sad felt the bark rough and scratchy against her skin. She scrunched her bottom until she felt safe and secure in Tree's branches.

Grandfather stepped back from the tree and smiled at Sad sitting in Tree like a bird.

"Would you like to get down?"

"No, Grandfather."

Grandfather walked away from the tree and into the house.

Sad was very happy sitting in Tree. Watching a tiny ant climbing up a branch, she asked, "How did you get all the way up here, Mr. Ant?"

The ant kept climbing and did not answer.

Sad looked down and felt afraid. It was a very long way to the ground. Then she saw Grandmother and Grandfather watching her from the kitchen window.

She very carefully stood and looked up into Tree's top branches. A Little bird with red on its chest sat there watching her. "Hello, little bird. Sing me a song please."

But Bird only winked an eye, and then flew away.

Sad wrapped her arms around Tree. She felt the scratchy bark on her cheek. "Tree, you remind me of Grandfather and his beard when he kisses me. I will always love you, Tree."

Grandfather came out of the house. "Are you ready to come down?"

"I think so."

Inside the house with Grandmother, Sad was quiet. Grandmother was making bubbly cinnamon toast and oatmeal for Sad.

Sad drank in the sweet smell of cinnamon and poked at the bubbly brown bread where butter and sugar and cream made a beautiful picture on her plate. She took a bite of the oatmeal, warm and gooey.

Grandmother sat at the table watching Sad eat. "When you are finished, we will wash your hair."

"Okay," replied Sad.

Sad loved the feel of Grandmother's fingers as she scrubbed her head under the warm flowing water. It made her feel sleepy. Later she sat between Grandmother's knees as she combed and brushed the tangles from Sad's hair. Sad felt love flowing out from Grandmother's long, slender fingers. They felt like fingers of sunshine stroking soft slices through Tree's nest.

"Now," asked Grandmother, "What is your name?"

"Not Tree," said Sad.

"Yes, you are right. I have taken away your nest."

"Sitting in Tree, I saw a bird with red right here." Sad put her hand on her chest.

"Then you saw a Robin."

"Robin can be my sister," replied Sad. "I think my name is Bird."

"Can you fly?" asked Grandmother.

"No."

"Then Bird is not your name."

"Okay," said Sad, jumping up and spinning in a circle.

"My name is not Bird, but Tree is my grandfather and Robin can be my sister."

Grandmother looked at Sad spinning in a circle, round and round. She smiled at the little girl. "You say it, then it is so."

Sad wished to keep spinning. For when she stopped, she knew Grandmother would take her back.

A Pig is a pig is a pig is a pig…

Sad soul, I take comfort,
nor forget that sunset never failed us yet.
~ Celia Leighton Thaxter ~

"Thunk! Crash! Splinkle!"

Those were the sounds that woke up Sad. Then the loud, angry voices. She opened her eyes and saw from her window that it was still dark outside. She raised her head and looked at her little brother sleeping quietly beside her.

Throwing back her blanket and stepping onto the cold, wooden floor, she shivered in her little T-shirt and bare feet. Looking again at the small bundle underneath the covers, she made a wish that he wouldn't wake-up or hear the angry voices.

Sad tiptoed to the door and very quietly cracked it open. She blinked in the bright light. Now she could see what made the crash noise. Her little piggy bank lay broken in pieces against the TV room's wall. She flinched when she heard the angry voice of the mommy.

"You idiot! Why did you do that? You almost hit me!"

"I should have hit you!" shouted the daddy. "Someone needs to!"

Sad started trembling. What was happening? Why were they shouting? She didn't care about Piggy. They shouldn't hit because of Piggy.

"So that's where you got the money!" said the daddy.

"I needed the money for cigarettes."

"And gin?"

"So what?" screamed the mommy. "You leave me here all day with these kids. What else do I have to do but drink?"

And then the daddy said a bad word that Sad wasn't allowed to say. She watched to see if the mommy would wash his mouth with soap.

Sad's legs shook so hard she thought she might fall down. She tried switching from foot to foot to stop the shaking, but it didn't help, so she crawled back into bed, under the blankets beside little brother. She put her fingers in her ears when the angry voices started again. She wished Moon would hurry and leave Sky so Sun would shine again.

Suddenly a bright light shone in the corner and filled the room. Sad sat up.

"Are you Sun?" she asked.

"No, I'm just a little girl like you," said the voice.

Sad liked the glowing light and got out of bed to walk towards it.

"Where did you come from?" she asked.

"I don't know. I was born on September 11, 2001. Sometimes I am called the *Face of Hope*."

"I don't know what that means," said Sad. "I'm going to call you Candle. Will you come with me to sleep in my bed?"

"Why?"

"Because I am afraid." Sad shivered, "can you hear the noise?"

"No."

"It's mommy and the daddy."

"I can't hear them, but I will sleep with you until Sun shines again."

"Thank you, Candle," said Sad, climbing back into bed and quickly drifting off to sleep.

Be not forgetful to entertain
strangers: for thereby
some have entertained
angels unawares.
Hebrews 13:2 KJV

Nippin' Things (Outside)

The human heart does not stay away too long
from that which hurt it most.
There is a return journey to anguish that few of us are
released from making.
~ Lillian Smith ~

Sad was hungry. It seemed like she was always hungry. It nipped at her belly button from inside. Sometimes she could hear her belly button grumble. It reminded her of the sound the angels made when they were bowling upstairs. This happened right before the clouds cried. Sad thought maybe they were crying because those old bowling balls were too heavy. Maybe the angel's tears leaked through the clouds whenever they lost the game.

Sad's belly button was grumbling again. Reaching down, she patted her tummy. "Since you make so much noise I think I will give you your own name." Sad put a finger against her lips while she thought. Sometimes, she saw Shirley Temple do that, and she looked sooooo cute in those telly shows.

"I'm going to name you *Grummy*!" she said, and pulled up her shirt and patted her belly button. Sad jumped down off her little bed and ran to look out the window. She squealed with excitement seeing the white blanket lying across everything. She ran to put on her little red snowsuit. Then she ran outside, closing the door very carefully. She didn't want to wake mommy.

The snow.

Wet and white.

Bringing tingles to her fingers and toes.

Nippin' at her nose like an excited puppy.

Sad walked through the white blanket, along the fence line, hearing the crunch her tiny shoes made as they bit the white blanket. She turned around to see her bite marks in the snow.

She looked up. The house was big, looming up suddenly. She was surprised to see it there.

"Where ya goin'?"

Sad noticed a girl, bigger than her, standing on the porch watching.

Sad didn't answer. She wanted to, but the whiff of baking cookies drifting out the door behind the girl, floated in a big fluffy cloud above Sad's head. The cloud had fists and punched *Grummy*. Sad wondered how a heavenly smell could have such a mean punch.

The girl took a slow bite of the cookie in her hand and showed scrunchy eyebrows at Sad. "Whatsa matter, can't you talk?"

Sad nodded her head, but her eyes were watching the cookie. Water filled her mouth. The smell was fighting with *Grummy*, making it do strange flips and flops. She shuffled her feet.

"Uhmm…can I have a bite?" asked Sad.

The little girl looked at Sad. She crossed her blue eyes and wrinkled her nose. When she tossed her head back, a pretty pink ribbon in her golden locks dangled droopily on top of her head. Sad thought the ribbon would like to be on a different girl.

"No, you little beggar!" The girl said and bit the cookie like she was mad. Then turning, she flounced back into the warm, golden house, taking the delicious smell of the cookie cloud with her.

The cloud, once above Sad's head, shifted and sunk. Now it seemed to be a dark, ugly thing, the color of soot. Settling like ash over Sad's little red snowsuit, making her heart feel dirty. Then floating, it sank, silent like a rock at Sad's feet. She kicked it.

Lit' l beggar.

She kicked it again.

Lit' l' beggar.

Lit' l Beggar, was the name of the rock she kicked all the way home.

Nippin' Things (Inside)

The room was warm. The sun slid down the wall, dancing next to the chest of drawers.

Sad was sitting on her bed, watching it dance against her brother playing with his blocks next to the wall. He sat half in, half out of the sun. Wondering if one side of him was warmer than the other, she jumped off the bed and went to put her hand on the cold side, testing.

It was a big mistake. Reminding him what they were trying to forget.

He looked at the door. Sad turned her back to him but knew what he would do.

He stood up and grabbed his weenie.

"I gotta pee-pee."

"No, you don't," she said, her voice hard, the way he didn't like.

He began dancing around, his fist still clenching his little weenie.

Sad sighed, "You know the door is locked."

"But I gotta pee-pee!"

Sad walked to the window and looked out. She spotted a red bird. "Come mere, look! A pretty red bird. He has an orange beak. Come look!"

Letting go of his pants, he came to stand next to her at the window. "Liff me up?"

"Okay but look fast. I can't hold you too long."

"Where? Where dis it?"

"See that tree next to the sidewalk? Right there."

"I seed it! Red's my favrit color."

Sad watched the bird, wishing the tree was closer. Maybe then she could climb out the window and go down to try to open the front door. When he began to wiggle around, she realized her arms were dead. She let him down onto the floor.

"I'm hungry," he said looking up into her eyes. Silky black fringe circled his dark brown eyes. They reminded Sad of two chocolate cookies.

"Me, too!" Sad went to the door again. Pounded on it with her little fists. "Mom! Mom wake up! We're hungry!"

She waited. Big, heavy silence pushed against the door. She imagined a big, cold blob of snow piling up against it, blocking them.

Looking again into his sweet, little face, she saw two fat teardrops fall from his big, chocolate eyes and drop onto his shaking chin.

Sad sighed. She walked over to the window and pushed it up. Placing the *Little Red Riding Hood* book underneath to hold the window up. Feeling the cool air kiss her face, she leaned out, looking for someone, anyone.

"Hello!" she shouted. "Hey, anyone there? HELLO!"

Sad kept calling until the lady who lived next door came out, looking up at Sad.

"Are you hollering out that window?"

"Yes ma'am."

"What's the matter?"

"My little brother is hungry."

"Where's your ma?"

"Sleepin'! The door's locked."

The lady in the yellow dress scratched her head. Watched Sad. Sad watched back.

"Do you have any jump ropes?"

"Yes ma'am."

"Do you like egg-salad sandwiches?"

"I think so."

"Okay, tie your jump ropes together and I'll be back."

The sandwiches were delicious and gone quickly. Sad went to look out the window again.

The lady came out of the house.

"Did you like the sandwiches?"

"Yes ma'am!"

"Are you still hungry?"

Sad nodded her head.

Sad and her brother sat in the middle of the floor. They were eating the last of the jellybeans, jump ropes spread around them like snakes at a picnic, when the bedroom door opened.

Doggie in the Window

It is such a secret place, the land of tears.
~ Antoine de Saint-Exupery ~

"Doggie in the window! Doggie in the window!"
"Again?" asked Sad's mother.

"Yes please, it's my favrite!" begged Sad.
"Okay, skooch over and let me in the bed beside you."

Sad scooted over and patted the space right next to her. Her mother settled in, and Sad lay back on the bed and closed her eyes. She didn't want to miss a word as her mother began singing with her movie-star voice. Sad was remembering how her Nanny said they always called Sad's mommy their little movie star, because she might someday grow up to be one. Just like Lucy on the *I Love Lucy* Show!

"How much is that doggie in the window?
The one with the waggily tail
How much is that doggie in the window?
I do hope that doggie is for sale

I must take a trip to California,
And leave my poor sweetheart alone
If he has a dog, he won't be lonesome
And the doggie will have a good home

How much is that doggie in the window?
The one with the waggily tail
How much is that doggie in the window?

I do hope that doggie's for sale

I read in the papers, there are robbers
With flashlights that shine in the dark
My love needs a doggie to protect him
And scare them away with one bark

I don't want a bunny or a kitty
I don't want a parrot that talks
I don't want a bowl of little fishies
You can't take a goldfish for walks
How much is that doggie in the window?
The one with the waggily tail
How much is that doggie in the window?
I do hope that doggie is for sale

(written by Bob Merrill, sang by Patti Page)

Her mother finished the song, and Sad lay there quietly. The room held its breath, hushed by such magical singing.

"Why is it your favorite song? Is it because we are in California?" asked her mother.

The spell had been broken, so Sad sat up and shook her head no. Quickly, she wiped away the tears escaping her eyes. She shook her head and sighed, "no."

"So why are you crying?"

"It always makes me cry."

"I don't understand. You always ask me to sing it. Why is it your favorite if it makes you cry?"

"I dunno," replied Sad. "I guess I think the next time you sing, it will be different. That someone will have bought the doggie."

Sad's mother laughed and her laughter tickled Sad, making her feel like sunshine had climbed inside her *Grummy*. She reached out and stroked her mother's soft hand. The color of her skin looked like coffee with a dollop of cream.

"Mama, why are you different than me?" Sad held her small hand next to her mothers', looking at the differences. "I want to be the same color as you," sighed Sad.

"Then stay outside and play in the sun more."

"Paw-Paw said if I drink coffee I'll turn black. Can I have coffee for breakfast?"

"No, you're too young."

"How old do I have to be?" asked Sad.

"I don't know, ask me when you're ten. Now go to sleep. First day of kindergarten tomorrow!"

Sad started wiggling around like an excited puppy. She couldn't wait to wear her new shoes to school and carry her brand new lunch box.

The room closed its eyes and Sad wondered if Moon would peek into her window.

She waited until she heard her bedroom door close, then jumped up to look for the man who lived in Moon. She suddenly had a great idea!

"Someday," she whispered, "someday little doggie, I'm going to come and buy you, then give you as a present to the man in Moon."

☽☽☽

Sad loved school! Her teacher, Mrs. Manners had a soft, crankily face when she smiled. She smiled a lot! Sad especially loved snack time because they got a little square box of milk!

The first day Mama had walked with Sad next to the gated fence to the little school. Now Sad came alone. She was a big girl, after all. Sad liked walking by herself. It was lots of fun except for the last part. The part right before the school. Her face became a thundercloud thinking about that last part. Alone sometimes, it made her cry. Even now, she heard the hateful voices singing in her head:

"Kindergarten baby,
born in the Navy,
walkin' down the street,
with a bald-headed baby."

Now the first graders were lined up next to the fence when they saw her coming. She couldn't understand why they sang that hateful song. After all, she didn't have a bald-headed baby! Hurrying past them, she ran all the way home and stomped into the house. Slamming her backpack on the floor, she entered the kitchen. The dirty look she had thrown the first graders was still on her face.

"Do you want your face to freeze like that?" asked her mom. "You look like a thundercloud."

"I wish I was," stormed Sad, "then I could thunder and lightning on those hateful first graders." She told her mother about the ugly song.

"Just ignore them. Say, sticks and stones will break my bones, but names will never hurt me."

Sad made her mother repeat the saying over again and again until she had it in her head. Like a lucky rabbit's foot, it was sure to work.

"I'll try it," said Sad, but she could still feel scrunchy eyebrows above her nose.

The next morning Sad practiced the saying all the way down the fence. Her steps got slower nearing the playground. She knew they could see her coming, and they ran to press their faces against the bars. Words sang out like sharp stones, raining on her head.

Standing before them, she waited for them to finish. She held the saying on her tongue, then threw it like a magic rock. "Sticks and stones will break my bones, but names will never hurt me." She flung it through the fence like a rock tossed into a lake.

A few first graders looked surprised and stopped singing. Then they blinked once and began singing the ugly song again, only louder.

Sad threw them her dirty look, walking away, wondering why their words still hurt.

Once in class, Sad smiled the rest of the day. Mrs. Manners gave her a hug! It wrapped around her like a warm blanket. Then at snack time, Sad decided to share her cookie with her favorite friend, Andy. She liked him best because his skin was darker than her mother's; his, the color of coffee without cream. Andy had soft, curly hair, and he liked to laugh a lot! Sad was sure his mom gave him coffee for breakfast, but maybe with a teaspoon of sugar, because when he laughed his teeth flashed so white, like little rows of sugar cubes.

At recess, Sad said, "C'mon Andy, let's play over here in the sun."

After their little naptime and coloring, it was time for Sad to start the walk home.

Waiting in the playground, she waved good-bye to Andy when his grandmother came to pick him up, then gave Mrs. Manners an extra hug. She played hopscotch one more time.

Walking to the edge of the playground, she looked towards the first-graders' fence. And then she had a grand idea! Turning around, she began to walk in the opposite direction. *This is pretty exciting! I'll just find another way to go home!*

She wondered if one of those little light bulbs was glowing above her head because of this new idea! *I've never been lost before. I wonder what that would feel like. Besides, if I get lost, won't Lassie come find me?*

She liked looking at the houses on this new street. Stopping beside a little tree, she reached out to pat it. She bent to smell a yellow flower in another yard. She saw a black and white purry cat and skipping towards it, she hoped it wouldn't run away. But the purry cat took off when it saw her coming.

Sad stopped.

She looked all around.

Turning in a circle, she looked carefully in each direction.

She couldn't remember which way she had come.

She didn't know which way to go!

Nothing looked the way she remembered!

Sad wasn't having fun anymore. She took off her backpack and placed it on the curb. She sat down and wondered if this was how the doggie in the window felt when he looked out the glass waiting for someone to come.

Watching an ant crawl along the crack in the sidewalk, she felt one fat tear drop out of her face and almost land on top of the ant! Soon her face was raining on the ant. She felt sorry for him and tried to stop the storm.

"Hello there!" said a voice.

A shadow grew big over Sad. She looked up.

A strange lady stood there. Sad was glad Sun wasn't hot on her anymore because Sun was behind the stranger.

Sad wasn't allowed to talk to strangers.

"Are you crying little girl, or just hot?" asked the lady. "Are you lost?"

Sad wondered what to do. Suddenly remembering her backpack, she nudged it towards the stranger. The lady picked it up and looked at it.

"I see! Your address is on your backpack! Come on then, I think I know where you live."

She reached up and took the stranger's hand.

Sad was disappointed. She wanted Lassie.

not gud wif frak-shuns

The apple sat on the center of the table.

Sad stood on tippy-toes to place it carefully in the very center of the table. She stepped back to look at it from all directions. Walking around it slowly, a small frown puckered her lips into a pout. A beam from the setting sun threw out a finger of light to caress the apple's skin. The apple glowed like a light had been turned on inside, reminding Sad of a shiny, round Christmas bulb tugging at the limb of a tree.

She wished it was Christmas now and that she could climb into Santa's lap and plead for one wish. She knew what that wish would be! Mama would come home with three more apples. Or even just one more apple would do. Yes, that's it! She would wish for one more apple and Mama! Closing the wish inside of her hand, she vowed to remember it tonight for the wishing star.

For now, there was work to do. She pushed the chairs away from the kitchen table. The chairs were heavy, and she hoped her two little brothers wouldn't be strong enough to push them back. The littlest one was a climber, always climbing where he didn't belong. She remembered the dresser with the mirror crashing down on top of him when he had climbed up to look at himself. She was so scared hearing that crash and his screams. She still shook inside when she thought of it, but his garden angel had protected him. At least that's what mama had said when they pushed the heavy dresser upright, and he crawled out without a scratch. Sad didn't know why he had a garden angel, cuz he weren't Farmer John or Old MacDonald, but grown-ups seem to know these things.

No, Sad didn't need any such clamities with mama away. Being in charge meant everything had to be okay, MUST BE OKAY, until mama came back. She looked around quick-like, hoping to catch sight of a garden angel that might be hiding, but instead four little legs rounded the corner into the kitchen. Four little eyes surveyed the room, one set blue, one set brown.

"Whatcha doin?" asked the brown-eyed boy.

"Stuff! Big girl stuff!" replied Sad.

"I wan mommy," said blue-eyes, running to the chair and trying to push it back up against the table.

"No! Stop it right now! Leave that chair alone," Sad said in her meanest voice, giving him the evil eye.

Blue-eyes immediately stopped. Looking over at the brown-eyed boy, he popped his thumb into his mouth.

Sad wanted to correct him but decided to let him suck his thumb this one time.

"I'm hongree," said the brown-eyed boy. He could barely see over the table, but Sad watched his eyes staring at the apple.

"Mew fru," muttered blue-eyes, around his thumb.

Sad knew she had to get their minds off the apple, so she crawled under the table and sat there cross-legged. Immediately their eyes lit up wondering what she would do next. They came towards her and she pulled blue-eyes into her lap. Too late, she realized he was wet again. He struggled against her, embarrassed that she had found out. He slammed his little fist against the underside of the table. Right in the center where Sad knew the apple must sit. Pushing him away, her own shorts smelly and wet with his pee, she sat for another moment, staring at them. They looked steadily back, no smiles on their faces now.

Sad closed her own brown eyes, then placed her hands over them and started counting, "one…two…three…" peeking through her fingers, she saw when the light returned to their eyes and happy to see smiles picking at the corner of their mouth.

"Four….five….six….you better run and hide, I'm coming to git you!"

Their delighted squeals of terror made her heart leap inside her, watching as they scrambled through the house looking for the best hiding place. She ran from the kitchen, running up the stairs, looking in imaginary places she knew they wouldn't be, hoping to make the game last as long as possible.

Could she make it last until bedtime?

Would they forget about the apple for one more day while she figgered it out?

She glanced back into the kitchen. The light was gone from the apple. Thankful the night was almost here, but, also a little bit scared.

Dark outside now. She walked around the room, picking up clothes off the floor and sniffing them. Surely she could find something clean to put on her and the blue-eyed boy. He was dry now, but she couldn't stand the smell of herself or him.

"Ah-ha!" She spotted some underpants he could wear for the night. Shuffling around some more, she finally found a clean pair of shorts for herself. They stood there watching and smiled when she held the clothes aloft.

"C'mon then, let's change clothes and get ready for bed."

"I'm hongree," grumbled brown-eyes.

"I wan mommy," said blue-eyes as she wrestled his underpants on.

"You ate a jelly samwitch this morning," she replied. She began tickling the little one to distract him. As if brown-eyes knew her intentions, he piped up behind her, "where's mommy?"

"Look, I tole you and tole you, she went to mail a letter! You know that! You was here when she said it."

He looked down at his feet and Sad was sorry for her harsh tone.

"C'mon, let's go to bed and I'll sing you a song."

"Otay," he said, climbing into the bed.

"I'll even tell you a story!" she added.

Finally, he looked at her and smiled. "Sing the doggie song, otay?"

"Okay."

Sad sat watching them sleep. They were so cute. She petted their faces and sang softly the last lines of the, *Yes, Jesus Loves Me,* song. She had already sung *Cookie Lend Me Your Comb, Jesus Loves All the Children,* and told them the story of *Goldilocks and the Three Bears.*

Quietly, she walked over and looked out the window. It was so dark out there. She couldn't even see the moon. She couldn't find her wishing star and that scared her even more. What would she do without her wishing star?

She ran downstairs to make sure she had locked all the doors. Mama had told her to lock the doors, don't let anyone in.

She went into the kitchen and looked in the pantry again hoping something was there that maybe she hadn't seen before. She opened the frigerator but the apple had been the last thing after the jelly samwitch.

She just had to figger it out. She went to the kitchen drawer and opened it up, looking at the spoons, forks and knives. She wasn't supposed to touch the sharp knives, so she got the butter knife out. Walking over to the table, she stood on tiptoe and grabbed the apple. She tried again to figger it out. She placed the knife this way and that across the top, but it was no use. Slowly she pushed it back to the center of the table and left the room.

Sad went upstairs to look once more for the wishing star. Outside the streetlights reflected back the quiet streets, the long row of apartment buildings across from her. She heard loud laughter down the street and suddenly a small group of boys came racing past her window. Behind them she heard shouts and saw people chasing. They carried bats and were waving their hands and cursing, saying words she wasn't allowed to say. She shrank back away from the window, terrified the crowd would come crashing in the door downstairs that she had locked so carefully. She shuddered behind the curtain, alarmed at a new set of fears crawling inside her window. She slunk below the windowsill, leaning her head against the wall. She would be alert and wait, wait for the wishing star to return.   Or maybe mama.

"Ow!" Sad woke to a sharp kick on her leg and looked up to see her little blue-eyed brother standing over her. She had fallen asleep on the floor! She suddenly realized sunshine was spilling across her shoulder and shining in the sandy locks of her little brother's hair. Sitting up, she swallowed the guilt. Opening her hand, she let the wish go for one more day.

"Ouch," she said rubbing her leg, "whaddu kick me for?"

"Sollee," he said and bent to kiss it better.

"I tole him not to," said brown-eyes sitting in the bed his dark wavy locks scattering crazy across his head.

They both looked at her and said, "We're HONGREE!"

"So, what's new!" sighed Sad, "Before we think about food we need to brush our teeth and brush our hair."

"No!" screamed blue-eyes and took off running out the door for the stairs, the smell of pee drifting back to burn Sad's nose and eyes.

She knew where he was headed and jumped up to thunder down the stairs after him. Hearing brown-eyes following close behind.

In the kitchen he stood under the table, his little head not even touching the surface. He angrily hopped and punched the table with his fists, trying to make the apple roll off.

"STOP IT! Stop it right this instant!"

"I wan afel!" he demanded.

"For such a little guy, you're pure D ol' mean!" said Sad.

Turning to look at brown-eyes, she saw a tear drop beneath his silky, black eyelashes.

Both set of eyes glued on her. No smiles again.

"Okay," she sighed, "we'll have the apple today. After brushes, after the kid shows on TV, okay?"

"Otay!"

Sad helped them brush their teeth and listened to their grumbles as she tugged a comb through their hair. She sang, *Cookie Lend Me Your Comb*, to distract them from the tangles, but her song was not as happy as it had been.

She had let them down.

She had fallen asleep waiting for the star.

And now she would have to break a rule. She didn't want mama to be mad.

She just couldn't figger it out.

"C'mon to the TV room. Sit on the couch, I'm going to find you a kid show."

She turned the knob on the set looking for one of those kid shows. Delighted when she heard, *'Hi! Ho! Silver, away!'* "Look guys, it's the Lone Ranger! You like that, don't you?"

From where they sat, eyes focused on the screen, they nodded their heads.

"Listen to me for just a minute." Slowly they turned to look at her. "You have to sit on this couch. You can't move. Pretend there are ally gators below you and you can't leave, okay? You watch the Lone Ranger and look out for ally gators. I'll be right back with the apple."

Both sets of eyes lit up at the word apple, and little blue-eyes peered over the edge of the couch looking for gators.

Sad walked backwards to the entrance to the kitchen. They were still watching her. "Ally-gators and rattlesnakes! Don't move until I get back and I'll chase them away, okay?"

Their eyes were big as saucers. They nodded.

Walking to the kitchen table, she stood on tiptoes and got the apple. She went to the silverware drawer and opened it up and studied the knives. She picked up the butter knife and went to the table. Criss-crossing the knife this way and that, but still she couldn't figger it out.

There was no other way around it. She would have to break a rule. She went back to the drawer and put the butter knife away, then selected the biggest, sharpest knife she could find. Knowing it was the kind the grown-ups like. Back at the door of the TV room, she checked on her brothers. They didn't turn her way, their eyes glued on Tonto and the Lone Ranger.

Taking a deep breath, she walked to the doorway that led outside and stood staring at the door holding the knife and apple. She heard again the voice of her mother before she left, "Watch your brothers. Lock the door and stay in the house. I'm going to mail a letter."

She took a deep breath, put the apple under her arm and unlocked the door. She slowly turned the knob and peered outside.

The bright sunshine hurt her eyes and she blinked, waited a moment, then walked out the door. She turned to the right and went to the first door. She held the apple under her chin to knock, then waited.

Sad was happy when the brown lady came to answer the door. She was soft and round and once had hugged Sad. She remembered feeling like the hug had swallowed her whole. She liked the lady with her smooth skin the color of apple butter. She also liked the way she smelled. It was like bacon cooking in pinto beans! Her stomach growled just thinking about it.

The brown lady stood staring at Sad. Her children crowded around her. Sad thought maybe they had just got out of bed because they still had their jammies on and their hair was sticking up all over their heads.

Sad carefully cleared her throat, "Ma'am, I was wondering if you could help me?"

"Chile, whatcha doing with that butcher knife?"

"Well Ma'am, I just need some help. I can't figger it out. Can you help me cut this apple in three pieces?" Sad lowered her head, ashamed to admit she couldn't do this one thing. "I just don't know how to cut it in three pieces."

The brown lady turned to her children, "Yawl go on back in the house. Go make your beds." She closed the door and stepped outside with Sad. "Honey, where is your ma?"

"She went to mail a letter."

"Well, let's go to your house and I'll cut this here apple for you."

Sad stood there for a moment, not sure what to do. This wasn't part of her plan. Would she be breaking another rule? It was too late to change her mind now; she already told her brothers they could have the apple. Sad looked up at the brown lady's face. She smiled and Sad thought she had the most beautiful smile. Her teeth were whiter than snow. This lady must brush her teeth four times a day! Sad handed the apple and knife to the lady and turning allowed the lady to follow her back inside the house.

The lady looked into the TV room and saw Sad's little brothers still sitting on the couch.

"Well, looka how sweet those angels are, just sitting so still and quiet on that couch!"

"Gators!" said the brown-eyed boy.

"Nakes," nodded the blue-eyed boy.

"Huh?" said the lady.

"Please ma'am, the apple?" reminded Sad.

"Sure, let's cut this apple for you." The lady turned to place the apple on the table, then went to the pantry and opened it up. Next, she went to the fridgerator and opened it up.

"There's just the one apple ma'am," said Sad.

"Uhm, I was looking for a plate to put the pieces on," replied the lady.

Sad pushed a chair to the cupboard, then climbed up and pulled a saucer out of the cabinet.

"Three pieces," she reminded the lady.

"Okay honey, let me show you. You have to cut the apple in half like this, then cut the halves into three pieces. Then you can have two pieces each."

"Ohhhhh, that's how to do it!" said Sad. "That's even better, right?"

She placed her hand on Sad's head and looked down at her. The smile was gone now. "Chile, how long your ma been gone?"

Sad looked back at the woman and shrugged her shoulders.

"Honey, you can tell me. I saw your ma walking down the street bout three days ago. Ain't she been back since then?"

Sad just stood there shuffling her feet. "Ma'am, I need to give my brothers the apple now."

"Okay honey, you do that. And I'm going to go next door and make you some sandwiches for later. You'd like that right?"

Sad knew they weren't supposed to ask for food, but this lady was telling her she would bring them food. That wasn't the same, but still Sad hesitated. There was something bothering her at the back of her head, but at least if she said yes, the lady would leave. Sad nodded.

When she left, Sad went to lock the door behind her. Running back in and grabbing the saucer of apples, she danced into the TV room.

"Ta-da! Ta-da!" Pretending to wave a magic wand over the floor, she chanted "All ally-gators and rattlesnakes must now leave! Shoo-fly! Be gone!" Placing the saucer on the couch, she climbed up beside her brothers and looked at the six pieces of apples cut evenly on the saucer. Her face broke into a big smile.

"Look! You each get two pieces of apple! Isn't that Grrrr..ate?!!!"

They sat on the couch, the three of them happily munching away on the apple. They finished watching the Lone Ranger and were watching Superman when someone knocked on the door.

Sad had forgotten all about the brown lady, but suddenly remembered the samwitches she had promised. She jumped up and ran to the door. Before she opened it up, she yelled out, "Is it you, Ma'am?"

"Yes honey, can you open the door?"

Sad opened the door and felt the smile slide right off her face. The brown lady was there but standing next to her was a policeman with a shiny badge on his hat and uniform. Sad didn't see any samwitches.

"Hello little girl. May we come in?"

"I'm not supposed to let in strangers," said Sad, her eyes turning to stare hard at the lady.

"Honey, it's okay. He's a really nice man. He just wants to meet your little brothers and talk to you a minute."

Sad stood back from the door. Walking inside, she quickly climbed up to sit between her brothers. She put one arm around each of them.

More rules were sure to be broken.

When my mother and my father forsake me,
Then the Lord will take care of me.
Psalm 27:10   NKJV

Pssssst...

Hey, it's me agin.
Bend yer ear down here
jest one more time.
I hafta tell you a secret.
Y' know that little gurl
name Sad?

Well it's realy me!
Ha ha ha, fooled ya!

The thing about it
is that sumtimes I think
she's my secret friend,
ya know?
like the invisible man on tv

so sometimes
she hasta tell the story
about us,
but most of the time
she lets me.

Part Two

His sadness began to accumulate like sand.
~ Tina De Rosa ~

The Elementary Years

Texas, New Mexico, Texas, Oregon,
New Mexico

1. Shiny Shoes

2. Superman vs. GOD

3. The Summy Day

4. The Smell of Safety

5. Tarzan Doesn't Carry Bullets

6. One Square per Girl

7. Trees that Wave and Teachers that Don't

8. The Dog Scout Days of Summer

9. Red Snow

10. A Day **NOT** to be Forgotten

11. Goals Set in Stone

12. Do-it-yourself Childhood

13. The Choosing

Shiny Shoes

I am the little girl named Sad.
Today I am six years old. I am all grown up.
The big people always say that to me.
They say I have sponsibilities
and have to set a sample for the kids.
I don't like setting a sample cuz
I have my Papa's moods.
The big people said that too.

Sometimes I get mad and don't talk to
anyone.
I want to be sweet and kind like Nanny.
She never says anything mean.

I don't know why it's mean when I say the
truth?
I don't want mom to be my mom.
I told her I wanted Nanny to be my mom.

Now I can't have the shiny shoes
Nanny bought for me.

Mom had monster eyes when
she whispered angry sounds to Nanny.
Nanny looked very sad,
but her eyes did not cry.
I stomped my foot. I pushed out my lip.
I did not cry either.

I did not get the shoes
my grandmother wanted to give me.
My mother marched away with
my angry hand in hers.

My heart turned back
and waved my other hand.

I did not know it would be this way.
To always leave the ones
I love and trust.

Superman vs. GOD

Sad sat at the kitchen table swinging her bare feet and wiggling her loose tooth with her tongue. She watched her tall, beautiful grandmother as she stood at the sink, her long dark wavy hair flowing almost to her waist. She was rinsing out a shiny, steel thermos to fill with coffee. The sink was taller than most kitchen sinks, built that way by her grandfather so Nanny wouldn't have a sore back.

Nanny turned to look at Sad. Her eyes, green and sparkly were deep set within the sockets, dark circles embracing her high cheekbones. Those eyes were orbits of rare beauty to Sad, jewels set in stone. She had dubbed them '*stranger eyes*' and no one knew why Sad called them that, but Sad knew. It was a term of endearment.

"That loose tooth a botherin' you?"

Sad nodded her head and wiggled it again.

"Want yer Pa-Paw to tie a string around it and yank it out?"

Sad shuddered and shook her head swiftly, making her long golden locks fly about her face. The mental image of a bloody tooth hanging by a string was enough to make her gag on the sweet, salty oatmeal in front of her.

"Where's Pa-Paw?" asked Sad, suddenly realizing she had yet to see him this morning. Sad had come to spend the night at Nanny and Pa-Paw's house. A rare treat and her favorite thing to do in the whole wide world!

"He's in his room," answered Nanny.

Sad knew this meant his CB radio room. Pa-Paw had built this himself. It was a room with windows all around so he could look outside and watch the birds. It opened up from their bedroom on one side and had a door so he could go out to the windowed porch on the other side.

Pa-Paw spent many hours in this room listening to his CB and police ban radios or watching TV. If he wasn't there, Sad knew he was outside. Maybe riding his lawn mower over the smooth green grass on the large corner lot. Sometimes Pa-Paw hitched a little trailer to the mower and took Sad or other grandkids for a magical mower ride. She loved how he kept everything so trim and tidy so the aunts and uncles could play croquet out on the lawn whenever they came to visit.

Nanny, noticing the dreamy look in Sad's eyes, held out the thermos she had just prepared for him, black coffee with lots of sugar.

"Want to take this to him?"

Sad nodded happily, then jumped down and rushed to grab the thermos.

"Don't bother him too long," Nanny added, smiling as she watched Sad swoosh down the hall.

"Pa...Paw?"

Sad looked quickly around the room, listening to the squelching, belching, staticky hiccup of the two squawking radios. She listened a second more in case one of them called out for *Tumbleweed* which Sad knew was her Pa-Paw's CB handle. Satisfied, she raced out the side door across the porch and galloped outside.

The Texas sun was already branding everything in sight with rays that packed a wallop. Sad raced up the gravel driveway and then stopped near the grassy edge to examine a huge red ant bed. She squatted there barefoot looking for horny toads. Sad loved horny toads with their tiny horned crown, scratchy dinosaur backs and soft little bellies. They were always near the ant beds munching on their favorite fiery feast. She wondered if ants tasted like jalapeno peppers to the horny toads!

Thrilled, she saw the tiniest baby horny toad! It was no bigger than the end of her thumb. With tiptoeing, trembling fingers she hovered over it, then quickly snatched it up by its little horny head. Then carefully, before it could spit tobacco juice at her, she turned it over and rubbed it softly on its belly. That was the best way to hypnotize them and Sad thought they rather liked the tummy tickling!

"Can't spit no baccy juice at me, you litl' horny toad!" She carefully placed it next to the ant bed.

"Now go on and gobble up those mean ol' stingin' ants so you can grow up big and strong."

She reached out grabbing the thermos she had left lying in the dirt.

"Ouch!" She drew her hand back from the hot surface, then rolled it around in the dirt with her foot to stomp out some of the heat. She scooped it up to continue her search for Pa-Paw.

Skipping her way to the carport, she slowed to savor the cool shade under the awning and quietly peered inside the door of the room built off the overhang. Fascinated she stared at all the odds and ends strewn about the little room. This was where Pa-Paw tinkered with things or built his birdhouses.

"Pa-Paw, are you in here?"

"Hmpf," she heard him grump, then saw him leaning over a half-finished bird house.

"Pa-Paw, I brought your coffee!" she said, holding the thermos up proudly.

"Why, thank you," he said peering into her light brown eyes. His eyes were the color of his coffee and his skin browned by the Texas sun was almost the color of the worn work table he sat beside. He removed the little silver thermos cup and poured himself a cup of the dark, sweet brew.

The scent floated through the air and snuck inside Sad's nose.

"Can I have some coffee too, Papaw?"

"Nah, it'll turn your feet black," he said.

Sad looked down at her own dusty toes the over at the scuffed and worn shoes that her grandfather wore. She wondered if his feet were black inside them.

"Whatcha doin'?" she asked, reluctant to leave his presence.

"I'm fixin' this birdhouse for the Purple Martins."

"Whatsa purple martin?" she asked, wiggling her tooth with her tongue.

"Want me to yank that out for ya?" he asked kindly, holding up a pair of pliers.

Sad's eyes widened and she backed away giggling, knowing by the twinkle in his eyes that he was just a kiddin' her.

He set the pliers down and slid off the seat of the stool that had him perched up high enough to reach his work bench.

"C'mon outside and I'll introduce you to the Martins."

Sad rushed to walk beside him, two steps to his one. They stopped beneath the tree Sad loved to perch in.

He pointed to a big birdhouse across the lawn, mounted high on a pole. It looked like a motel for birds.

"Stand still and don't talk. Keep watchin' and you'll see 'em."

Sad kept quiet as a church mouse on Sunday morning, barely breathing as she squinted at the house.

Waiting and watching with Pa-Paw.

Suddenly she saw them, swoop out, and then swoop back inside the tiny holes of the house. With one hand she lifted a finger, counting under her breath.

"You see them?" asked Pa-Paw, breaking the quiet so Sad could breathe again.

"Yes, I did! Four Martins."

"Okay then. Count to four in Spanish."

"Uno, dos, tres, qu…qu…. What is it Pa-Paw?"

"Cuatro. Bueno! Very good! Do you know why Purple Martins are important birds?"

Sad shook her head, waiting to learn something new. Pa-Paw was good for that.

"It's because they eat mosquitoes and every year they send out a scout to find the best houses to build their nests in and have their babies."

"Pa-Paw, I know you build the best houses," said Sad proudly.

Her grandfather smiled and walked back into the carport. Sad followed close behind him, reluctant to leave but kept hearing Nanny's words in her head.

Pa-Paw reached into a rusty looking coffee can and took out two shiny square objects and handed them to Sad.

Sad looked down at them, heavy in her hand.

"What are they Pa-Paw?"

"They're magnets! You can pick up all sorts of things with them." He turned the can filled with nails, nuts and bolts towards Sad and showed her how the magnets would grab things. Sad was beside herself with joy at this tiny little gift and its power.

"Now go on outside and see what you can find with your magnets. You might even find things in the dirt."

"Thanks Pa-Paw!" Sad started to leave then ran back to give her grandfather a quick hug and kiss. She stood there looking into his coffee-colored eyes, then asked in a quiet little voice, "will you do one thing for me? Pretty please with cream and sugar." She flashed him her best dimpled smile.

"What is it?" he asked gruffly, but his eyes twinkled.

"Will you play Woody-Woodpecker? Just one time?"

He reached behind him and picked up his steel guitar. Grabbed the coffee can of nails and dug around until he found a guitar pick.

Sad stood there enraptured as he strummed out the sound that Woody Woodpecker made on the cartoon. *Uhhhh aaa uuuhhhh uh, a uuuuhhhh, uh!*

Sad beamed. Her heart was full of him. She could hardly wait to tell Nanny and show her the treasures. She turned to run out then peeked back in to look at her grandfather.

"I love you Pa-Paw."

"I love you too," he said gruffly and winked.

Inside the house, Nanny was standing at the stove stirring a big pot of bubbling peanut brittle. She heard Sad come in and called out cautioning her.

"Don't come near the stove. This stuff is hot enough to take your skin right off."

Sad shuddered at the thought but the heavenly scent of karo syrup, sugar and butter banished the image from her mind.

Jiminy Crickets! Could this day get any better?

"Nanny, guess what?"

"What?"

"Turkey squat!" said Sad laughing.

"Not really! Pa-Paw played Woody Woodpecker for me; and showed me the Martins and gave me two magnets!"

Nanny looked over and smiled at Sad's happy expression. Sad watched her ladle the hot, bubbling peanut-filled golden lava out onto the waxed paper. She spread it around and the scent made Sad's mouth water and her stomach growl loudly.

"Want a nanner?" asked Nanny.

Sad looked over at the bunch of bananas lying on the counter, counted them quietly under her breath. Visions of the eyes of her brothers and sisters at home stared hard inside of her. There were only three bananas.

"No thank you," replied Sad. She sat there quietly at the table thinking about Woody Woodpecker and playing with her magnets. She remembered another of her favorite shows on TV.

"Nanny, how much do you know about God?"

Nanny looked up, puzzled at Sad's question. She came to sit down across from her, noting the serious expression in her granddaughter's eyes.

"Well, let's see. I know a few things. Why do you ask?"

"Because, I have some questions about Him and Superman."

"I see," replied Nanny, her green eyes sparkling but serious.

"Well, ask away and I'll see if I know the answers."

"I've been wondering, is God as strong as Superman?"

"Yes, He is. Much stronger!"

Sad sat thinking about this new revelation. "Wow! That's really strong."

"Well, can God fly faster than a speeding bullet? Can He leap over tall buildings? Can He do all the things Superman does?"

"Actually, He can do more than Superman. He can be with you when you're sleeping. He sees all things, knows all things. He loves you very much and can protect you if you ask Him."

Sad sat there taking in this new information, comparing the two in her mind.

"Nanny, I think I love God even more than Superman."

"Well, I think you are a very smart little girl! Now when this brittle cools, you can help me break it up and we'll take some out to your house when I drive you home."

Sad's face fell at the mention of home. She wanted to help Nanny with the brittle. She was very happy to hear that they were taking some to the other kids.

Nanny noticed the slumped shoulders, the spark gone from the little brown eyes.

"What's wrong Honey?"

"Nanny, why can't you be my mom?" demanded Sad, her face in a pout. "Everywhere we go, people say you look young enough to be my mother. Pa-Paw can be my dad."

"I can't be your mother, Sweetheart. God decides who gets to be the mothers and who gets to be the grandmothers. He picked your mother out special just for you and she loves you very much."

"Well, can't we ask GOD to change it around?"

"No Honey, we can't. He knew what He was doing when He made it that way."

Sad looked into the sympathetic green eyes of her beautiful grandmother. She jumped off her chair and ran around to throw herself into her arms.

"But I want you for my mother," she whispered sadly, trying to stop the sobs cradled in her throat. Her grandmother bowed her head on top of Sad's little one, the dark locks of her hair mingling with the golden strands.

Silence enfolded the two and Sad pressed tight against Nanny's heart. She wished Superman could fly her up to God. Perhaps then He would grant her wish. She would ask 'pretty please with cream and sugar'.

My Favrite Easter

I wanta tell you about my favrite Easter.
It starts with all the aunts bein here.
My redhead aunt with her little boy,
my big-city aunt with the fancy-smancy fingernails
that match all her clothes,
with her daughter and boys,
and then my aunt with so many kids
that she don't know what to do,
kinda like the lady in the shoe.
They are gonna cook up some tater salad and
nanner puddin and maybe some ham samwitches!
Yummy!
So all my Nanny's daughters are together
and they laff and talk so much that
the kids can't even get a word in the edge-wise.
We don't really care cuz we're all
playing freeze tag,
and hide and seek, and runnin around like
chickens or ducks or bunnies
with thar heads cut off.
And that's the other bestest part.
The baby bunny !!!

Now all us kids have to take a pretend nap,
so's the little kids will think the Easter Bunny
came to hide the eggs.
Then we run outside like crazy folk
with a pail or sack
or sumpin to carry all the eggs in.
I don't like the wrapped candy ones that
have nasty tastin marshymelow in the middle,
but I get them anyway
cuz they'll be good for tradin later.
I trade the white part of the boiled egg
with my brother for the yellow part.
He says he has more that way.
And I like the yellow.
So, then jest when I go to grab an egg
hiden behind a mesquite tree,
I see a tiny baby bunny,
all furry and brown.
He was a lookin at the Easter egg,
sniffin it like it was sumpin he cud eat.
I start to yell to tell the other kids, but then I got
worryed they might hurt it,
so I jest call the kids in my family over to see it.
they know more bout things out here
in the contry and how portant they are.

The Summy Day

November 22, 1963

Darkness cannot drive out darkness; only light can do that.
Hate cannot drive out hate; only love can do that.
~ Martin Luther King Jr. ~

Sad skipped down the street singing a song she made up as she went along.

"I'm soooooo glad,
No longer mad
Now that the mumps
Have gone to the dumps."

She remembered looking in the mirror. Her face all swole up like Chip and Dale gone crazy on a peanut picnic in the park. Missing two whole days at the new school made her worry and she almost fell when her feet missed a beat between the skip and the song.

Their rattlily old station wagon left Texas for New Mexico, and Sad had cried when she thought no one was watching. She hated leaving Nanny and Pa-Paw, her tears a river at the thought of leaving them.

She didn't want to go to a new school and leave her 2nd grade teacher, Mrs. Robinson. Sad loved Mrs. Robinson! After all, it was she who had taught Sad how to write in cursive. She smiled at the thought of practicing her letters. She was trying to decide which one was her favorite. Today she was leaning towards the letter ' *L* '.

L for love, learn, listen and laugh!

Sad couldn't understand why they had to leave in the first place. Perhaps it was so the dad could live near his mother for a while. Sad guessed it was his turn.

It was hard leaving behind people she loved, like the red-headed aunt that had lots of freckles. This aunt seemed almost like an older sister to Sad. She remembered something her aunt said to Sad before they left. A strange thing.

"When you were born, you were already 42!"

Sad cocked her head sideways and looked at the aunt.

"What does that mean?" Sad asked, not sure whether to get mad or thank her.

"Don't worry about it," her aunt replied. "You'll figure it out someday."

Sad shook her head at all these thoughts, wiped the sweat out of her eyes and smiled at the sun before walking up the last few steps to the school. She hoped she wasn't late and slid in her seat just as the school bell rang.

Sad looked around for her friend, Elizabeth. She didn't see her anywhere and Sad decided when school was over, she would ask her mother if she could go visit Elizabeth who lived just a hop, skip but not a jump from Sad's house.

Thinking about Elizabeth reminded Sad of another peculiar thing that an adult said. This from the grandmother in New Mexico. The dad's mom.

Sad sat practicing her letters, thinking about grownups and how strange they were sometimes. She compared her two grandmothers. In her heart she knew she loved the Texas grandmother more.

But why?

The New Mexico grandmother always had something good cooking on the stove.

She had a very clean house too, and when they first arrived, they spent a few nights with her and the grandfather. The dad had said this grandfather wasn't his dad, but they could call him granddad anyway.

And she wondered why her mom didn't like the grandmother.

They were nice to each other, but Sad knew something was wrong. She saw it in her mother's face, when her mouth twisted up and lines grew above her nose. She heard it in the politeness of her mother's voice.

The first night was very interesting. The grandmother opened a hall closet and Sad stood there amazed! Never had she seen a closet like this. There were plenty of towels, wash cloths, pillowcases and sheets all folded neatly and lined in rows. Blankets too! The grandmother took some down to make the beds.

Sad stood there studying the closet for a long time.

Such a wonderment!

She determined to have a closet like this someday. A closet you could just open up and take things out, everything lined up neat and folded, just waiting for company to arrive. She smiled and turned to follow the grandmother.

Another surprise awaited her.

They were going to get two sheets on the bed!

Sad could hardly believe it! They never had that at home. Most times they didn't even have one sheet.

Sad remembered sliding between the delicious coolness of two sheets, knowing her dreams would surely be good that night.

Soon they moved into their own house and the grandmother came to visit. That was when Sad wondered about the grandmother and the strange thing she had said.

It was about Elizabeth.

After school, Elizabeth and Sad had walked home hand and hand. They were skipping and singing songs.

"Want to come home with me?" asked Elizabeth, when they stopped in front of Sad's house. "We can play hopscotch on my sidewalk."

"Okay, but I have to go ask my mom first," replied Sad. "Come with me to ask."

"No, I'll wait here. I can't go inside unless I have permission."

Sad rushed inside and noticed her grandmother had come over for a visit. She gave her a quick hug.

"Mom, can I go play at Elizabeth's house?"

The women looked outside and saw the little girl waiting outside. Sad's mom started to nod her head, but the grandmother leaned over to whisper to her. Sad heard every word the grandmother said.

"You shouldn't let her go. They are dirty people."

Sad looked at her mother's face. She noticed the little lines above her mother's nose and the scrunchy mouth.

"Sure, go play," replied Sad's mom, "but come back in a few hours."

Sad bounded out the door and looked at Elizabeth's beautiful, brightly flowered dress. Sad didn't see a spot of dirt. She laughed as they skipped away, Elizabeth's neatly braided long, dark hair bouncing against her back.

Inside Elizabeth's house, Sad looked around at the clean swept floors, the tidy kitchen counters with the dishes washed and neatly put away. A wonderful aroma floated up out of a pot on the stove.

Elizabeth's mother had the same color of skin as Sad's mom. She spoke to her daughter in Spanish and welcomed Sad with a hug.

"So is this your new friend, Mija?" She is muy bonita!"

Sad smiled up at Elizabeth's pretty mother, but secretly thought her own mother more beautiful.

The girls got a cookie from the cookie jar and went outside to play hopscotch.

"What did your mom say?" asked Sad. "Will you teach me to talk in Spanish? In Texas, my Pa-Paw taught me how to count. But that's all I know."

"Si, that means yes. How far can you count in Spanish?"

** 1,2,3,4,5 **

Suddenly the school bell rang, and Sad realized that she had been day-dreaming. It was already time for lunch. She ran out the door and started skipping towards her house.

After lunch, Sad walked back to school. She kept thinking about Elizabeth. Thinking about what the grandmother had said. Wondering why she would say something mean that wasn't even true. Maybe the grandmother wasn't taught, like Sad, that it was better to not say anything if you couldn't say something nice.

She walked inside the school and stopped quickly, as if her shoes had brakes in them.

A teacher was crying in the hallway! Another teacher hugged her, patting her on the back.

Sad wondered what was wrong and noticed other teachers standing around in little groups, talking close-like. Their faces looked worried. Sad thought their frowns need to turn upside down, like the Brownie song at Girl Scouts.

Her stomach did flip-flops when she looked at her own teacher's face. Her eyes looked all wet and watery. Her head hung down low and her voice sounded like there were tears in her throat when she told the children to take their seats. Then she stepped out into the hall.

Sad looked around at the other students, but none of them looked scared. But she knew something was very wrong when the teacher came back.

"Class, this is a very unhappy day for America," she said, and tears ran down her face when she talked.

"We are letting everyone go home early. Bus students line up at the door."

Outside, Sad looked up to see if the sun had stopped shining. Nope. She thought it would be cloudy from all the tears inside.

She started skipping home, but the songs were not in her heart. She fell down and skinned her knee. She looked at the scab from the last time she had fallen and saw it had broken open. Yuk! It was bleeding.

"Jiminy Crickets!" she said and kicked a rock the rest of the way home.

When Sad opened the door, she saw her mother sitting in front of the TV. She was crying too! Peering at the black, white and gray figures on the TV, Sad couldn't see
anything that might cause her mother to cry.

"This is some kind of Summy Day!" exclaimed Sad.

"What are you talking about?" Asked her mother.

"You know, a sunny day but everything is gloomy all around. I made it up." Sad smiled, hoping her mother would smile back.

She didn't.

Sad went to sit beside her mother on the couch.

"Mom why is everyone crying?"

"Because our President has been shot," she said, not taking her eyes from the TV.

"Oh." Sad sat there wondering who that was.

"Well, did everyone love him or something?"

"Yes. He was a great President. And he was so very young." She sniffed and held up a tissue to blow her nose.

"Well I guess that explains it!" answered Sad.

"Explains what?"

"Explains why the whole world is crying," Sad said in a whisper.

The Smell of Safety

Sorrow was like the wind. It came in gusts.
~ Marjorie K. Rawlings ~

Sad was happy. Perched high, sitting on the wheel well, in the back of the old pick-up truck, she loved the feel of the wind as it whipped past her face, lifting her long locks of golden hair, spinning crazily about her head like silky strands of spun gossamer. The last rays of the setting sun caressed her skin, sending delicious waves throughout her body.

She turned her head to survey her little kingdom. Being the eldest gave her certain privileges; like not having to sit on her bottom when the truck was moving, as the others did. There was her, then two boys and two girls.

She studied her brothers and sisters once again. Their hair was much darker than hers and freckles spattered across their faces. Somehow the differences went much deeper, to places inside her she didn't understand. Wondered countless times about it, having considered the possibility of being adopted. But that was where she hit the brick wall. Who in their right mind would allow teenagers of 15 and 17 to adopt a child? She glanced into the pickup window at the two people who called themselves her parents. She often felt more like a sister to her mother. And the dad, well…, something was missing between him and Sad.

A little sigh escaped her lips. All eyes turned towards Sad.

Sad smiled at them, "tonight will be fun."

"Really?" Asked the brown-eyed girl.

"Oh yes! We'll play games," answered Sad.

"And tell ghost stories?" Exclaimed the boys in unison, their eyes sparkling.

"I no want ghost stories," quivered the littlest blue-eyed girl, "I get skeered."

"You can hold my hand," soothed Sad.

"Otay."

Yes, tonight would be good. Yip! Yip! Hooray!!! They were back in Texas and on the way to Nanny and Pa-Paw's house so the grown-ups could play 42, a Texas domino game.

Yep, tonight there would be no beer cans, only coffee and tea and Dr Pepper.

She rubbed her head where it still hurt reminding her of the most recent event. She had thought since she was bigger now and stronger that she could fight back when the dad went to hit her mother. After all, she had always been able to protect the kids, so maybe she was letting her mom down by not trying to save her as well. She had listened on the other side of the bedroom door. The kids were safe huddled inside. The voices were getting louder now, angrier. And when she heard the smack, she raced from the room.

She jumped right between them and screamed in his face, "leave her alone!" Before she even knew what was happening, he grabbed her by the hair of her head and pitched her straight against the wall. Gathering the kids, they left in the truck without him, to Nanny's house. When her mother began crying to Nanny about it, Sad put her 2 cents worth in as well. She was rubbing her head and said, "and then when I tried to save Mom, he pulled my hair and threw me into the wall!"

Nanny looked shocked, and held me close, but Mom turned, her face an angry mask and screeched, "THAT'S WHAT YOU GET FOR INTERFERING!"

#&$@+

Just then the truck hit a bump and almost knocked Sad off her perch. The other kids looked over at her while she regained her position.

Yes, tonight would be different.

No loud screaming, no hiding the kids, no wondering how to make everyone safe and happy.

Tonight, she could pretend. Pretend to be a kid. Play with the kids. They would play *Hide and Seek*, *Simon Says*, and *Freeze Tag*. They would catch lightning bugs winking at the moon, huddle close together and listen to her made-up ghost stories. And then, before they went into the house, they could all wish on a star.

They would all be tired from playing games when they trooped into the beloved house. They would stretch out on the floor in front of Nanny and Pa-Paw's new color TV! It was great watching *Bonanza*, *The Fugitive* or *Walt Disney World* in color!

She would listen to the comforting clakidy-clack while they shuffled the dominoes, their words lulling her into a sense of calm.

"Whose shuffle is it?"

"What's yer bid?"

"Hey, J-Dub shot the moon!"

She would listen to the laughter, watch smoke swirl around their heads like a silvery fog trapped on a moonless night. She would smile, watching them drink iced tea, coffee and Doctor Pepper. She would look for a wink from Pa-Paw and long for a touch from Nanny's hand, soft as bedroom slippers, slipping through Sad's tangled hair.

Then when the evening began to slip away, she would listen for the clues. Clues that would be her signal to sneak onto the couch, turn her face to the back of it, and pretend to be asleep.

She would squeeze the light from her eyes, slow her breathing. She would suck in the scent of stale cigarettes, but most importantly, the scent of Nanny's hands. A soothing smell captured in the threads of the crocheted comforter tossed haphazardly across the couch to hide the cracks and tears. She would allow her body to melt into the couch and drink in the smell of safety.

Slowly she would try to fall into real sleep, not pretend sleep.
But she never could. She could only lie there praying that this time they would leave her here. Just one quiet night in the blessed house. She knew she was too heavy for them to carry to the pickup. And too old. Already nine. Anyway, she would have to help them carry the little ones.

So she stretched out on the couch and breathed in deep, treasuring each moment.

Tarzan Doesn't Carry Bullets

We could never learn to be brave and patient
if there were only joy in the world.
~ Helen Keller ~

"Ahh a-a-a ahhh a-a-a-ahhhhhhhhhh!" The blood-curdling yell of Sad's cousin tore through the air. Fascinated she watched him pound his chest, then race towards her.

"I'm coming Jane! Tarzan will save you!"

"Hurry Tarzan, the elephants are stampeding!" A quiver of excitement raced down Sad's spine as her brave hero made it just in time to save the day.

She was braced against the tree, her hands stretched behind her, the imaginary ropes held her tight. Tarzan swung through the trees on huge snake-like vines and made it to her just in the knick of time.

"Quick Jane, grab the rope and hang on!"

"Okay Tarzan, but don't let go. I don't want to fall in the raging river."

"Don't worry Jane, you're safe with me!"

Sad beamed up into her cousin's two-tone face. One side red splotches that covered half his face and throat, the other a honey gold from the Texas sun. Her heart swelled with love for him. She remembered as a little girl asking him what had happened? Had his mother slapped his face? The family had laughed good-natured at her childish question. Then explained it was his birthmark. Secretly she envied him having such distinguishing marks. Her own birthmark, a tiny mark outside her left eye was hardly noticeable. He had always been her hero. When she was three and he was five, he fished her out of a baby pool by the hair of her head where she lay floundering in the water. He loved telling this story to any who cared how he had saved her life.

The two were in the backyard behind his house. Sad loved coming here! His home always a beehive of activity with five kids from Sad's family and eight from theirs. Kids, kids everywhere! Sad watched as the littlest boy, shaggy blonde hair and big, bright-blue eyes approached them.

"Tan I pray wit ou?"

Sad looked down at him, puzzled. He was so cute. A face like an angel.

"Can you pray with me?"

"Oh…" interjected my cousin, "he means play. He turned to glare at him. "No! Go play with the little kids, we're busy here."

Sad watched as he shuffled away towards the house, chin thrust upon his chest. She turned back to her cousin.

"You want to play Knights of the Round Table and damsels in distress now?"

"Sure, but we need more people. Let me go get some of the other kids."

She watched as he ran in search of their older cousin, the dark-haired boy and the dark-haired girl just under Sad's age. It was an unspoken rule. The big kids played with the big kids and the little kids played together; a clear division that needed no discussion.

She kicked a pebble across the red Texas dirt and wiped sweat from her brow. She leaned against the clapboard house and watched enchanted as the yard transformed from thick jungle forest, tall trees alive with vines and roaring brook into soft, velvety green rolling hills, a tall gleaming castle with a moat sparkling in the setting sun. She would be duly dressed with blue gown, lacy bodice, and a circle of white daisies adorning her hair. Her younger cousin would wear a red gown to accent her dark features and a crown of yellow roses. The knights of course would be arrayed in clanging armor with shiny swords to protect them from fire-breathing dragons.

The first twinkling stars hunted the moon before we gave up our games. Lightning bugs blinking tiny lanterns chased them as they trooped in, dirty and tired; the roar of the cicadas left behind to sing their raspy songs.

The living room now dotted with sprawling kids. Some settling on the floor in front of the TV, little hands and tiny feet draped across the couch and chairs.

Sad walked into the kitchen looking around for her mother. Her aunt was clearly the only adult left in the house.

"Where'd Mom go?" Sad asked.

"She left with your uncle's wife."

"Do you know when they're coming back?"

Her aunt shrugged, unsmiling, and turned away towards the kitchen sink. Sad sensed something was wrong but was hesitant to ask more questions. She turned to join the other kids in the living room. Suddenly the back door off the kitchen crashed loudly inward startling them both.

Her uncle stood there, lurching unevenly in the doorway then crossed over to search the living room.

Sad's muscles tensed up. A small trembling began in her belly. This was not the uncle she loved. This uncle distinguished by a mean scowl and a huge beer belly that now blocked her view into the other room. She could smell the foul odor on his breath and knew not to look into his red, piggy eyes. The memory that lingered in Sad's mind was of one of their dogs that hated him and the knife-slashed coat of brindled fur.

"Where is she?" he bellowed.

Sad stood there.

Silently waiting.

Watching.

Watching to make her dash into the next room the moment he moved.

Her aunt answered him as she stood beside the kitchen sink. "She's not here." Her voice tight and her eyes looking anywhere but at her brother.

He swaggered forward and yelled louder this time.

"Well then, WHERE THE HELL IS SHE?"
He lunged forward, "Somebody better tell me!" his speech slurred.

Sad tried to dart past him, but with one beefy hand he reached out and grabbed her by the shirt, dragging her back into the room. He jerked her roughly and too late, she saw what was in his other hand.

BIG.   SHINY.   SILVER.

"She's with yer ma, ain't she?" he shook her, his fingers digging into her flesh.

"WHERE. DID. THEY GO?" he punched out the words.

Sad didn't want to look at him.

She felt the blood drain from her face.

She didn't want him touching her. Her skin felt cold and clammy.

"LET ME GO!"

"You know where they went," he snarled, his voice low and mean.

He placed the barrel of the gun right above Sad's left ear and pressed.

Hard.

"Tell me!" he demanded. "Tell me now, or I'm going to put a bullet through your rotten little skull!"

Sad stood there and felt the silence fold her up like a heavy blanket. The shaking inside her stopped.

She wondered what it would be like to die at the age of 10.

To die because she didn't have the answer to a question.

Finally, she tilted her head, shifting in his grasp. The gun not on her now, but still felt like it was boring a hole inside her. She knew she didn't care if he shot her.

She wasn't afraid of him anymore. If she had known the answer to the question, she still wouldn't tell him.

She wondered what had made him so mean. What had turned him into another bullyboy? A coward who picked on people littler than himself.

She looked into his eyes. "I DON'T KNOW where they went."

The room held its breath, listening to the clock tock.

Abruptly, he let her go; lurching out the door, he slammed it hard behind him.

Sad walked slowly into the living room. So many pairs of little eyes following her.

Crossing to the window, she peered out.

Looking for the jungle with its swinging vines and…

…. Tarzan.

One Square per Girl

He was gentle and sweet and shy.
Sad didn't know he liked her until one day
in the school lunchroom.
The boys always sat at tables with boys.
The girls sat at tables with girls.
That was just the way it was.

Sad was eating her lunch and
talking to her friends
when a boy tapped on her shoulder.
"Ike said to give you this."
Then he put a chocolate M&M in her hand.
It was her favorite.
Looking at Ike, she popped it in her mouth.
All the boys started tittering behind their
hands.

Sad walked over to the boy table and
stared at Ike.
"Why are they laughing?" she asked.

Ike couldn't meet her eyes,
and a slow, red flush crept up his neck.

The boy who had handed her the M&M
piped up,
"Ike kissed the M&M!"

So that's how Sad and Ike began going
steady.
Which just meant that he liked her
and she liked him.
Whenever Sad thought of Ike,
she saw a square.
Solid and strong with straight lines.

One day, during Christmas break,
there was a tap at Sad's door.
When she opened the door, Ike stood there,
a carefully wrapped present in his hand.
He shuffled his feet, then handed it to her.
It was a beautiful bracelet with dainty
charms.
The best present ever!!!

A few days before school was out
for the summer
there was a square dance.
Along came Tod.

Whenever Sad thought of Tod,
she saw a circle.
Shiny and round,
moving quick on the ground.

She left Ike behind.

Sad didn't know
that there would be many Tods,
but
never
another
boy
like
Ike.

Trees that Wave and Teachers that Don't

Solitary trees if they grow at all, grow strong.
~ Winston Churchill ~

Sad had a friend named Aubree.
They shared a secret.
They shared the code of silence.
It was the same unwritten code of silence
that all children of alcoholics, drug addicts,
and abused children share.
They share the same common ground, yet
rarely know it because the code is so strong.
Binds their lips.
Binds their lips and heart as surely as if duct
tape was used.

Sad wondered sometimes about Aubree. She thought about her when she was walking to school and waving at the trees. Sad loved trees! The trees always waved back! They were constant. A lovely presence in an often-unlovely world.

Whenever Sad left to start her walk home from school, she also waved good-bye to Aubree.

Aubree always stood by the flagpole.

Waiting for her mother to come pick her up. She knew Aubree sometimes waited for hours after the school closed. Standing by the flagpole. Sometimes her smooth dark hand grasped the pole and she twirled around it, her long dark hair flying out like a flag, or a kite in the breeze.

Waiting. Always waiting.

Wondering.

Waiting for a mother who forgot so many times that Aubree had stopped counting.

Wondering what state of mind she would be in if she remembered to pick her up.

And wishing. Always wishing.

Wishing for a life that never seemed to change.

Ω Ω Ω

Sad walked up the hill towards the school. She had a lot on her mind and barely noticed the wind as it whipped her hair about her shoulders. She waved at the trees but didn't give them her usual undivided attention. Didn't stop to beam up into their branches, with her dimpled smile.

The signed report card burned a hole in her backpack, calling out to her with an accusatory tone. The same accusatory tone the dad had used when he looked at it and saw the "C".

C for cursed, c for crappola, c for CRIMINEE!

Sad had never had a "C" on a report card before. First, Second and Third Grades were all straight "A's," the dad reminded Sad.

Sad remembered how the dad had bragged to his Fireman buddies when she came to slide down the pole at the firehouse.

"A straight 'A' student, that one!" he said, pointing at Sad when she slid down the pole and ran past him to climb the stairs, then slide down one more time.

Well, he won't be bragging now, she thought, listening to what he said to her mother as she passed by, head hanging low.

"She's getting low grades because she's discovered boys!"

Sad knew that wasn't the reason for her lower grades. She couldn't quite figure out the reason for the 'C'. She had always liked boys. No big discovery there!

Sad walked up to her teacher and handed her the signed report card. The teacher didn't nod, or even turn to look at her.

She took her seat and noticed Aubree sitting towards the back of the room, her head lying on her desk.

"Aubree, sit up straight!" demanded Mrs. Phoney Macaroni.

Sad turned around to give Aubree a sympathetic smile, but then Mrs. Phoney Macaroni yelled at Sad to turn back around.

Sad knew the teacher didn't like girls like her and Aubree. Girls who wore wrinkled shirts that smelled like their parents overflowing ashtrays and greasy potato sandwiches.

Mrs. Phoney Macaroni liked girls like Brenda. Sad and Aubree liked Brenda too, with her neatly ironed calico dress and shiny shoes. Brenda always knew the answers to the questions that their teachers asked. Brenda was part of their secret singing group at recess. The one they were sure that Elvis would someday discover if he would only pass by and hear them singing. Then surely he would make them stars!

Brenda's hair smelled like flowers and sunshine. And Brenda always had plenty of paper and sharpened pencils.

Once when Sad only had a tiny stub of a pencil left and they were taking one of those tests where you have to darken the circles with plenty of lead, Sad had leaned over to ask Brenda if she could borrow one of her freshly sharpened pencils.

Mrs. Phoney Macaroni stomped down the aisle and scrawled a big fat, red zero on Sad's paper. Sad had looked down at her test, horrified! Her pleas fell on phoney, close-minded ears and Sad wasn't even allowed to explain.

Sometimes when Sad went to school her stomach would start hurting, hurting like it often did. The doctor had told Sad's mother it was a worry ulcer. Sad tried not to worry, but sometimes it was impossible with so many things weighing on her mind. And now a "C" to add to it!

She hoped it wouldn't start hurting today, because Mrs. Phoney Macaroni wouldn't allow Sad to call her mother. She knew this because it had happened before.   Sad doubled over in pain, had to wait until math class and ask Mr. Tallend if she could go to the nurse. When Mrs. Phoney Macaroni found out, she yelled at Sad in front of the class. Sad went home crying that day and told her mother what had happened. Her mother marched to school to talk to the principal. The principal was very fond of Sad's beautiful mother. But it sure didn't make things any easier between Sad and Mrs. Phoney Macaroni.

Sad sighed. *"C"* stood for complications too!

The bell finally rang, and Sad could hardly wait to go home. At home she could hug her dog, Scout, and wave at the trees.

Outside the wind whipped even harder, and Sad knew a thunderstorm was on the way. Aubree stood by the flagpole and Sad walked over to stand next to her.

"Hey Aubree, what time's your mom coming?"

"I dunno," shrugged Aubree, and began swinging around the pole.

Sad looked up, worried as the sky began pouting and puckering, turning unhappy shades of black and gray.

Sad grabbed the pole and twirled around with Aubree, her golden strands of blonde mingling with Aubree's dark, wavy locks. Two storm-tossed flags flying free.

Plop, plop, plop danced drops of rain while the two girls twirled around and around.

"Honk, honk!" Came the sound that startled them both.

Two sets of eyes looked up at the same time, happy to hear a sound that meant Aubree's mother had arrived.

Except it wasn't Aubree's mother.

Sad stared into the eyes of the strange man. She had never seen him before, and he looked at the girls. To Sad he looked like he was hungry.

"Would you girls like a ride home?" he asked.

Sad backed away from the pole, shaking her head no, but Aubree stood still and silent. Looking inside the car at the man. At the dry, smooth leather. The clean, empty seat. The smiling face of the hungry man.

"C'mon Aubree," said Sad, "let's skip to my house and maybe my mom can drive you home."

"No. It's okay," she said. "I think I've seen him on my street before."

A crack of thunder made them jump and lightening streaked the sky!

The man ran quickly around and opened the door. Sad could see why he did it.

There weren't any handles on the inside of the car door.

Aubree turned to wave at Sad as she climbed into the car.

Sad walked home slowly.

Her stomach beginning to hurt.

Not stopping to wave at the crying trees.

The Dog Scout Days of Summer

Tears are words the heart can't express.
Anonymous

Sad lifted one wooden leg, then the other. Holding the stilts steady, she tried doing a little dance step. "Taa Dah! Now, the amazing Pippi will defeat the stairs with death-defying leaps of danger!"

She imagined her ponytail flying behind, a brilliant carrot red, instead of golden brown. A monkey perched precariously on her shoulder as she practiced her stilt dancing. Pippi Longstocking was Sad's favorite heroine, and she wondered if she could talk her parents into getting her a monkey.

Fingers white, teeth clenched, she started up the backstairs of the house. First the left leg, then the right. A furry flash of white and gold suddenly bounded up the steps in front of her.

Sad flung herself off the stilts, grabbing the wiggling ball of fur. Pressing her face against his furry one, she enjoyed each sloppy lick from his pink, wet tongue.

"Scout, you came back! Uhhh…. again," she looked around quick-like, wondering if she was the only one who had seen the bounding ball of fur. She put a finger to her lips to still his excited whimpers.

Slam!

She jumped, hearing the sound of a door closing around the front of the house. Nervously, she tried to shield Scout from view when the dad came running around to the car parked under the carport. He backed the car up to the curb in front of the house and left the driver door open with the engine idling. He noticed Sad and waved her over.

"Do me a favor?" he asked, his eyes twinkling, then he noticed the wiggling dog beside her. "Heh, now what's this mutt doing back?"

"Please, please let him stay this time," begged Sad.   "I promise I'll take care of him. He can have part of my supper."

"Well, I reckon you might as well keep him. It's his third trip back from the dump. Probably wouldn't do any good taking him off again," he said, scratching and shaking his head as he looked at the dog.

"Did you hear that, Scout, you can stay!"

"All right, now do me a favor and hold the front door open for me."

Sad walked around to the front of the house and did as he asked.

"You might want to stand behind it," he added marching inside.

Sad didn't know what was going on but was thrilled that she could keep Scout. She clicked in her throat, patting her leg for the dog to come sit beside her. Thinking back to the day she found him.

Actually, he found her! Sad and Katie were both Girl Scouts and had been selling cookies on a warm and sunny day.

The little dog had wandered up to them and both girls dropped to their knees, lavishing love and praise on the bedraggled canine. He was sandy brown and white, a short haired terrier-mix dog with perky ears and a happy-go-lucky smile on his face. When they continued on their way, he followed along, determined to stay with them as they went door to door. No amount of shooing him away did any good. They decided to name him Dog Scout, and he wagged his tail when they tried it out on him.

They knew they had a problem when Katie's folks flat out refused to let her keep Dog Scout. At Sad's house, the dad said they couldn't afford another mouth to feed. She fought the urge to cry when he drove away taking Scout to the dump, assuring her that he would find plenty to eat there. Sad wasn't so sure about that and worried what would become of the friendly-faced dog.

Sad smiled again at Scout. Suddenly hearing a swoosh, the dad came flying out the door, her mother screaming and yelling right behind him. He flew down the steps, jumped into the car, then slamming the door he sped off down the road, laughing maniacally.

Sad looked up to see her mother standing in the doorway with her hair dripping down around her face like lumpy, wet noodles.

"I'll get you for this!" she screamed, glaring down the road and waving her fist in the air!

Sad wanted to laugh but held it in. Instead, keeping a blank expression she said, "What happened?"

"He dumped a bucket of water on me while I was sleeping!"

Sad could see she wasn't as mad as she pretended to be.

"Why did he do that?"

"Oh, he wanted me to get up to go look at a house in the country."   She went back inside and Sad left to go look for her stilts.

Feeling a blurring streak of motion whipping past her, Sad turned around. Her little brother sped past, grabbing her swinging ponytail, jerking her head forward.

"OUCH! I'll get you, you little beast!" she yelled.

Her brother laughed, his wicked blue eyes crinkling, and an evil grin plastered his face. He was well out of reach. She would have to plan a sneak attack for later.

"Brothers!" she swore, patting Scout on his head. "Why can't we have dogs instead of boys?"

Tired of the stilts, she went inside for a drink of water. Her mother was getting dressed and pointed to a stack of books.

"Do I have to?" asked Sad.

"C'mon, just practice walking for ten minutes. Don't you want to win the Beauty Contest?"

"I guess," she said, reluctantly picking up the stack of three books and placing them on her head. She started pacing the room, balancing the books. If they dropped, she had to start all over. *This is a waste of time, but it'll make Mom and my grandparents proud if I win.* She thought about the last beauty contest where she had only placed third. She had been so embarrassed that day.

Mom kept reminding her to smile at the judges when all she could think about were the gaps in her snaggily mouth where all her baby teeth were missing!

"Snaggle-tooth, Snaggle-tooth," called the kids at school, taunting her. Thinking about it had made her run off the stage after smiling at the judges. The judges said that was the reason she placed third. This time she was determined to get it right and satisfy her mom. She glanced in the mirror flashing a smile, thankful there were no gaps now. Her teeth shining back at her like tiny little soldiers waiting for orders.

She shuddered at the other horrors in store for her: strips of cloth around her long golden hair so it would fall in ringlets, big prickly curlers all over her head that made sleeping impossible. She sighed and the books slid off her head.

"Dammit!" she said, then looked around quickly. Whew! No kids were around to hear. She had to set a good example, so she picked up the books and started over.

When she finished balancing with the books on her head, she was shocked to see what awaited her next! Walking into the room she shared with her brothers and sisters, her mother was sitting on the bed, a little white brassiere next to her.

"What's that?" Sad demanded.

"You have to start wearing this," said her mother.

"I don't want to!" Sad turned away embarrassed, crossing her arms across her bumpy chest.

"You have to. Don't you want to be a young lady?"

"Not if it means wearing that," said Sad pointing to the offensive garment. "I like feeling free."

Sad's mother looked at her like she was a Martian or something.

"It's uncomfortable," she pouted.

"Well, you have to start wearing them," concluded her mother, standing up to leave the room.

"Can I just wear …. it…." she picked it up and held it away from her as if it was infected with creepy, crawly critters," ….to school and not around here?"

Her mother heaved a heavy sigh, "okay, but this is the last…. 'free' …. summer, so you better enjoy it."

After her mother left the room, Sad threw herself on the bed. Life was so unfair! Books on her head, curlers in her hair, and now this awful thing! She stuffed the offensive garment under the bed, then ran outside to tell Dog Scout how lucky he was to be a dog!

***

In spite of the obvious inconveniences, that was a very happy summer. Sad won first place in the beauty contest, making everyone happy. Then the family moved out of the little two-bedroom house in town to a ramshackle, country house. It was the first time Sad could ever remember having her very own bedroom. It was delicious having a private space to read, dream, and cuddle with Dog Scout. The house sat on several wooded acres, which the five kids loved to explore.

After settling in the dad sent away for a huge box of baby chickens. Next they added a deaf Shetland pony and a spooky ol' mare quarter horse. It was just like a little farm and, perfectly complete when an adorable, freckle-faced calico kitten joined the family. Sad knew right away what to name her. '*Freckles*' loved to tiptoe in between the horse's legs whenever they were outside. They all watched, captivated as the little kitten happily marched between the clip-clopping hooves. They couldn't understand why the horses never trampled her but instinctively knew that a teeny-tiny kitten was prancing between their legs.

With all these things going right for them, Sad thought it a bit strange when the dad and Sad's favorite uncle decided to take off hitch-hiking to Alaska late that summer. She didn't understand it one bit and hoped it didn't mean another move was looming in the future.

The new place even boasted a tree house, with a slide on one side and a ladder on the other! It was the best clubhouse ever! Sad climbed up beneath the leafy branches of the tree house and yelled for the other kids to join her.

"C'mon y'all! Let's see if the dogs can climb up here." When all five kids were packed inside the tree house, they began whistling and calling the dogs to try and master the ladder.

"Wow," they said in unison, when Dog Scout carefully pulled himself up the ladder. Tyke, their dad's yellow-hair dog, had to be helped a bit. They slid down the slide laughing with delight when the dogs slid right down behind them.

"I know what we can do!" said Sad. "Let's pack a lunch and let the horses carry it for us. We'll go exploring!"

"Yahoo!" hollered the blue-eyed boy.

"Great idea!" announced the brown-eyed boy.

"I'll help you pack the lunches," volunteered the brown-eyed girl.

"What can I do?" inquired the littlest blue-eyed girl.

Soon they had bologna and bread packed in a bread bag and water in a milk jug. Next, they had to try and convince the skittish mare to let them put a lead on her. The little Shetland would follow them once the mare was caught. They never rode the horses. The Shetland bucked them off as soon as they got on him and the mare was scared of everyone, especially men. It was just fun having them along on their expeditions.

They were all lined up, kids, dogs and horses with *Freckles* the kitten marching proudly, the belly of the mare shadowing her.

"Okay now, I'm going to teach you some hand signals that you need to pay attention to when we're out here exploring," said Sad, looking intently into each set of eyes. They nodded their heads, quiet and focused on her directions.

"When I hold up one finger, it means be quiet. Two fingers mean to look around carefully. If I flatten my hand, it means to duck down. If I flip it backwards, you need to hide quick!"

Sad looked at her troops, "You GOT it?"

They nodded, a little uneasily, so she decided to test them.

"What does two fingers mean?"

"I know, I know," piped up her little blue-eyed sister.

"What?" asked Sad.

"It means to duck down."

"No it doesn't," said the blue-eyed boy. "It means to look around, ya silly girl."

"Don't be mean," said Sad. "Look, I'll go over it again when we get in the woods."

"Yay!" Everyone cheered and they began marching towards the line of mesquite trees.

In spite of the cramping in Sad's stomach, she figured it was that ol' worry ulcer acting up again; they had a great time in the woods. They challenged danger around every bend, and practiced the new hand signals until even the littlest girl knew them all by heart. Sad was finally satisfied that she could take them into the deepest forests of any jungle and keep them safe using their new sign language.

Finally, they were tired and sat around in a circle munching on bologna sandwiches and passing around the water jug.

"I miss daddy," said the littlest girl, "when ya think he's coming back?"

"I don't know," said Sad. Secretly she liked him gone but had an uncomfortable feeling when she thought about his absence. She didn't want to leave this happy place.

She stood up abruptly, the pain in her stomach almost doubling her over.

"Come on, let's head back. We'll practice the signals on the way home."

Once they arrived back at the house, Sad's mother stood in the living room holding a letter in one hand and something that looked like tickets in another. Sad noticed her face shone with happiness. Sad marched right past her to the bathroom and closed the door, leaning against it, suddenly worried. Happy news for her mother wasn't always happy news for the rest of them. Her stomach tightened inside her like a clenched fist and Sad went to use the toilet. She glanced down as her white shorts settled around her ankles.

"Well dammit to hell anyway!" She swore under her breath, glaring at the bright beacon of blood staining her shorts. She felt the tears start up behind her eyes. She knew what this meant. Something to do with babies and becoming a woman. She had heard about it from her mom and at a class for girls at school.

She rested her head in her hands, overcome with this new tragedy in her life. She kicked the offending garment off her foot where it flew underneath the claw-foot bathtub.

"I'm only ten!" she sniffed, burying her face between her clenched fists. "I don't want to be a woman! It's not fair!!! Why wasn't I born a boy? They have all the luck, all the privileges in life. Never have to wear uncomfortable contraptions around their chest, can run all around without a shirt, don't have blood pouring out of their guts! It's NOT FAIR!!! It's just not fair," she sobbed.

Suddenly there was a knock at the door.

"I gotta pee," said the brown-eyed boy.

"TOO BAD!" she shrieked, "Go do it outside!"

Another thing boys get to do! Sad sat quietly sobbing for another five minutes, then heard the brown-eyed girl on the other side of the door. "Mom says you have to come out."

Sad hurriedly wiped away her tears, "Tell mom to come to the door," she said, suddenly feeling tired and defeated.

She heard footsteps run through the house, and soon her mother was at the door. "What is it? What do you want?"

"It's happened," said Sad, her voice barely audible.

"What? I can't hear you?"

"I said

IT….

HAS….

Happened!" Another small sob escaped as Sad sat overwhelmed by the injustices thrust upon her.

After a lengthy pause, her mother said, "Oh." Then, "Well are you okay? Do you want me to come in?"

"NO!" shrieked Sad. Then in a quieter voice hoping no one else was near her mother, "Uhm…do we have those things I'm supposed to use?"

"Oh... well.... I don't think so. Use some toilet paper for now and I'll call Nanny and have her bring some."

"Okay," sighed Sad, knowing her life was over as she knew it before. She felt a surge of hatred towards her brothers and all the freedom they enjoyed and a new wave of sympathy towards her little sisters.

Suddenly a lightning bolt thought crashed through the black cloud in her mind. She jumped off the toilet, rushing to press her ear against the door.

We don't have a phone! So... how... NO, she wouldn't! Would she?

Too late, she heard the statticky, hiccup of the CB radio. She cracked the door open just in time to hear her mother calling her grandmother over the radio. She heard her grandmother reply back.

"Can you bring us some Kotex? We have a new woman in the house." Sad listened in horror while her mother told Nanny that Sad had started her period.

Sad felt a primal scream build up in her throat! Instead of letting out the scream she slunk into a fetal position, a quivering heap on the floor! Never again would she be able to show her face in town, much less school. Now everyone in the entire world knew her pain and humiliation.

She began praying that all the blood in her body would flow out leaving only a shell to bury in the red, sun-packed dirt of Texas.

Red Snow

A wound heals but the scar remains.
Proverb

Sad sat facing front watching the bus pull away from the school. The gentle rocking of the big yellow bus almost made her sleepy. The sound of a song floating from the back of the bus, jostled her awake!

"Home, home on the range…

Where the deer and the antelope play…

Oh give me a home…"

Sad turned and smiled at the singers, then joined in, *"where the buffalo roammmmmmm, and the deer and the antelope play."*

"Hey, Texas, did you have buffalo running around in your yard when you lived there?" asked a redhead boy.

"Nope, just a longhorn steer or two!" Sad quipped, turning back around to face forward.

She smiled. They were teasing her, but she loved it! Didn't that mean they had finally accepted her? She had always been told that when someone teased you that meant they liked you.

She sat thinking about that other bus trip. The one they had ridden for four days. Sad, her mom, and the kids. A tiresome trip coming by Greyhound all the way from Texas to Oregon to join the dad. The scenery was beautiful through the Colorado mountains, and into Oregon, but she thought they'd never reach their destination. She was still resentful of all she had to leave behind. Nanny, Pa-Paw and Scout.

Scout! Her very best friend in the whole world. His soft yellow fur pressed against her face when she told him the news of their leaving, his heart surely breaking just like her own.

Sad stopped her thoughts.   She didn't want to think about Scout. Didn't want to chance a tear floating out of her eye and get the bad kind of teasing.

Besides, Nanny had told her to look for the rainbow behind every cloud. Pa-Paw had said it would be an adventure moving to Oregon.

Sure 'nuff, Pa-Paw had been right. She stared out the window at the graceful, gently swaying pine trees. She sucked in their scent from the cold air blowing in from the half-lowered window. It was delicious and tickled her nose, all the way to the back of it. She swayed to the left when the bus swerved around the corner and began the incline up the mountain where she lived. Another thing Oregon had that Texas didn't, mountains, lots of them. Big and bumpy!

Sad sat thinking about the question the teacher asked her at school today. An odd thing for a teacher to say. Surely a teacher should know the answer to that silly ol' question.

"Did you ride horses to school in Texas?" asked Mrs. Simpson.

Sad looked hard at the teacher, thinking maybe she was a' trying to pull her leg, or make fun of her like she was a hillbilly or something. But the teacher only stared back, serious-like, no twinkle in her eye, waiting for Sad to answer.

"No, Ma'am. I usually walked to school. Tweren't far," replied Sad, thinking about her Waving Trees.

"Well then, were there shoot-outs in the street?"

Sad couldn't believe her ears. Was this teacher even educated? She acted like Texas was the wild, Wild West.

"No, ma'am," Sad replied and turned to take her seat, hoping to waylay any and all future questions from this silly woman.

That incident reminded Sad of the neighbor girl who had come to meet her when she moved into their house.

"Hello!" she said, "or should I say 'Howdy'?"

"Hi or howdy is fine by me," replied Sad.

"I thought you would come to the door with cowboy boots and a hat."

Sad laughed inside herself, shaking her head at such nonsense. "No, I don't even have a pair of boots. Wish I did though."

Sad thought Oregon people were a bit strange. They often teased her about her Texas drawl, but she didn't mind.

The bus rattled to a stop and Sad jumped off and started down the gentle slope towards her house. Bonnye Bank it was called. Sad tossed the name around in her head, liking the sound of it. Before approaching the house she looked for the little yellow VW bug that was her mother's car. It was there. Sad opened the door and called out to her, waiting to hear her voice.

Her voice would let Sad know how many beers she had drunk and whether to enter the house on guard or relaxed.

"I'm in here!" Came her mother's reply.

Whew! Sad relaxed. She hadn't started drinking yet. Perhaps today would be a good day after all.

The school week passed quickly and before Sad knew it, she was facing another weekend. She loved school, and sometimes felt fretful facing the uncertainty of the weekend. She felt warm, safe and happy inside the school walls and really enjoyed the school lunches. The thoughts that made her unhappy didn't press against her head so much when she was at school.

Sad jumped out of bed shivering when her bare feet hit the cold wood floor. She tiptoed into the kitchen to see if anyone else was awake. The dad stood next to the coffee pot pouring a cup of coffee. Sad went over and found a cup and poured herself one too. Black. Sad had been drinking it that way since the age of 10. Mom said cream and sugar would make her fat. She warmed her hands against the cup inhaling the wonderful aroma.

"I'm glad you're up," said the dad, "I'll try to wake your mother and you can wake up the kids. Tell them to dress in their warmest clothes because today we're going to Mt. Hood!"

Sad nodded, smiling. This was great news! If they were going to Mt. Hood, they would take the red plastic flying saucer to slide down the snow slopes!

She took a quick sip of her coffee then ran to wake the kids and tell them the good news!

Sad ran into the bedroom she shared with her little sisters. "Hey, wake up sleepy heads!" she said and bounced the bottom bunk where the youngest sister slept. She opened her eyes and looked up at Sad.

"What is it?" she asked.

"We're going to Mt. Hood today!"

"What does that mean?" asked the brown-eyed girl, turning sleepily over and looking down at Sad from the top bunk.

"You remember that mountain we always see that has the snow on top?"

Both girls nodded their heads.

"Well, we get to go up there and take the flying saucer and slide down the mountain! It's going to be great! Now get dressed and bring lots of extra socks to keep your hands warm. And wear two pair on your feet," instructed Sad as she ran to fly down the basement stairs to wake her brothers.

In nothing flat, the family was packed in the car and headed towards the beautiful snow-peaked mountain. An air of excitement whirled inside the car, while their favorite songs pierced the cold mountain air. They merrily sang all their favorites: *I've Been Working on the Railroad, Michael Rowed the Boat Ashore, Just a Boy and a Girl* and they started *99 Bottles of Beers on the Wall*, before they reached the mountaintop and the sledding slopes.

The mountaintop was beautiful! Sparkling white as far as the eye could see. Glittering like stars when the sun kissed the snow. Sad had never seen so much white!

They ran around as happy as Yogi Bear at a

picnic. Running here and there, flinging themselves into the soft, sunny snowbanks. The day flew by as if it had the wings of angels while they trudged up the hill over and over again carrying the saucer. They patiently took turns, flying down the mountain on the red flying saucer, screaming in delighted fright!

Sad stood waiting at the top of the hill and watched other families with their sleds. She noticed one particular slope that looked like a longer ride. It was the littlest sister's
turn, and Sad took her over to try out the new hill.

"I think this way will be more fun," Sad instructed and gave the little one a push off.

Sad watched in shock as the saucer gathered speed then hit a bump, throwing her little sister high into the air flying head over heels, her black boots sailing in one direction and the red saucer flying solo down the hill! Sad, terrified, went running down, slipping and sliding to check on her.

She lay crying in the snow and looked up at Sad, her blue eyes the color of the sky, only now filled with rain. Sad grabbed her and held her tight, miserable that she had been the one to send her down the hill.

"I'm so, so sorry! I didn't know it would do that. Are you okay?"

By now the parents had joined them with the other kids, all looking in concern at little *Sky Eyes*.

"Why did you send her that way?" demanded the dad.

"What were you thinking?" echoed her mom.

Sad stood there unable to meet their eyes.

"I…. I just thought it was a better slope," she stammered.

"Well then, you should have tried it out yourself!" Said her mother and stormed away. Leaving without a backward glance at her children left behind in a snowy snarl.

Sad knew her mother was right and swallowed the tears clogging her throat. The blue-eyed brother held out *Sky Eyes'* boots, and Sad sat down in the snow to help her put them back on her feet.

The day had lost its magic for Sad, and the kids attempted a few more half-hearted slides down the slippery slopes before calling it a day. Tired, cold and damp, the socks on their hands frozen into stiff Popsicle sticks and their feet feeling like blocks of bricks, the family trundled back into the car. The sky was gently closing her blue eyes, turning the mountain into a foggy, distant gray.

The drive down the mountain was quiet and an unsettling air filled the car.

Traffic was heavy, cars in front, cars in back, and they only moved a few feet at a time. Sad could hear the dad cussing under his breath, and she noticed her mother nodding off in the front seat beside him. Sad knew the parents had been drinking and this made her uneasy. She looked at the little kids, softly slumbering, unaware.

Watching the slow-moving cars, she wondered if they would ever get home. Dark descended like an avenging angel, hovering over the traffic inching its way down the mountain.

Suddenly, red lights flashed like embers of fire from hell, and the car in front of them braked hard! The dad swore and stomped on his brakes almost crashing into the car in front of him and sending their sleeping mother crashing against the dashboard! She screamed out in pain as she bashed her head, then started crying and moaning, trying to climb out of the car.

The dad wrestled her back, then yelled at Sad to climb over the seat and get in the front.

"Quick, sit between her and the door."

"Jump out, jump out of the car," moaned her mother, leaning hard against Sad.

Sad's eyes were big in her face. She had never been so nervous as they inched slowly down the mountain. She knew without turning around that all the kids were now awake and quivering.

"Jump out!" demanded her mother again.

"Mom, stop!" said Sad.

"NO!" Jump out of the car," slurred her mother, "we have to get away." She pushed Sad hard against the door frame, trying to reach across and grab the door handle.

Sad was terrified! What was wrong with her mother? Why did she want to get out? Sad had been so busy playing on the mountain, that she hadn't watched to see how many beers the parents drank.

"Jump out NOW!" her mother screamed.

"NO," screamed Sad, "STOP pushing me!" she grabbed her mother's prying fingers as they tried to reach across for the door handle.

Suddenly the dad swerved the car to the right and pulled off the road away from traffic. The tires crunched as they bit into the crusty snow.

He jumped out of the car and rushed over to Sad's passenger door, jerked it open and dragged Sad's mother out of the car, across Sad. Her mother screaming as she fell out the door. Sad saw the dad jerk her up by the hair of her head and then he slammed the car door, blocking Sad's frightened eyes. But Sad's ears weren't blocked as she heard the screams and the hard hurtful sound of fist hammering bone. The screams that slammed through the dark sending the night creatures running for their lives. Sad wished she could run too.

They sat trembling and terrified inside the car, the cold and damp whimpering alongside them while they waited, not knowing what new horror the dastardly night might bring them next.

Evil brought its foul breath inside the car, when the dad opened the door and shoved her mother back inside.

The saturated smell of blood and alcohol made the inside of Sad's head turn red and black, black, black.

Black the night.

Black the silent bundle huddling unconscious beside her.

Black the color of guilt racing through Sad's veins.

Red the color of the snow left behind.

Red the color of the taillights in front of them as they entered the stream of cars, winding their way down the mountain.

White the halo of distant lights, inching towards the city.

My Favorite Christmas

There was a time when I liked the dad.
It was a Christmas in Oregon.
I was 11 years old.

When we left Texas, I still loved to hold baby dolls
and play like I was their mama.
I thought I was a good mom,
so I almost cried when we had to leave
all our toys behind.

Sometimes, I would roll up a towel,
hold it in my arms
and sing songs to it, pretenden it was my baby.
I knew deep down I was too old
to be still playing with dolls,
but sometimes I just couldn't help it.

I will never forget that Christmas morning.
When we woke up and ran to see what Santa
(I knew the truth, but the kids didn't)
put under the tree.

Well, the first thing I saw was a beautiful
hand-made, wooden baby bed with rockers
so you can rock a baby to sleep.

I stood stock still, knowing in my heart
that it had to be for my little sisters,
cuz I'm way too old for such things.
I wanna be happy for them,
but I sure did want that bed !

Little Sky Eyes ran to sit down beside it,
pushing it gentle to rock.
The dad said, "no, that's not for you,"
and then he turned
smiling at me.

I couldn't even believe it !
He built it with his own two hands.
Just for me!

I thought in my heart that maybe he did like me,
just a little bit.

A Day NOT to be Forgotten

March 19

Sorrow makes us all children again, destroys all difference of intellect. The wisest knows nothing.
~ Ralph Waldo Emerson ~

Sad rolled over slowly, thankful not to have any sisters still lying about in the bed with her. Fuzzy with sleep she struggled to recall what day it was. Saturday! Great! No school, no insulting glances thrown her way. She was the new girl, yet again. They had left Oregon in the middle of the night and, once again were living in New Mexico.

She still wondered about that quick getaway, as if they were fugitives on the run, leaving everything behind except a few clothes.

Sitting up, she stretched, luxuriously relishing these few stolen moments of time, smiling, thinking about yesterday and the boy who smelled so delicious.

She went over each little moment, playing in the back of her head like a love story on TV. The casual stroll down the street. Her headband placed just right; golden blond hair brushed until is shone like store-bought honey. The dab of cologne she had stolen from her mother's dresser, carefully placed behind each ear and a dot on each wrist as she had watched her mother do when she was going out. She ran out of the house before anyone could detect her newly scented skin or stop her to do a chore.

Sad had walked slowly down his street wishing fervently he would see her this time and perhaps even say something.

"If wishes were horses, beggars would ride." She recalled her mother saying this on numerous occasions. This saying always haunted her dream making.

Well, today let me be a beggar! She inhaled the sweet scent of honeysuckle growing wild along the fence line. His house fast approaching, she stopped to examine her reflection in a puddle from last night's rainstorm. Brown eyes flecked with green stared back. High cheekbones thanks to Nanny and the Cherokees, and a small pointed chin completed her face. She adjusted the headband once more and tugged at the too small T-shirt, faded and worn. Standing tall, she threw back her shoulders, sighing in exasperation at her fast-budding chest that was already a huge inconvenience and embarrassment. Most of the girls in school teased her, accusing her of stuffing; the boys staring at her in weird ways talking in whispers behind their hands.

He's never going to look my way. She thought about Chevonne and Delia with their fancy clothes and brand-new tennis shoes. She turned to go back home.

"Hey there! Where ya going?"

Startled, Sad whirled around and came face to face with him. She felt the quick heat spread across her face and chest and wished the ground would open up a hole and swallow her up.

"Ummm… I …. uhhhh… was just out for a walk. Looking for my brother," she answered with sudden inspiration.

"You're in Mr. Fredrick's math class, same as me, right?" he asked.

"Yes, yes that's right." She smiled, a little bubble of happiness floating inside her knowing that he had remembered.

She noticed the broad band of sprinkled freckles running like a marked path across his nose. His hair glistening and wet, stood straight up and stubby in a fresh crew cut. His eyes the smoky blue of a sky preparing for rain.

"C'mon, I'll help you." He said turning to walk next to her.

"Help me what?"

"Look for your brother," he chuckled.

Suddenly embarrassed at having been caught in the lie, she shuffled her feet, then thought better of it, not wanting him to notice her holey, old sneakers.

"Oh, he'll find his way back. He always does. Do you have any brothers or sisters?"

"Yeah, just one. An older brother, but he's a pain in the a- -," he stopped talking and glanced sideways at her.

"I know what you mean," she replied, smiling at him warmly, knowing he was feeling awkward at the near slip.

"C'mon then, I'll show you where I live instead. It's only two doors down."

"Okay," replied Sad, happy that he didn't know she had almost been stalking him.

They sat on his front steps talking about school and brothers and so many inconsequential things. She was thankful for the fresh spring breeze that constantly blew his masculine scent under her nose. A smell of spicy soap, fresh cut grasses and woods. The next hour was a heavenly 'beggar' moment to Sad. Knowing with dishes to do and siblings to watch she had been away too long, but the scent of him kept her glued to the steps, wanting to draw out the moments.

Reluctantly she stood. "I better head back."

He stood with her and looked deep into her eyes. They walked towards the gate and he followed her out to the sidewalk. Now it was him scuffling his feet, feeling awkward.

"You know," he said, "you have beautiful eyes."

Sad stopped and turned to stare at him, hardly believing what she heard.

Swiftly he leaned forward and kissed her! On the lips! Before she could react he turned and ran back through the gate, up the steps and into his house.

She didn't know what to say but sucked in the scent of him and then taking his lead, turned and fled up the street towards her house.

~♥~

Sad sighed, relishing those moments, then reluctantly jumped out of the bed, still dreamily thinking about that kiss. Her very first boy kiss! She touched her fingers to her lips deciding to put off washing her face just one more day. She pulled on her jeans and T-shirt and walked into the kitchen.

Scrounging in the sink looking for a dirty cup she could wash for a cup of coffee, she suddenly heard the murmur of angry voices coming from the next room. She sighed, feeling that old familiar sinking sensation. It settled like a solid lump of cold clay sitting squarely between her shoulder blades. Turning away from the sink feeling the tension thick as jam on a soggy piece of toast. It was too early for this. It usually came at night, rarely in the morning.

That's why the kids didn't wake her. They're hiding somewhere outside. She quickly fled to the bedroom to grab her tennis shoes, to go outside and check on them.

She had just pulled on her shoes when she heard the door slam. Loud! A signal and not a good one.

Jumping to her feet, she fled in that direction. Outside, the kids were playing in the dirt with a broken dump truck, but stopped, staring as their mother came bolting out the door. Sad opened the door to follow her out, the door silent in her wake.

"Get in the car," her mother said through clenched teeth.

The kids scrambled to their feet and looked at Sad expectantly.

Sad shivered. She heard the slurred speech, but it didn't make sense. It was morning! How could she already have slurred speech?

"I said, GET IN THE CAR!!! NOW!!!" Her mother screamed at them.

Like puppets on a string, all the children jumped up, and scrambled for the car. Sad looked fearfully at the door of the house, half expecting the dad to come running after them with a butcher knife.

Why else could there be such urgency to flee in the car? She jumped into the front seat as her siblings piled into the back. They were pulling out of the driveway when the dad opened the front door screen and peered out at them. He called out to their mother, demanding her to come back. Sad saw his clenched jaw and the look on his face was murderous. She had seen that look before. She saw it now, mirrored on her mother's face; her hands gripping the steering wheel.

Her mother peeled out of the driveway, churning gravel. The tires burned rubber shrieking their protest against the road. Sad quickly glanced in the back seat, peering into each little face, each pinched white and silent. They looked at Sad, question marks rising frightened above their heads.

Turning back around, she looked at her mother's hands, gripping the steering wheel, white knuckled. Tears were streaming down her face. Suddenly she started accelerating, letting go with one hand, beating her other against the wheel.

"What's the matter?" Sad asked quietly, reaching out a tentative hand to place it on her shoulder. "Mom, what's wrong?"

"WHAT'S WRONG, you say?" she shrugged off Sad's hand, shrieking the question back into her daughter's face.

Sad turned away and faced forward, watching the road more intently. She gasped terrified, when her mother veered into the ditch, still driving fast...even faster. Watching as they drove jaggedly through the ditches, their bodies jouncing hard against the seat. Then she turned the car, heading up the median driving straight at the approaching traffic. Cars swerved and honked, trying to get out of the way.

"MOM!" shouted Sad, "STOP the CAR! STOP IT NOW!"

Her mother ignored her and continued to careen madly forward, ranting as she raced towards oncoming cars. The faces of the people in the cars a mirrored reflection of their own, while scrambling in every direction.

Sad was clutching the window jamb with one hand, the other gripping the back of the seat. Loosening her death grip, she turned to make sure the kids were alright. They peered back at her, tears streaming down their faces. It seemed they had been in the car with her for hours, yet Sad knew it had only been moments.

Moments of precious life.

"What's WRONG?" muttered her mother. "All of you are what's wrong!" said her mother seething between tears. "It's all your fault, every single one of you!"

"What is Mom? Tell me, what have we done?" begged Sad.

"We're sorry, Mama."

"We're sorry, Mommy."

"We promise not to do it again." Tremulous pleas uttered from the little ones in the back.

Turning around, Sad shook her head at them, putting a finger to her lips, motioning them to remain quiet. She had to find a way out of this and needed their silence.

Her mother turned and headed into a residential area. Probably worried about cops following them, thought Sad.

"Mom, what did we do?" she asked again.

Her mother slowed to a stop, turning, looking straight at Sad.

"Not one of you," she sobbed, "not one of you…" she continued pounding the wheel. "Not one of you remembered my birthday."

Sad looked incredulously at her mother.

In the back seat, little voices piped up in unison.

"We're sorry Mama."

"Happy birthday Mommy!"

"We won't forget again. We love you Mommy."

While Sad's mother continued to sob pounding the steering wheel, the car was momentarily stalled in the middle of the street.

White hot rage screamed loud inside Sad's head. Her face carved in stone, she turned to her siblings in the back. "Get out of the car." They sat still, crying and shaking, snot running from their noses, leaving a snail's trail down their faces.

"GET OUT OF THE CAR NOW!" Sad screeched. "Quickly," she said, softening her tone.

Jumping out, she slammed the door with as much force as she could muster and began pulling them from the back seat, the littlest one barely clearing leather, before her mother put the car in gear and rolled a few feet forward.

Sad pulled the kids into a little shelter of her arms, patting and prodding as she herded them away in the direction of the nearest house.

Scared and shaking, they followed in silence, except for little hiccupping sobs, escaping from time to time.

With resolute steps, she marched up to the first house on the street. Standing tall beside them, clustered in the shade of her shadow, they watched the car now beginning to lurch forward.

Sad knocked loudly on the door.

A plump, white haired lady answered, her startled eyes asking questions of the group of children at her door.

"May I use your phone?" asked Sad politely. Seeing the doubt leap from the lady's eyes, she quickly added, "I need to call the police. Our mother is drunk and trying to kill us."

The lady looked down the street at the car driving jerkily away. Opening the door wide, she ushered them safe inside.

Sad walked inside, the cold, clammy cement that had rested between her shoulder blades that morning now a pendulum of guilt swinging heavy between her breasts at the thought of what she was about to do. She knew she would wear it forever.

Looking at the faces of her brothers and sisters, she quickly picked up the phone.

Goals Set in Stone

A sadness in those eyes like water seeping into
a hole you've dug in the earth.
~ Joyce Carol Oates ~

Sad could remember the day she chiseled out two goals for her life. She set them in stone. It was the same day she knew the name of her brother, the brown-eyed boy.

She saw them standing there.

The dad towering over his son. His face like a black thundercloud. His words like hailstones hurling down on the tousled black curls that crowned his son's head. The upturned look that framed the boy's delicate face, soot-black eyelashes circling chocolate brown eyes threw Sad backwards… to a moment, frozen in time.

It was many years ago when she was five and he was three; the look he gave her then haunted her through the years. Even now the memory clouded her face red with shame.

He had made her mad about something that day. She couldn't even remember why. Her body trembling with anger, her hand slashing out almost by itself, like a snake striking its victim, lashed out, striking him across the face. He looked at her then, with the same look he now had facing the dad.

She remembered his silky eyelashes wet with tears beginning a slow trek down his little face. Sad's heart had broken in two, then, not caring if their mom heard his cries or if she got into trouble. She only wanted to undo the hurt she had caused him. Reaching out, she crushed him to her chest, kissing away his pain, his tears.

She had never wanted to see that look again. Not on his face!

Not on anyone's face.

But there it was again.

Now.

Seven years later.

This time put there by the dad. The brown-eyed boy could no longer be called a boy, really. He was trying to learn the way of a man, ever struggling to find the way of things.

They stood in the distance. A tall man, leaning hard over the boy. The words hurled like stones about his head.

Black tendrils of hair dripping down his neck, wilting just over his collar as the words pelted down. His head bowed, thin shoulders hunched, and fingers dangling dejected towards his toes.

Not looking up.

Not saying a word.

Not crying this time.

Sad waited for the dad to stop. To reach out crushing the boy to his chest as Sad had done.

To kiss away the damage.

To soothe away the hurt.

Instead he turned and walked away.

Walked away from the damage he had done.

Sad knew as she stood there watching that it could never be undone.

The damage.

The hurt and the shame. The name.

It was permanent.

Set in stone.

Chiseled in his heart.

The words flew around like angry bees in search of a nest.

Never

    Amount

        to Anything

            Boy finally looked up.

He saw Sad standing there watching him.

He looked at her.

Looked at her with old man eyes in a broken boy's body.

Do-it-yourself Childhood

I didn't know
when I was a little girl
that there would come a day
that I would question my parents.

That I could and would
fall quite out of love with them.
That I would wish I could divorce them
and become an orphan.
That I might even feel hate towards them
and question each and every
decision they made.

I was little then and accepted
the grown-up responsibilities
that they decided I must carry.

I didn't know at the time
that it would mean
having a do-it-yourself childhood,
and sacrificing the art of play.

Doing grown-up chores and
making grown-up decisions
way before I was grown-up.

I didn't know that this
would mold me and shape me,
burn me and brand me
in so many ways
that later in life
I would continue trying to overcome
fears and habits instilled in me during
those years.

I didn't know that children
could have PTSD
and that no one would ever know.

The Choosing

*Loneliness and the feeling of being unwanted
is the most terrible poverty.*
~ Mother Teresa ~

Every little girl wants a father. A father that thinks the sun and moon sets in his little girl's eyes. A father that will look after her and protect her.

Sad knew that wasn't the case with her. She wasn't even sure if the dad liked her. She often resented him and thought he was a bit of a bully. Wondering why he did certain things, like kissing her on the lips the night they slept at the blind lady's house. Sad hated that kiss and was old enough to know it was weird.

He had taken the five of them to the blind lady's house the day after Sad put her mother in jail. Up until then, Sad hadn't even known about the blind lady's existence. *What were they doing here?*

The dad was impressed with how the woman cleaned her house. He told them how she swept the floor, barefoot, so she could feel crumbs and dirt on the floor.

When night slammed shut her eyes, Sad slept on the couch in the living room. She guessed the dad slept with the blind lady. It was on that same couch where the hateful kiss took place. Early morning. What was he thinking? Sad pushed him away. Gave him her dirty look! Scrubbed her arm hard across her mouth.

So, when the time came for *'the choosing'*, Sad had already made her choice. It wasn't a hard decision for her to make.

But it was so much harder for the others.

Extremely hard for the blue-eyed boy.

It happened on a sunny day when the sky was blue with white fluffy, cottontail clouds floating high above them. Better to be remembered as a sullen, sorrowful night when lightning streaks across the sky and thunder booms his reply. Better to be remembered like the parting of the Red Seas or *'stepping on a crack* **to** *break your mother's back.'*

Sad's mother was out of jail, but Sad could hardly look her in the eye. She thought there should be some way to make up for what she had done, for being the cause of her being put there. And now the parents were splitting up, going their separate ways.

There they stood.

Five kids lined up in the middle between the two parents.

Lined up like victims of a horrible holocaust.

Toeing the imaginary dotted line.

Worrying and waiting.

Fear slipping from their sweat like drips from a rainspout. Indecision making little toes twitch to a very unhappy beat.

They had to choose.

Which parent?

Who did they want to live with?

Who did they want to leave behind?

Sad knew she had to go with her mother. She knew someone needed to take care of her. Besides, she didn't really trust the dad. She was hoping the other kids would follow her.

Poor doe-eyed, *Little Bird* was next to make a choice. Tears trickling down her face when she stepped gingerly across the dotted line to join Sad. Stretching shaky little fingers towards *Sky Eyes,* the baby of the family, and to her brothers.

The dad shook his head and motioned for *Sky-Eyes* to join him. She didn't get to choose. Sad was puzzled about that.

Never Amount to anything boy was next. He needed to go with the dad. He knew the mom didn't really like him sometimes. Besides, it would even it out. Now with an opportunity to be the oldest child and the family divided, he would have a better chance.

A chance finally to be loved! To prove himself!

That left the blue-eyed boy. The one with wavy, sandy-colored hair, freckles sprinkling across a snubbed-up nose, his big blue eyes already filling with tears. He stood straddling the line. Torn tennis shoes bouncing from one foot to the other.

Squirming and wiggling like he had ants in his pants.

'I'm only eight,' he thought. *'Why do I have to choose?'*

Hurriedly wiping his face of tears lest the dad see a big boy crying.

He looked up at everyone. Everyone was waiting to see what he would do. The family already divided in half.

I have to choose, he thought, *but how?*

Indecision knitted his brow as he snuck a peek around him.

Can I leave my sisters and mom? I love them so much. But I love my brother, dad, and baby sister too. Sure, sometimes we fight, but don't all brothers fight?

How can I choose between them?

His shoulders slumped.

He knew they were waiting on him, but he could barely lift his head, feeling like the sheriff in a new town facing a pack of gunslingers in the OK Corral. There was nothing OK about this day! He turned to look at his mom.

He felt his tears start up again.

She was his refuge.

She didn't get mad at him for crying.

"Men don't cry!" his father had said.

In spite of the hard man he knew his father wanted him to be, he needed to cry sometimes. And his mother understood and loved him anyway. She often kissed away his tears even when the dad wanted him to be strong and brave.

So, should I choose her?

I'm a boy, should I go with the man? Isn't that the way everyone did it? When other families split in half, was that how they decided?

I don't know! I just don't know.

The back of his throat felt raw from swallowing so many tears. He knew his inside cheek was bleeding from where he had bit it. His teeth were clenched tight, shut. He could barely breathe and wished the floor would crack open like a mouth and gobble him up in one bite!

I have to decide!
Now!

Decide before he passed out on the floor and an ambulance came to pick up his dead body. *Would they care then? Care about the damage they had done?*

Would things be better for them when they split up?

Would there be less fighting.

Perhaps that was the one bright star on this dark and gloomy day.

Slowly he lifted his head. Looked at his father. Thought about his littlest sister standing there silent, not understanding what this was all about. *She reminded him of one of the baby bunny rabbits they found on Easter. Out of the ground running around without a mother or sister to protect her.*

He took a step towards them. Afraid to look back at the mother he loves or the two sisters he would leave behind.

Little Boy Blue walked across the line.
Facing forward, his hands clenched at his side.
Not looking back.

Knowing if he did it would bring the tears.
The tears he would no longer be allowed to cry.
Tears that had to remain inside him,
with no mother to kiss them away.

I will not leave you orphans;
I will come to you.
John 14:18 NKJV

APR . 56 
APR . 56

Okay,

This is how it is,
WE ARE TEENAGERS!!!
(Sad and me)

Danger, Danger,
look out boys!
I don't even need to tell you
how difficult and complicated
our life has become.

Sometimes I can't even tell where
she stops and I begin.
Sometimes I am more her
than me.
And every now and again
I allow her
to tell my stories because
it's the only way they will get told.

When the hurt is too deep
inside me
and a lump the size of Texas
is in my throat,
well….
I just can't see the pages
and I don't want them all soggy.

Besides, I believe she's a better
storyteller than me.

PART THREE

There are times when sorrow seems the only truth.
~ Oscar Wilde ~

The Teenage Years

Texas, Oregon

1. A Nest to Fit

2. Regular Kids

3. Things that go Bump and Baptists

4. Rattlesnake Soup

5. Pancakes and Paraphernalia

6. No Beer Allowed

7. A Dunk in Holy Water

8. A Dance in the Emerald Forest

9. O is for Oregon and P is for Pot

10. The House of No More Shadows

11. Doodle Rock Island

12. Things That Go Cold in the Night

13. Soldier Boy, oh my little soldier boy…

14. If Only and Alligator Bites

15. A Sister that Cries and a Suitcase that Flies

A Nest to Fit

There are as many nights as days,
and the one is just as long as the other
on the year's course. Even a happy life
cannot be without a measure of darkness,
and the word 'happy' would lose its meaning
if it were not balanced by sadness.
~ Carl Jung ~

I knew life would be different and times would be hard, but I didn't realize how much I would miss my brothers and little sister. Watching *Little Bird* sleeping peacefully in the only chair in our small apartment, I thought how her usual timid smile seemed to have flown away. Had she even smiled since the split?

Perhaps the separation was harder on her than me. *Little Bird* and *Sky Eyes* often band together when the boys were bent on bullying, but *Little Bird* also paired off with *Boy Blue* for an adventure or two. It's no wonder her usual sunny disposition seemed so cloudy. I pushed back the lock of hair covering her eyes and thought how the split had brought us closer.

Outside the night was tarry black, the lights in the city stealing the shine from the stars. Almost as if the night wore paint splattered cloak on an unfinished canvas.Perhaps that is what I am feeling. Hopeless. I complain about being a big sister, often fantasizing about what it would be like to be an orphan, but this new lack of responsibility was unsettling to me, making me feel fidgety, with too much time and not enough to do. Cooking and cleaning up after the three of us wasn't hard, though there wasn't much to cook, because the leftovers Mom brought home from the restaurant seemed to be our main food source. Just thinking about those yeasty rolls was making me drool, but still…

I miss hearing *Sky Eyes* giggle and *Boy Blue's* constant teasing. I even miss *Never Amount's* awkwardness. I miss the constant motion of them, trying to stop their daily battles. But one thing I will never miss is the battle between the grown-ups. It's much easier to deal with one drunken parent than two.

Hearing a sudden noise, I held my breath. Being in charge was unsettling. What if someone breaks in? Thankfully it was just Mom.

"I see you're still up. Is your sister asleep?"

"Yeah, she's in the chair and I didn't have the heart to wake her."

"Okay. I'll put her to bed."

"How was work?"

"It wasn't busy tonight, so the tips weren't great. I think we'll have to find another place to live. It's too expensive here."

"Oh," I paused on the way to the kitchen with the bags Mom brought in, sniffing to catch a whiff of yeasty rolls, "if we have to move, can it at least be somewhere where we can see the stars at night?"

Mom paused by window and looked out, "Why, I think that's a great idea!"

I smiled back, happy to hear praise and feel included in her plans. Just before I opened the bag of leftovers, I had a weird thought. Could she be as unhappy as Little Bird and me?

I guess we were all a bit like little birds flying around to find a nest that fit.

"Oh, my goodness, will you look at the size of these sunflowers!" I couldn't believe how big they were. My entire hand was dwarfed next to them.

"I know! I've never seen any this big! Can we eat the seeds?" asked *Little Bird*.

"I don't know. We have to make sure this field doesn't belong to anyone, and then I have to learn how to cook them."

We were out exploring the streets around our new little house in the country. It wasn't really the country, but at least it was in a one-horse town, so it felt like the country. There were lots of trees and open fields and even a drive-in movie theater right down the street!

It took Mom only two weeks to find the perfect place for us. It was further for her to drive to work, but the school was within walking distance for *Little Bird* and I can take the bus to the Junior High in the city. The house was small, but just right for the three of us.

I stole a sideways look at *Little Bird* and smiled. Her eyes were crinkly, and her giggles reminded me of a springtime shower on fresh flowers.

We cheerfully waved at the neighbor who lived down the street as we passed by. Recently she had shown us a fig tree in her yard explaining that we had one in our yard as well. I had never heard of a fig, much less a fig tree, but was always excited, discovering new things! I had learned that from the dad, to *always be willing to try new things*, even if it was a nasty ol' octopus. Which was what we tried when he said that to us.   So, the first time I bit into the soggy, sweet fruit, I thought, it's okay if there isn't any other fruit around. Or maybe if we were extra hungry. Now I knew why I didn't really like Fig Newtons!

"Hey, let's walk to the drive-in and see what's playing tonight? Maybe Mom will give us some money to see a show!"

"Okay!" said *Little Bird*. "I'll race ya!" She put one foot in front of the other, getting ready to take off running.

"On your mark, one, two..." I sped away, laughing at her complaints trailing behind me.

"No fair, you cheated," she said, laughing at my prank.

There was nobody manning the booth for the drive-in theater, so we walked right on in to have a look around. I was hoping there would be a merry-go-round and swings like the drive-in we went to when I was a kid and the dad was a fireman. We had some happy times back then, but I shoved that thought right out of my mind. I didn't want to think about the time when we were a whole family and not a half of one.

"Hey look, this is different!" I was standing under the awning of an outdoor seating area next to the concession stand. The wooden seats were connected together all in rows and a large awning sheltered the audience from rain. "The theater we went to before didn't have this."

Little Bird looked over but was more interested in checking out the swings.

I heard some chatter in the distance and noticed three other kids about my age heading our way. Nervous butterflies were flapping around inside me and I was hoping they were friendly. After all, it would be great to have someone my age to talk to.

While waiting, I was checking them out from the corner of my eye but pretending to study the stands. There were two boys, one blond and one redhead with a dark headed girl walking between them. Their walk made me think they were acting as if they owned the place.

"Hello," said the girl taking the lead. "I'm Julie and this is Alex," she nodded to the blond. Then she turned towards the redhead boy, "and this is Earnest but we call him Stretch. We all go to school together, but I don't think we've ever seen you before."

"We just moved here," I replied, introducing my little sister and myself. *Little Bird* had rushed up and now stood solemnly beside me.

"Most people think this is a dead-end town, but it's not really a bad place to live," said Alex.

I thought Alex was kinda cute but blushed when he kept staring. "I'm sure we'll like it okay. Do you come here often? We were just checking everything out."

"Sure, we do," said Stretch, "only thing to do in Dullsville." He kicked at a dirt clod then bent over, grabbed a rock and hurled it at the fence.

Julie smiled and turned her back on Stretch, "so where do you live?"

"Do you know that little blue house down the road right before the end? We just moved in this weekend. Our mom works in town."

"Oh yeah, I know exactly where you mean. It's been empty a few months. I live one street over."

"That's great! It will be good to know someone when school starts. Well, I guess we should head back."

"We'll walk with you," replied Julie. Alex and Stretch quickly fell into place.

When they passed the tall sunflowers bending low under the weight of seeds, Sad remembered *Little Bird's* request. "These sunflowers are fantastic and humongous! I didn't know they grew this tall. Do you know who owns them?" I asked, turning towards Julie.

"Only God and Texas!" answered Alex. We all laughed and then Julie said, "That's right and just wait till you taste them roasted and salted!"

"So, we can pick them? Julie, will you tell me how to cook them?"

"Sure, it's simple! Here, let's pick some now and I'll show you."

Sad and *Little Bird* pulled a batch of roasted sunflower seeds out of the oven just as their mother walked in the door.

"Well look at this," she exclaimed, sniffing the air, "Where did you get these?"

"Just down the road. We picked them ourselves, want to try some?" I asked.

"Maybe later, I'm going to change and go out again."

"How are you feeling?" I said remembering her recent car accident. "Do you have to go back to work? Why are you leaving so soon?"

"No, I don't have to go back to work," she said giving me a look which meant shut-up and mind my own business.

"Guess what? We met some kids about my age and they want to know if we can meet them at the drive-in theater tonight. Do you have enough tips so we can go?" I was hoping that since she was *going out* she would feel guilty and more willing to fork over some cash.

"Sure, I guess so, just be sure to watch your sister."

"Oh Mom, don't I always?"

"I'm a big girl," piped up *Little Bird*. Her eyebrows were bunched up like thunderclouds, her big brown eyes looking like a storm approaching. She put her hands on her hips and said, "I can watch myself!"

"I'm sure you can, but I need you to keep an eye on your big sister as well."

I started to protest, then changed my mind, gratefully accepting the dollar bills and loose change she handed me. Stuffing them in my jean pocket, I looked at the clock. We would barely have enough time.

"C'mon," I said to *Little Bird*, "if we race we can get there before the cartoons."

We beat feet and headed down the street.

I looked up once then stopped still in my tracks. It was quite heavenly to see the stars shining like little beaming beacons guiding our path. A delicious shiver ran through me and I felt thankful to be out of the city and running down the road by star-shine.

We made it to the theater just as Road Runner was trying to out-bird Wile E. Coyote. Remembering that it was the dad's favorite cartoon, I hoped it wouldn't remind *Little Bird* of everything we left behind. Perhaps she didn't know it was his favorite. I followed her just to make sure and we sat on the merry-go-round, pushing it around with our feet, eyes glued to the big screen. The playground area was right up close to the screen and it was uncomfortable tilting my neck so far back to watch the movie.

"Do you want to go sit in the stands with me?"

"No, I think I'll stay and play awhile." I could tell by the sound of her voice she was thinking about the other half of us. "I'll stay here with you, if you want." I looked over at the chairs, but it was too dark to see if Julie, Stretch or Alex was there. "How bout I push you on the swings?"

"Okay." she said and jumped up.

I pushed her until all the cartoons and previews came to an end. Finally, I felt like my big sister duty was done. "Hey, I'm going to go sit down and watch the show. I'll be right over there and can still see you. Look, why don't you go meet some of those kids on the merry-go-round? When you get tired of playing, come find me. I think I've got enough change to get us popcorn."

"Okay," replied *Little Bird,* looking doubtful towards the group of kids.

I left knowing she was shy and probably wouldn't initiate a conversation, but I wanted to see if my new friends were here.

It was still too dark to see in the rows of chairs beyond the first set of seats. I didn't want to look stupid standing there peering into the dark, so I took a seat in the middle of the first row where I could see the playground.

The seats were wooden but felt oddly comfortable like hundreds of bottoms had worn them smooth and snuggly. The scent of popcorn from the nearby concession stand tickled my nose and made my stomach growl. We really hadn't had much to eat that day, a fig or two and sunflower seeds about summed up our meals.

I looked up at the screen just in time to see a car being chased, swerve wildly then fly into the air flipping over onto its side. What was this movie? I realized that I hadn't bothered to look at the title on the sign in front of the theater. Staring at the upside-down car, my thoughts went right to where I had been trying to keep from going all week. The memory I didn't want to think about. Not here. Not now. It was hard to believe it had only happened a week ago.

We had gone to our aunt's house for the weekend. She lived a few towns away, and I was there to babysit my cousin while mom moved our stuff into the new house. Then she would return to get us in a couple of days.

I remembered the knock at the door. There was a cop standing at the door and I felt a lump as big as Texas form in my stomach. Somehow, I knew that he wasn't an ordinary cop, definitely not the kind you can send your little sister to get help from. This was a bad one, with small beady eyes and a huge beer belly that covered the belt he didn't need to wear. Those pants weren't going anywhere! His belt buckle was swallowed up whole by his gut. He wore a white cowboy hat. Did he think it would fool folks? After all, only good guys wore white cowboy hats. My shoulders tensed waiting for whatever blow he came to deliver.   I didn't speak, just stared back at him like he was an alien from the planet Mars. Though I don't think Mars would want him either.

He stood silent as well, staring at me, his beasty eyes moving up and down my body like he was looking for a tasty snack.

"Yes," I finally said, forcing steel into my voice.

"Are you the daughter of," he asked, using my mother's full name. Fear clawed at my throat and I found it difficult to swallow. So, I just nodded.

He waited another moment, looking at me with that greedy glint in his eye. "Well I'm here to tell you she's been involved in an accident," and then as if he had just given the weather report, he turned and strolled off the porch toward the police car in the driveway.

"But… Wait!" I called. "Is she okay? Where is she?" He didn't even turn around and I hated him like I had known him forever.

I barely recall the next few hours. Somehow between my aunt, and me, we found out where mom was being treated. We were told she had fallen asleep at the wheel on her way to come get us, and plowed into another car, totaling the one she drove. Her injuries included a cracked rib, a slight concussion and deep bruising where she bumped against the steering column. Sliding into the floorboard under the dashboard had probably saved her life. She only stayed one night in the hospital, then came to get us the next day.

Secretly, I wondered if she had been drunk and passed out, but I didn't want to think bad thoughts about her when she was in the hospital and in pain. We would have more problems to deal with now because she didn't have any insurance.

She just has to get better I thought, feeling selfish for thinking about myself. I just couldn't bear the thought of living with the dad again. Mom wasn't half bad when she didn't drink and maybe we could get the other kids back somehow.

Sighing deeply, I was jolted back to the present when I heard giggling behind me. Turning, I saw Julie's smiling face! Stretch and Alex were sitting right next to her.

"We wondered when you'd notice us," said Julie, "you were really spaced out with that car scene!" She laughed, "By the way … he wants to ask you something," she nudged Alex, "don't you Alex?"

Alex glared at Julie but smiled at Sad. "I was uh… just wondering if you minded if I uh…"

"Oh puh…leese!" said Julie. "He's wants to know if he can sit by you?"

"Well sure, I guess, but I probably should go check on my sister. Oh, I see her!" I waved at *Little Bird* while Alex jumped over the seat and settled in next to me.

"Well, I'm glad you made it tonight," said Alex, "want some popcorn?"

"Nah, thanks! I'm going to get some later when my sister gets here. It's nice of you to offer though." My heart was jumping in my chest while I searched for something to say.

"No problem. Do you like the movie?"

"Yes, well…uh, it's great." I hoped he wouldn't ask me anything else about it because I still didn't know what we were watching.

"It's great to be out of the house for a change."

"Yeah, I know what you mean. There's not a lot of action around here."

"Well, I bet you're happy to have this theater!" I replied, hoping the dark would cover my flaming face. Talking wasn't very easy with the movie blaring and trying to keep a lookout for *Little Bird*. Even though my heart was doing flip-flops, inside I was smiling.

Suddenly, feeling something nudge my left arm, I turned to see what it was, then jerked back around, my face flooding with heat when I realized Alex had put his arm around me. I heard muffled snickering behind us and suddenly felt embarrassed. Were Julie and Stretch laughing at us? I didn't know what to feel. Honored? Embarrassed? Indignant? It was the first time a boy had put a move on me, and I sat there feeling a swarm of strange emotions.

Thankful for the distraction, *Little Bird* came running up and plopped down next to me. I was secretly relieved when Alex quickly removed his arm.

"I'm ready for some popcorn now!" announced *Little Bird*.

"Okay! Let's go get it." Turning to Alex, I smiled, "We'll be right back."

Later that night with *Little Bird* settled in bed, I lay in the dark trying to figure out that weird mixture of emotions when Alex put his arm around me. I was flattered by the attention, but in another way it bothered me. *Why?* Perhaps because I didn't really know him very well. I felt like he was doing it on a dare instead of knowing who I was and really liking me. *Well, he won't get the chance to do it again until I decide if I like him.*

Satisfied, I turned over and tried to sleep. I was just drifting off when I heard a car door slam, and then another. The sound of two car doors alarmed me. Sitting up in bed, ready to get up and check it out, I heard Mom laugh. Followed by the deep rumble of a male voice.

Hearing them enter the house, I laid back down pretending to sleep. I had left my bedroom door open and now heard someone close it quietly. Sitting up, I felt my heartbeats quicken and felt totally ticked off at her. What is she doing bringing a man home? Perhaps he's just dropping her off because she drank too much. Lying back down, I closed my eyes. It was quieter now. What could they be doing? Then I heard bedsprings squeak and unmistakable noises. Gross! Noises I didn't want to hear.

I put my pillow over my head hoping to drown them out, but suddenly heard a gasp of pain. That brought me back up, listening intently. There it was again, another gasp, a cry of pain, then Mom's voice crying out, "Stop! You're hurting me! Stop now!"

Leaping out of bed, I threw my door open and ran into her bedroom. A man was on top of her as she gasped and cried out in pain.

Smashing my fist against the door, I yelled, "Stop! You're hurting her! Leave her alone or I'll call the cops!"

The man stopped immediately shocked that anyone else was in the house. I raced out the front door searching for a place to hide. Running to the scrubs that bordered the house, I crouched down waiting to make sure he left before I went to call the cops.

Only a moment later he ran out the front door, buttoning his pants. He looked left, then right, before jumping in his car and speeding away.

I collapsed on the ground feeling like my legs were made of mush. My heart was pounding, and I could actually feel it thumping inside of me. Thank God, Mom is safe. My sister is safe. Still trembling head to toe when Mom came to the front door calling for me, but I didn't answer. I was absolutely furious! What kinda mother puts us in danger with some jerk like that? What if he comes back? Besides, Mom sounded mad. She's probably drunk, and I just didn't feel like dealing with her right now, so I waited in the dark trying to decide what to do.

The cicadas and the whippoorwills were the only witnesses to my stifled sobs. As the night crept along, the moon with her audience of stars were trekking a slow crawl across the night sky. Immune to my pain.

Feeling steady enough to stand, I finally decided the car wasn't coming back. I hadn't heard a noise from the house and decided to go check on them. Stealing softly into our bedroom, I could see my little sister hadn't moved, still sleeping in the same position as before. *Little Bird* slept the sleep she deserved. Now I was so thankful the playground had worn her out and she wouldn't have another bad memory to add to the others.

I went to look for my mother. She was passed out on the commode. The scent of blood and alcohol assaulted my senses and I stumbled away from the door. Dark ribbons of memories flooded my head, and I felt faint standing outside the bathroom door.

Turning, I fled from the house out into the uncomplicated night, running up the street, without a direction. The cocoon of darkness enveloped me now, making me feel safe, even though the stars and moon hid their faces from me. Almost as if they too felt the shame. I felt so alone. Walking down the road, angrily brushing away my tears, white, hot rage feeding the anger churning inside my guts. Furious at my mother! Furious with God, with everyone and everything! I couldn't figure out where to go or what to do. The scent of blood might mean she is seriously hurt, but what can I do? I don't want to call the cops. Again. The guilt of the other time still haunted me.

Also, remembering the last cop I met didn't give me any hope for help. So I ran down the street and stopped in front of the house of the fig tree lady. Trying to decide what to do. A light was on in her house. Could she be up at this time of night? I had no clue what time it was. Time seemed to have stopped and I felt like this night would never end. Taking a deep breath and before I could change my mind, I walked as if in a dream up the stairs to knock on the door. Taking in deep breaths of the cool night air, I tried to stop shaking and crying before she answered.

The fig tree lady looked out the window, then quickly opened the door. "What is it, dear? Please come in and tell me what's wrong."

With a sigh of relief, I stepped inside, knowing I couldn't tell her everything, but just enough so she would check on my mom and make sure she was okay. To my horror, I found myself sobbing out the whole terrible story. At the end all I could say was, "Would you please go check on her?"

"Do you think we should call the police?" asked the lady.

"No. I am sure he's gone. I just don't know if my mother is okay."

"Okay dearie, let's go."

"I don't want to go inside with you ma'am. I'm afraid my mother will be mad at me for coming to get you. If you don't mind, I'll just wait outside while you check on her."

"All right, whatever you say."

I waited outside while the woman went in, knots kneading my shoulders as the knowledge hit me that I was a coward and a traitor.

After a time the fig tree lady came out and walked up to me, "She'll be fine now, she's just bruised up a bit. I have her settled in bed."

I swallowed the lump in my throat and nodded.

"You did the right thing y'know. I'm sure your mother loves you."

Thanking her, I watched her walk down the road to her house. I lingered outside watching the dark, wishing for the comfort of the moon and her captive stars.

People seemed to be always telling me that my mother loved me, but in my heart, I knew that I didn't believe them. How can she do the things she does and still love me?

The little blue house stood there all aglow, with every light turned on inside. It had been a nice little nest for a while, but I knew we wouldn't stay. Perhaps that's why birds have wings.

They are
only meant to fly.

Regular Kids

In our sad condition, our only consolation is the expectancy
of another life. Here below all is incomprehensible.
~ Martin Luther ~

I sat on my bottom with my back pushed against the round, steel wall. A single ray of sunshine poured through the small opening above me, spreading out like liquid gold glazing the few strands of straw scattered on the floor. Like strands of gold waiting for Rapunzel to pick up and sew into a shiny rope in which to escape her tower.

Opening my arms, I pressed the palms of my hands behind me, pushing against the grain bin's circular steel wall. It felt wonderful. Silent. Cold. Safe. When I looked back up at the sunshine, I sneezed. The noise exploded, echoing within the walls. I wanted to laugh but remained quiet.

There were grains of seed scattered on the floor as well. Seed and straw were all that was left behind. Being alone with grains of the earth was a nice feeling. Yes, this suits me just fine. It's always a luxury to be alone with my thoughts and I knew it wouldn't be long before they found me.

Inside this circle, I can be whatever I want to be, sad with no one to tell me to smile, happy and not share the reason why. I can cry and let the tears and snot run from my nose without worrying about questions, or dream of a life far away from them.

A different life.

One with regular meals in a regular bed sitting at a regular table.

A life where my stomach won't seize up with worry and knot into an angry fist that doubles me over in pain.

A life where I can have a chance to become anything.

Perhaps the writer I know I'm meant to be, or a mother with two boys and two girls and a husband kind and gentle who tells grand jokes that makes us throw back our heads and scream out loud with laughter. A man who sits at the supper table with us smiling as he listens to our problems that day. Yes, anything is possible inside this hard hunk of steel.

Outside, life is much different.

"There you are!" I heard the little voice pipe above me, "Can we come down?"

I looked up and saw the freckled face of *Sky Eyes* peering down at me. I knew *Little Bird* would be close behind her. They had been inseparable since the family had gotten back together.

"Sure, but first see if y'all can find an old wooden box or something that will make it easier to get in and out of here. Tell the boys to help look for one."

"Okay!" she said running off to search and relay the message.

Fantasy time was over. This huge, empty grain bin behind the house is the only positive thing about the new shack we were calling home. Come to think of it, *home* is stretching it a bit too far. This house has to be a hundred years old and miles from town and without indoor plumbing. I hated it already, having to use that stinky old outhouse. But at least we have running water so I can wash my hair, I thought, always trying to look for that elusive silver lining.

I figure they'll have to buy an old wash tub for us to take baths in and I hope we can keep clean enough for school. With Junior High starting in two weeks we'll have to ride the school bus to town. I was determined to find a way to fit in with regular kids who lived regular lives.

"We found one," hollered *Boy Blue*. I reached up to grab the wooden crate he handed down.

"This is perfect!" I said and was rewarded with his quick, quirky smile.

"We're coming down now."

I watched as one by one the kids lowered themselves into the bin, balancing on the wooden crate before jumping onto the floor.

"You're right," said *Sky Eyes*, "this is easier."

Once they were all inside, I sat back down in my spot. They each found their own space with their backs up against the wall. Now we were sitting in a circle facing each other.

"This is great!" smiled *Never Amount*.

"A regular clubhouse," agreed *Boy Blue*.

"Our own secret hideout," whispered *Little Bird*.

"I wish we could live in here forever," piped *Sky Eyes*. I laughed and so did they. We were all just happy to be together again and safe.

"This is the perfect place to tell ghost stories. Once it gets dark," I winked.

Little Bird shivered and *Sky Eyes* looked nervous, but the boys nodded in agreement.

"But what are we going to do till then? Asked *Never Amount.*

In unison four sets of eyes turned to look at me.

⇆ ⇄

School started before we had hardly blinked and our sheltered days spent in our clubhouse were numbered. The first ride on the school bus, I got up extra early for the hour ride to town. Our house was one of the first stops, so I studied the boys and girls as they climbed aboard wearing brand new clothes and shoes. I hoped they wouldn't notice that my clothes weren't new. Besides, it didn't really matter. There's been a few times when we had money for new clothes and school supplies, this just isn't one of them.

Better to remember those days and be thankful for the things I have now. No use crying over spilt milk like Nanny would say. I cocked my head to one side, trying to puzzle out if that's the right saying for this particular situation.

One thing I was thankful for was that Nanny lived in town and hopefully we could see her more often. My aunt, uncle and little cousin also lived near them. The last time I babysat for them, my uncle gave me a Louis Lamour book to read. I read it in two days and could hardly wait to borrow another. I loved his stories about Indians and Cowboys and days spent on the trail. I was learning valuable things like never to sit with my back to the door and never to stare into the fire when out on the trail.

I was hoping that someday I could meet a man like Louis Lamour. He believed everyone was equal, the Indians just as good as the Cowboys. He even mentioned other books that I wanted to read by authors named Shakespeare, Yeats, and Thoreau. People I'd never heard about and he talked about the Bible a whole lot too! I was learning from his books how to be a better person, and since I wanted to write, I thought that perhaps it would help me learn to write better just by reading his books.

The dad had done one thing right by moving us closer to kin. Even if it was to a house without a bathroom. Ever since he had come back to Mom, I tried not to treat him with the cold shoulder, but it was hard sometimes. Anger seemed to boil up inside me like a beast with a burning fever when I least expected it. Just last night while I was spooning beans into bowls for the kids, I turned to look at my mom and said, "Why can't we eat around a table like a regular family?" I was thinking about *Father Knows Best* and *Leave it to Beaver*. They always sat around a table and talked.

My mother just gave me a dirty look and I was quick to return it. I was always giving them dirty looks and getting scolded a lot, but I REALLY DIDN'T CARE!

Besides, most of the time I felt more comfortable at school with the regular kids and regular adults. I had classes to attend, a locker to keep my things inside, all neat and tidy, and a hot lunch in the middle of the day.

Hmmmm…. I guess school was a bit like the grain bin, only larger and I had to share it with more people.

Things That Go Bump and Baptists

Sorrow and joy have the same Lord.
~ Charles Reign Scoville ~

The relationship between my mother and me was not improving. I felt I had slipped on a gravelly road and was forever picking bits of dirt and rock from my skin. Pieces of flesh that used to be a part of me with names like respect, trust, and love now plucked out and discarded. I didn't have the necessary iodine or Band-Aids to make it better. And if I did have a Band-Aid, would I even bother pulling off the protective slip to apply it?

The relationship between her and the dad had improved, however. The best part is: HIP, HIP, HOORAY, we are moving to a house in town!!!

Pulling into the driveway of the new house, I could hardly believe my eyes. A regular house! I was so excited running inside with the kids, all of us ignoring our parents calling out to grab something to help unload.

I HAD to get first dibs on the best room and raced upstairs. Wow! I stood at the upstairs landing looking around in amazement. A whole bathroom upstairs just for the kids and me! Heavens to Betsy, I could hardly believe our luck and quickly checked out each of the three bedrooms.

I knew at once which one I wanted. It was a room with two windows letting in plenty of light and overlooking the driveway so I would know who came to visit. What luxury to have a room all to myself!

Twirling happily, I listened to the excited chatter of the kids arguing over the other two rooms.

I ran out to join them, "C'mon, let's go help them unload our stuff," I peered into each excited face, "isn't this house cool?"

"I love it here already!" said *Little Bird*.

"We've got the whole upstairs to ourselves!" exclaimed *Boy Blue*.

"No more stinky outhouse," said *Never Amount* coming out of the bathroom.

"Yeah except when you come out of it," replied *Boy Blue* and then dodged the punch aimed at him.

Sky Eyes giggled and went hopping down the stairs singing, "Yippee, skippy, do-dah."

"I'm so happy that I don't have to ride that dumb school bus anymore! I can walk to school," I said.

"Aunt and Uncle only live a few blocks away so you can walk over there to baby sit for them too," nodded *Little Bird*.

"That's right! I think this is the perfect house for us. I hope we never have to move again."

Everyone agreed and we rushed out to help unload the truck.

The rest of the house was perfect, too. There was a large master bedroom off the living room with a bathroom and huge walk-in closet. The kitchen, dining and living room were large and roomy. The dining room had floor to ceiling glass doors, but they didn't open up to anything. I thought that maybe now we could sit down and eat at a table like a regular family since we had such a fine house.

There wasn't much of a yard out front and the back had a deep gully running behind it that shortened the yard, so not much room for the kids to run and play, but I didn't think they would mind. Right next door was a grocery store, which made me think that since the dad could afford to rent this fancy house, we might have more money to spend on food.

The only thing I didn't like about the house was that to reach the upstairs, we had to tromp through the master bedroom. Whoever set it up that way was kinda stupid, but all in all, I loved everything else.

School had been great lately! I was making lots of friends and a couple of boys had asked me to go steady with them. That really just meant we liked each other. I mean, it's not like I can go out if they ask me, because the parents said I couldn't date until I was sixteen. I didn't care about dating anyway but argued that I was mature for my age. It seemed like we were always arguing about something.

A few nights after we settled in, the parents decided to go out on the town meaning I was stuck with the kids while they went off drinking somewhere.

I didn't really mind because I could put on some music, my kind of music, and have the house all to myself after the kids went to bed. I was listening to *Paint it Black* by the Rolling Stones. I owned a few of their 45's and wanted to hear them first and save my favorite record by the Monkey's for last.

I sat down on the couch and drew my legs up beside me. I was thinking about Joey, the cute guy I had decided to go steady with, when I heard a loud thump. I almost jumped out of my skin. I didn't think the noise came from upstairs, but it seemed to echo all around the room.

I held my breath, my ears straining to hear and suddenly nervous about those glass doors in the dining room. They didn't open but made me feel exposed, so I turned to look in that direction. I couldn't believe what I was seeing! The doorknobs on the glass doors were turning back and forth like someone was trying to get inside.

Goose pimples popped out all over me, dancing around like Mexican jumping beans! I was wondering if the hair on my head was standing straight up as well. My breath was caught in my chest and my body frozen to the couch. All I could think was, what could I do if someone comes through those doors? How will I protect us?

Looking frantically around for anything I could use as a weapon, wishing fervently for a baseball bat, I knew I didn't have time to run upstairs and search. A kitchen chair stood between the door and me so that wouldn't work. I felt exposed with all the lights on in the house and windows all around me. Without a plan or a hope against whatever was out there, I silently prayed for God to protect us.

The Rolling Stone's weren't *painting it black* any longer and the silence was eerie. Nothing more happened, but I couldn't move from my spot, and sat there like a piece of petrified wood until the parents finally walked in the door. I was so relieved to see them that I didn't even care how much they had to drink.

They looked surprised to see me sitting there. "I thought you'd be in bed by now," said Mom.

"Is everything all right?" said the dad. "You look weird."

"I am so glad you're home. You'll never believe what happened!" I quickly told them everything.

"How long ago did this happen?" asked the dad.

"Maybe 45 minutes to an hour ago."

"I'll go outside and take a look around."

My mother and I just stared at each other, waiting for him to return, breathing much easier when he came back in.

"I didn't see anything," he said. "Why don't you go on up to bed?"

I was more than happy to hand over the responsibility and started up the stairs to my room. Behind me I heard him say something in a lowered voice to Mom that stopped me in right in my tracks and made goose pimples jump across my skin again.

"Those two doors don't have any knobs on the outside. The knobs are only on the inside," he said. "She must have been imagining things."

The hair on the back of my neck was a reminder that I hadn't imagined anything. Walking into each of the kid's rooms to check on them, I knew sleep would be a long time coming. Nor would it be the last time our family would be counting goose pimples.

****

Sitting sullen and silent on the mattress on the floor, I stared out at the gray, ugly fields and scraggly mesquite trees that lifted their bare branches as if imploring God for a taste of warmth and color.

Gray grass, gray trees, seems like the cows grazing off to my right should be gray as well. They half-heartedly foraged, searching for one spot of green in this ugly, cold world of winter.

I hate January! And I wasn't any too happy about moving back into the country and leaving our nice house. So, what if the house in town was haunted? At least it was in town! And the ghost hadn't laid a single bony finger on any of us. Why couldn't we just share it with him? Or her? Probably a him though, since he liked to peek in at mom in the tub and open closed bathroom doors. He also liked making a ruckus upstairs, so the dad thought the kids were up and playing around.

I thought it was kinda funny, myself. Besides, I knew that God was stronger than Superman, so I figured He was in control of the ghosts as well. The way I look at it is, any visitors I can't see are much easier to deal with than the ones I can see who have too much beer in them.

My bedroom at this house isn't anything like the pretty, little bedroom left behind; it was more of a half room, really. The best things about it were the three tall windows that spilt light inside to warm my mattress. I didn't even need to put a blanket up to cover the windows because the road was a ways off so no one could see inside from there.

I did put up a blanket for privacy, hanging between me and the girl's room, the blanket acting like a door. Their room was large enough for an old iron post bedstead, but I preferred my mattress on the floor.

"Knock, knock," called *Little Bird,* tapping on my imaginary door.

"Who's there?"

"Orange."

"Orange who?" I said half-heartedly, already having heard this joke 100 times.

"Orange you going to let me in?" she said, busting out laughing.

I pulled back the curtain and looked at her. Little sisters were so annoying sometimes. "What do you want?"

"The boys wanted me to ask you if you were going to fix breakfast."

I glanced at the little alarm clock next to my bed and saw it was already after eleven o'clock. Our mother rarely got up before noon, so on the weekends, I usually try to rustle up something for us to eat. "Oh, all right, I'll be there in a minute, but someday one of you is going to have to learn to cook. I'm not gonna stick around forever!"

I threw back the curtain, walked through their bedroom, down the hallway and into the kitchen. Without looking, I already knew what food was left in the fridge. One can of Pillsbury biscuits looking pretty lonely, but they wouldn't have time to be lonely for long because they were today's breakfast!

On the other side of the kitchen was the entrance to the laundry room and the boys slept in there. *Boy Blue* poked his head around the corner. "Whatcha making?"

"Something good." My bad mood was drifting away and my mouth already watering at my plan. "Climb up on the counter and get me the Crisco."

"Okay," he said and hopped up quicker than you could say 'jiminy cricket'. My brothers always move at lightning speed when food is involved. "Here," he said, handing down the can of Crisco.

"Before you jump down, see if there's any Hershey's cocoa up there?"

He quickly found the can and handed it over, enjoying his monkey stance on top of the counters, but before he could start swinging from the curtains, I made him get down.

Plopping big spoons full of Crisco in the pan, I turned on the heat and picked up the can of biscuits.

"Wait, I wanta pop it open," he pleaded, turning those baby blues my way.

"Oh all right."

"Are you making what I think you're making?" he asked.

"I don't know, what do you think I'm making?"

"Donuts?" His eyes lit up and his smile was hopeful.

"Yep."

"Whoopee!" he shouted, and they all piled into the kitchen at the sound of excitement. They stood around watching me put a hole in a biscuit with my finger and stretch out the dough, careful not to tear it, then plop it into the hot grease. It only took seconds for each donut to cook and I was careful not to undercook them. I had learned the hard way once before and we had to eat some doughy donuts.

Once the donuts were cooked, I tossed them into a bag of cocoa and powdered sugar so we could have chocolate donuts. This was the first time I had thought of using the cocoa and the kids were delighted. There were ten biscuits so we each got two apiece and secretly I was glad mom stayed in bed, so we didn't have to share. We went outside with our donuts to sit on the front porch.

I was thinking about the poem I had been working on for my writing class. It was personal, though, and I wasn't sure I could share it with the other students or the teacher.

Looking up I noticed the sun had pulled through the clouds and the day was finally warming. We didn't even need a jacket today. Living in Texas, you could sometimes play with your toys wearing T-shirts on Christmas day. January had a mind of its own, though. You could be hot as a grasshopper on a fishing pole, one day, and freezing cold the next, with the wind whittling a hole through your clothes to nestle right next to your skin. Sometimes, both of these things happened on the very same day.

Sky Eyes looked over, her face smeared with chocolaty powder, "When do you think Daddy will come back?"

I could see sadness behind her eyes. I thought she probably missed him more than the rest of us did. The dad seemed partial to her and was often hard on the boys. I think they secretly enjoyed the break, but *Sky Eyes* had been closer to him since that first split.

Now here we were facing another split, only this time everyone was left behind. In spite of his leaving, Mom had been curiously happy. She hadn't gone out drinking much either, but with very little money for food I knew she didn't have any for beer.

Finally I answered her since she sat looking at me so hopeful, "I don't know. You miss him, huh?"

She nodded and I saw her eyes fill with tears. Jumping up, I said, "C'mon y'all, let's go exploring."

♥ ♥ ♥

January slipped on out the door and Valentine's Day was almost here. The dad, still incognito. I liked that word and mulled it over and over in my head. In Cog Neeto!

Sitting at the table, I was helping the kids with their Valentine cards. Nanny had bought some of the store-bought packages for us to take to school and we were thankful for that. After all, it was embarrassing to show up empty handed.

"Look at this one," said *Sky Eyes*, "I'm gonna give it to Nick."

"Ohhhh, is that yer boyfriend? You love Nick! K. I. S. S. I. N. G., you and Nicky sittin' in a tree," teased *Boy Blue*.

"I do not love him! I only love Daddy!" she said, looking at me.

"Leave her alone," I scolded.

Mom walked out of the kitchen with a book in her hand. "You kids need to treat each other better," she said, "This book I'm reading, *The Power of Positive*

Thinking by Dr. Norman Vincent Peale says anything can be accomplished with positive thinking."

"Yeah sure, whatever!" I said rolling my eyes.

"I'm serious," she stopped beside my chair, smiling. "There's even this prayer in here that says if you pray it for thirty days and believe it, your prayer will come true."

"So why do you wanta believe someone you've never even met?" I asked. Sometimes I wondered about her mental health.

"Will it bring Daddy back?" asked *Sky Eyes*. We all paused to look at her. She sat there a valentine in one hand, a hopeful expression painted across her face.

"I believe it will, and I'm going to start praying that prayer today."

I couldn't believe my ears and looked at my mother. Sometimes I could happily strangle her. How could she do this to a little kid? Getting her hopes up like that. I gave her my dirtiest look, which she ignored, turning to leave the room.

"You should try thinking positive sometimes," she said with a backward look.

All I could do was shake my head. I sure wasn't going to try some silly prayer by some guy I had never even met. Besides, I didn't know if I wanted the dad back, but looking at *Sky Eyes* I knew I shouldn't wish that.

She held up a valentine, "I'm saving this one for Daddy, it's the prettiest."

The bitter, cold days slowly left our state and I wondered what had come over Mom. She walked around with a smile on her face and began taking us all to church. I didn't know what to make of this new mother and secretly mistrusted her. Whenever we all felt sad and blue, she would lead us out on the porch and we would sit there singing church songs.

The kids were happier, looking at her with adoring eyes, but my eyes stayed true brown, full of distrust. I had listened to her promises my whole life long. Didn't I have the right to refuse to believe them? Santa died a long time ago and I certainly did not believe in Saint Mom.

One Saturday morning there was a knock at the door. The kids were sitting around watching cartoons and we stared at each other, startled. We never had visitors and kinfolk always walked right in. When I went to answer, three men in suits stood there.

"Hello there," said one, "is your mother home?"

"Just a minute," I replied and closed the door right in their faces. I rushed to my mother's room and knocked on the door. "Mom, there's three guys wearing suits at the door."

"Oh crap," she said sitting up, "I forgot they were coming."

"You know them?"

"Yeah, they're from that Baptist church we've been going to and I agreed to let them come by to talk to us. Invite them in and I'll get dressed."

"Well hurry up," I said, alarmed to have to be alone with them. What would I say?

I yelled for *Little Bird* and when she came running, I said, "quick, take the ashtrays to the kitchen. Hurry!" I scanned the room for any other signs of sin. Going back to the door, I let them in, "My mother will be with you in a minute. Would you like some coffee or tea?"

"No thank you," the leader replied. I figured he was the leader cuz he was the one doing the talking. They sat down on the couch and I stood there looking at them nervously. They reminded me of penguins at a duck pond, and I tried hard to not burst out in nervous laughter at the thought.

"It must be nice living out here in the country," said the youngest guy with spiky hair.

"It's okay," I said looking frantically around for my mother. Where is she? I felt like cussing, standing there waiting for her and suddenly wondered if they could tell I wanted to cuss.

Finally, she walked into the room, a warm greeting for each of them. She acted as if she knew the leader, so I began inching my way towards the door when she looked up, "Why don't you pull up a chair and sit with us?"

I felt trapped but couldn't think of an excuse and knew I couldn't argue in front of them, or give Mom my dirty look, but I sure did want to.

The leader began, "Sistah, the brothers and I have been delighted to have you and your family attend our church services."

I wondered why he was calling her sister and looked at the others a little closer.

They didn't really look related, so this must just be the way Baptists talk. I had my feet wrapped tight around the rungs of the chair and my hands felt icy cold. I opened my fists and laid them on my thighs to warm. My mother was chatting and telling them the story of the miracle we had last Sunday.

"Yes," she continued, "we were on the way to church and noticed the gas gauge was on empty. I was very worried we wouldn't make it and then we had a miracle!" She looked over at me to confirm it. I nodded, praying she wouldn't make me talk.

"What happened?" asked the leader, his eyes riveted on her face.

"Well, I asked my children to sing. Singing always seems to help us not worry and to be more positive. We watched in amazement as the gas gauge moved back up and we made it to church and back."

They all beamed, nodding and looking at me. I smiled back because what she said was true. I was feeling a little more relaxed.

Then the leader, with warmth filling his eyes, turned to look at me, "Are you saved, child?"

"Uhhh…" I started to squirm in my seat and felt hot all over. This must be what they mean about sitting in the hot seat, "welll…. uhhhm, I'm not sure what you mean." I gave my mother a look that clearly said 'help', but she just sat there smiling sweetly while all eyes turned my way.

"I mean, I uh… love God and I read my Bible," I said, but that didn't seem to get me off the hook.

He continued, "but do you have Jesus in your heart?"

Now this was something new to me, so I just looked at him hoping he would explain, because I really didn't know what to ask.

"You see, the Bible says that we must admit to being sinners, ask forgiveness for our sins and allow Jesus to fill your heart and life. Then, He can help you to live a better life." He pulled out his Bible and showed us John 3:16 which says, *"For God so loved the world that He gave His only begotten Son, that whoever believes in Him should not perish but have everlasting life."*

He quoted more scriptures and explained that we were all born in sin since Adam and Eve, but that Jesus' death on the cross was to pay for those sins and whoever asked Jesus into their hearts would be saved and receive eternal life.

I sat there thinking about everything he said. It didn't sound like a bad deal at all. Sure, I knew I was a sinner. I had bad thoughts every day, especially where my mother was concerned. Sometimes I even snuck a bite of food or a drink of milk. That was probably considered stealing. I hated lying, but what about all those little white lies? Hmmm…. I was wondering what else I could get from this deal he was offering.

"Okay," I finally said, looking straight into his eyes. "If I ask Jesus to come into my heart, will He help me to understand the Bible better? Because sometimes I really have a hard time with it."

They all beamed and nodded their heads in unison.

"Okay, I'm ready. What do I have to do?"

They led me in a little prayer. "Jesus, I admit I am a sinner. Please forgive me for my sins and come into my heart. Help me to be a better person and help me to understand Your word and use it as a light unto my path."

Afterwards I felt warm all over, clean and strong. They told me I was a new creation and today was like a birthday. I wanted to believe them and not think they were pulling my leg like the Easter Bunny, the Tooth Fairy, Santa Claus or Saint Mom. I knew in my heart that I had loved God since I was a little girl, and I would love to have more help here on Earth, but could a prayer that simple make a difference? I didn't know but was willing to try.

Now, everyone was standing around and hugging. The leader said, "The next time you come to church, it would be good for you to declare your love, your new birth publicly so others can share in your joy. Then, when you are ready, we can baptize you."

I knew my face reflected my shock. I just knew there had to be a catch. I felt the smile slide right off my face, horrified at the thought of walking down the aisle in a room full of church people. Everyone dressed in their Sunday best, while none of us had any church clothes.

Perhaps the leader could see some of my thoughts because he looked at me with kind eyes, and said, "you can do it whenever you feel comfortable. You have the

Holy Spirit now and He will guide you. You don't have to be afraid anymore."

I don't have to be afraid anymore. Those words were like cream in coffee or my Nanny's cinnamon toast. They warmed me right up inside. Those words sounded even better than 'In Cog Nito,' so I grabbed them right up and placed them tight inside my heart, right next to Jesus.

****

As the weeks passed by, I tried hard to get the hang of this thing about being a Christian and a new creature and all that stuff. It wasn't easy, believe you me, because one minute I would be smiling and happy and the next I was hating my mother. Did Christians hate people? I wondered sometimes if maybe it just didn't take with me and I'd have to do it all over again. I was having such a hard time with that one commandment that said to 'honor your father and mother'. Did I really need to obey all Ten Commandments?
One good thing was that while reading my Bible, I was really beginning to understand it better than before. I figured that was the Holy Spirit helping me. What puzzled me most though, was why there were so many different churches?

My Nanny sometimes went to the Witness Hall, and we were going to a Baptist one and my aunt and uncle didn't go anywhere most of the time. My friend Sassy went to the Church of Christ, and Mom was talking about checking out the Seventh Day Adventist Church. It seemed to me if we were all Christians, shouldn't we get along enough to go to the same church? After all, wouldn't we all be in the same heaven? Like the song I loved to sing that said:

"Jesus loves the little children,
all the children of the world.
Red and yellow, black and white,
they are precious in His sight.
Jesus loves the little children of the world."

Mom continued praying her 30-day Norman Vincent Peale prayer. Her and *Sky Eyes* believed he'd be walking in the door any day now. Secretly, I was still wondering if I wanted him home. What if Mom changed back into the drinking Mom? I was slowly getting used to *Saint Mom* and had to admit life had been much easier for us kids without the fighting and drinking. Food was scarce, but that was okay. We got by somehow.

****

The prayer worked.

But I really don't want to talk about it anymore.

The good part is I got my dog Scout back! He had been living with the dad's kinfolk. It was great to have my old, furry-faced friend to listen to my troubles.

And *Sky Eyes* had someone to give her valentine to.

And my poem, well I decided it was too personal to share in class.

Made this Way

You ask me why
I don't go out to play
well someone has to stay

There are meals
to be made
and before I put
the kids to bed
they might have
to be hid

from fighting and fists
that fly in the night
I am needed here
to put things right

Don't ask me why
I don't go out to play
for your tempers
and tantrums
made me this way

Ask me why
I choose not to play
and pray for you
to go away

Ask me why
I cry in the night
and with every adult
put up a fight

For peace and silence
is all I crave
instead of blows
and rants and raves

DON'T.

ASK.

ME.

Rattlesnake Soup

A low grade sadness coursing through me like a virus.
~ Greg Bottoms~

"Hey, you kids come in the living room and watch this. It's history in the making!"

"What is it?" I asked the dad as we all gathered around the TV set.

"Man's first step on the moon!" he said excitedly, his eyes never leaving the set; we watched with him as the astronaut stepped out of the rocket ship and out onto the moon. He took huge, bouncy steps.

"Is this for real?" asked *Never Amount.*

The dad nodded and we all sat motionless, staring in wonderment of a man walking on the moon.

"But it's not dark outside," said *Sky Eyes* and we turned to see what he would say about that.

"It's dark in other places around the world, now listen. This is an important time for our country and someday you can tell your own kids how you watched a man take the first steps on the moon."

Later that evening Sad sat in her room writing in her diary, when she heard them call out. "Watch the kids!"

She nodded, quickly writing the last lines, not bothering to go out and watch her parents as they hastened out the door to the truck.

It wasn't a question, really not even a demand; just part of her normal routine, long established as guardian in charge. She had the power to decide what to scramble up for supper, to issue orders like a gym teacher, even wield a belt when necessary. Most often she just picked it up and threatened. Or gave them one of her famous 'dirty looks.'

Sad carefully placed her diary under the mattress, which lay, on the floor. Satisfied that her diary didn't make a noticeable bump, she sat wondering about the challenges Kipling, Twain or Astrid Lindgren had faced on their way to becoming famous writers. Had they ever been the oldest in charge of a pack of kids? She realized that she had really been in charge since about the age of five.

She had just finished writing in her diary about the dynamite. The power of it. It began after the dad blew up the *tank*. People in Oregon didn't even recognize that word. They called it 'the pond'. A tank was like a pond, a small body of water, not as big as a lake.

That wasn't the only thing he had blown up, but she knew she couldn't write about that incident in her diary, since he had filed down his boots and buried them in the dirt afterwards.

Instead, she asked him why he threw dynamite into the tank, but when the fish popped up floating on the top, she knew. There were enough fish to feed a hungry family of seven. She never complained when they had meat. They had all had meals from rabbit, frog legs, quail and the occasional poached deer. She had even had armadillo stew once at her grandparents' home. That wasn't her favorite in the list of things she had eaten, but when you're hungry, you *ALWAYS* eat what's put in front of you.

Sad glanced out the living room window, watching the dust clouds settle behind the old Chevy truck as it rattled down the driveway. They had almost made it to the cattle guard. She waited, watching for the blinker. Waiting to see if it blinked to the left or right. Left towards town, right towards trouble.

"Damn!" Right blinker. She looked around, hoping none of the kids heard her swear. She was always telling them to use their imagination to come up with their own swear word instead of the ones other folks use.

Her personal favorite was, "Hector Heathcote,' (a favorite character in Tennessee Tuxedo cartoons) and said with enough vengeance, it was a great swear word! Lately though, *damn* seemed to slip out now and again.

She thought about the dynamite again. Knew if she had some, she'd go *right*, like that blinker. *Right to Buster's Beer Joint! The first one on her hit list. How many sticks of dynamite would it take to blow up every single beer joint in town? Save a heck a lot of folks some heartache.*

Sad stood up, her diary now forgotten, and walked to the kitchen to look into the fridge. Quickly noticing the carton of milk on the first shelf, she grabbed a glass and sneaked just a tiny taste.

Not enough for anyone to notice.

Wonderful elixir!

Not for her, nor for the kids. She looked at the avocado sitting on the second shelf. Another item they weren't allowed. She had watched the parents split it in half, sharing it between them. Longing for just one bite, but knowing it wasn't for them.

Did these luxuries help him toss those sticks of dynamite? Hmpf... Sad didn't think so.

The fridge was just about bare. A half-eaten pot of pinto beans. They were all sick of beans and out of mayonnaise. And sick of trying to find ways to make the beans taste better. Mayonnaise was their new favorite thing to add.

In the cupboard was some USDA cheese and USDA spam. Perhaps she could figure out something new to make with that junk, maybe toss in some cornmeal and onions and fry it in a pan. *Oh well, I'll figure it out later.*

She went outside and sat on the porch to get away from the stifling heat inside the house. Watching and waiting for the sun to take its scorpion tail out of the day. Her hair felt like a wet blanket on her neck and shoulders, so she swept it up and twisted it into a bun.

Wonder where the kids are? She hadn't heard a peep out of them for a while.

She stood and scanned the fields where the cows grazed. They weren't allowed to spook the landlord's cattle anymore, so they probably hadn't gone in that direction.

Smiling, she remembered how they had scared the cows back and forth between the fences until they had plunged through and broken down one of the gates.

They had run away, scared at what they had done, but took the punishment it brought. *Lordy, it had been fun!* Served those cows right for following her one Saturday and scaring her silly when they lined up on the ridge above her. It was things like that that broke up the monotony of living so far out of town.

Suddenly she saw them coming towards her! Four little, bouncing heads of hair, marching in single file, heading for the house. Way out in the north field, coming from the direction of that spooky ol' graveyard. They were carrying a long, dark rope slung between them. She wondered what they had dug up this time.

When they got closer, she noticed the smile on each of their faces. Heads that were held high and proud, two sets of blue eyes, two sets of brown.

When they reached the porch, Sad looked down at the six-foot rope strung out between them. "JIMINY CRICKETS!" she shrieked, jumping back in alarm. "Drop that rattlesnake NOW!"

Four sets of puzzled eyes turned in her direction. Their eyebrows making arched bridges spanning freckled noses, puzzled by the look of horror on Sad's face. They dropped it reluctantly, unwilling to relinquish their prize.

Boy Blue struck a defensive stance, glaring back at her.

"Are you kids crazy?" Sad yelled, motioning towards the dead snake.

"No," answered *Never Amount*, looking around at all of them as if to make sure.

"Don't you know how dangerous it is to touch a dead snake?" Sad demanded, trying to soften her tone. All she could think about was venom in an open sore. She quickly scanned their faces looking for signs of poison.

"Oh… but…" piped the soft voice of *Little bird*, wanting to make everything right, "it wasn't dead."

Sad felt faint. "What?"
"Yeth…" piped up *Sky Eyes*, all innocence, "we stuck sticks down its mouth till it died."

Pancakes and Paraphernalia

However long the night, the dawn will break.
~ African Proverb ~

Sassy and I liked boys! A lot! Sometimes that was all we talked about.

The day '*he*' mounted the hill, stalking across the school lawn, the word "boys" had a whole new meaning.

The girls standing in front of the Junior High School, huddled within their cluster of tight little groups, reminded me of hens in front of a hen house. Occasional clucks and pecking, with much tossing of feathers and furtive whispers behind their wings when the roosters passed by.

Sassy and I happened to be in the middle of a serious conversation involving.... I could never remember what, when we saw *him* for the first time.

He wore black cowboy boots and skintight black denim jeans. A black turtleneck hugged his body stretching taut, as if begging to bust loose and free the bulging muscles rippling across his chest and arms. The first image that came to my mind was of a panther on the prowl. I watched the sun glinting off his wavy curls of coppery, golden hair curling down to rest on his shoulders. The sun shone on the huge, gold medallion that rested smug upon his chest, which made me think that he was, perhaps, more like a lion. Definitely predatory, though, with his confident stride. Prowling with the marauding stalk of a jungle cat. He was different from the other "boys" and so was his name.

The ripples carrying it along almost melodious, like a chime carried by a breeze. His name whispered from the lips of each and every girl. A name long and mystical that rolled off the tongue like a song.

Now, a few days later we were standing in the hallway before class and *he* was passing our way again.

Broad shoulders, narrow hips, and jeans that hugged his butt just right. You would think that was enough, but the guy had a cleft chin, sparkling green eyes and a smile that took your breath away. His after-shave was spicy and seductive, and he **did** need to shave, with a stubble of beard, (a violation of school policy) that never hid that cleft. His scent trailed behind him like a beckoning finger. (Or claw).

I felt a bit faint, hot and cold at the same time and glanced over at my best friend, Sassy. She was standing smack dab in the middle of the hall with a dreamy smile covering half her face, not even trying to hide her furtive look as *his highness* prowled down the hall.

He stopped at the entrance to the Biology class and looked back at Sassy and winked!

Damn! I buried my head in my locker. *He'll never wink at me.* I looked at my boring ol' jeans and unremarkable T-shirt. Sassy stood there looking like the cat's meow in her hot pink pantsuit, and white go-go boots. The boys seemed to think so too. The pink pants were cut short, but that didn't stop her from hiking them up further to show off her legs. The silky top pushed her breasts up like they were standing for the pledge of allegiance. I couldn't blame the guys for looking and sometimes saw that some of the male teachers snuck a look too.

Grabbing my biology book, I slammed my locker door. The noise broke the spell and Sassy finally looked over at me. That dreamy expression was still on her face which made her broad smile lovely as ever. Her chestnut hair was cut shoulder length and hung straight down. Another difference between us. Sassy never had to iron her hair. A throaty giggle escaped and she licked her lips as if she had just taken a bite of her favorite chocolate bar.

"My, my, my, my…. my! Did you see him wink? He actually winked at me! I'm going to have to make sure I'm in the hall when he comes out of class."

"But Sassy, how are you going to do that? You've got P.E. next. You have to shower and change and …"

"Don't worry, I'll manage. Just keep an eye on him for me, will ya? Let me know who's flirting with him."

Slinking to the back of the biology class, I stuck my head in my book, determined not to keep track of all the girls who flirted and passed notes to *hunka-hunka, burning love*. Sassy could keep her own tabs!

A hard, fist-of-a-knot settled in my stomach and I turned my attention to our handsome biology teacher. He was young, witty and lots of fun and I loved his class even if he was married. I caught myself laughing a little too loud at his corny jokes, but when the conversation actually turned to biology I drifted back into my own troubled thoughts.

Even though I had decided to ignore *j.c.*, as I had dubbed him, *j.c.* for jungle cat. No caps for him! After all, he wasn't Jesus Christ! I tried hard to ignore him, but he seemed to always be just on the edge of my peripheral vision, his presence floating around me like an enigma. I was proud of using words like 'peripheral' and 'enigma' even in if only in my thoughts. After all, as a budding writer, I had to continually work on improving my vocabulary.

The bell rang and I slowly gathered up my books, determined not to be in the hall to watch Sassy flirt with that damn *jungle cat*. Instead, I thought up a question to ask the teacher so I could linger until I knew the hall was almost clear and students began coming in for the next class.

Out in the almost deserted hall, I rushed through the door of my algebra class just as the bell rang. Shoot! I forgot to stop and pick up my book. I stood up to ask permission to return to my locker, when I heard the words we all hate to hear.

"All right, class, put away your books. Pop quiz today!"

I didn't see Sassy until right after lunch. I scoured the lunchroom looking for her, but it wasn't until I walked outside that I saw her, perched like a queen bee on the balustrade, (another word for my vocabulary list) against the hedges.

She was surrounded by boys. Okay to be fair, there were a few girls there too, but *j.c.* stood apart from them, occasionally tossing out a word or two, like the King of the Jungle tossing a few scraps of meat to his subjects.

Sassy had her eye on him, all the while swinging her white go-go boots like a banner in the wind. She barely heard my approach and when she looked down at me she had that goofy, dreamy smile on her face.

"I've been looking for you. I thought you were going to meet me in the lunchroom," I said, trying not to let my irritation show.

"Oh…. well…. I um, decided to skip lunch today, I thought I'd get a breath of fresh air instead."

"Really? Is that what you're calling it?" I asked angrily.

Sassy looked puzzled, but the dreamy smile came back when *j.c.* tossed out another morsel of meat.

"So, are you secure on that little perch of yours?"

Sassy ignored me, continuing to look wistfully at his royal highness. Finally, she said, "Hmmm…. what did you say?"

"I said, are you secure on your perch?"

"Oh, yes… why?"

I don't know why I did what I did next. I think my arm had a mind of its own as it reached out and shoved Sassy! A gentle shove, just for a joke. Then Sassy was all flailing legs and arms, a ball of hot pink pantsuit and flashing white go-go boots, flying backwards into the hungry teeth of the green, prickly shrubbery. She screamed out in pain and *j.c.* and another boy rushed to help UN-entangle her from the bushes.

"Oh my gosh, Sassy, I'm so sorry. I didn't mean to…." My face was flaming red with shame. Everyone turned to stare at me, their faces registering shock.

But it was Sassy's eyes that haunted me. I watched as a trickle of tears trailed down her face, which felt like a white-hot poker through my heart. Her voice was filled with anguish when she asked, "why did you push me?"

"Sassy, I'm so sorry. REALLY! I didn't think you would fall. Are you all right?"

Sassy looked down at her torn nylons and we noticed trickles of blood forming angry welts across her legs and thighs.

"C'mon Sassy, I'm really, really sorry. I'll go with you to the nurse's office."

"I can manage by myself," she said, and brushed away my touch. The crowd gave me one more hateful stare, turning in unison to walk with Sassy to the nurse's office.

I stood there a moment longer, my burning face flaming with shame knowing I had let my best friend down. Possibly even injured her. What kinda friend does that? I thought she would probably never speak to me again.

The rest of the day slugged by like a snail without a trail. I barely listened in the rest of my classes and was thankful that Sassy and I didn't have any together. How could I face her again? Another friendship down the tubes and this one _not_ because I had to move again.

For the first time in my life I wished we were moving. Tomorrow! I mean, we've packed up before in the middle of the night and left town. It could happen again. I felt hope, but it quickly left when I thought about that furtive move in the night when we left Oregon the last time.

I still remembered coming home from school with the biggest smile on my face. I was eleven at the time and had just discovered my calling that very day! My teacher had told the class to write a story about anything at all. When the time came to read my story out loud, my voice trembled, my legs felt weak but soon I was caught up in the tale of my own creation.

I was amazed hearing laughter at the funny parts and sniffles from the kids when I read the tragic ending. Everyone applauded! The teacher gave me an 'A', and even asked to read it to another class. I knew from that moment that my destiny lay before me. Wanting to be able to reach out and touch others with my stories. It felt amazing discovering the power of words.

After all, hadn't reading a book allowed me to escape my own life? I loved being carried away whenever I opened the cover of a book, becoming one with the character I identified with most. Or learning about new lands, other faraway places and people I might never have the chance to meet. Books were the best way to escape and learn at the same time! What greater calling than to become a writer!

Coming home that day with my incredulous news, I watched as my world, my news, my wishes fell by the wayside as everything came unraveled once again.

We were moving. That night! We had to pack one bag each because we were leaving when night fell.

Mom told me to make tea for the trip, and when I carried the boiling water across the room, I slipped on a piece of tomato someone had dropped on the floor, spilling the water and burning my hand.

To add to my misery, they refused to let me take the guitar I had been given for Christmas. I had begged for one the entire year and was just beginning to learn how to play. They insisted that there was no room in the car even though I pleaded, arguing that I would hold it in my lap the whole way. Still they refused. Everything must be left behind.

Always wondering if there was more to the story, that maybe they owed money for our possessions, but I never asked. What difference would it make?

We drove off in the dark of night. Me sitting in the back seat holding my throbbing hand against the cold window for relief. A guitar, my friendships, and a soft bed to sleep in, gone like the stripes on the road.

The bell ringing startled me, bringing me back to the present and signaling an end to the day. I gathered my books and headed to my locker, still lost in the memory of that eleven-year-old girl. How many towns, how many schools, how many friendships had been lost since then? But not my hopes and dreams! Never my hopes and dreams. I bit my lip determined that if I had anything to do with it, not my friendship with Sassy either!

On the bus ride home, I tried to figure out a way to make it up to Sassy. Stepping off the bus and walking across the cattle guard to begin the long walk to the house, I was so lost in my thoughts that I didn't remember if I looked to see if any calves were trapped under the cattle guard. That happened last week, so I turned to look back.

That had been interesting, watching the farmer try to get the calf unstuck. Living in the country gave me some great ideas for short stories.

Thankful for no cows in unsavory predicaments, I stepped into the house, nerves always on edge, until I could hear Mom's voice and determine the daily situation. Would it be a two-beer or two-sheets to the wind day? Kinda like preparing for war.

"I'm home! Is anybody beer, whoops, I mean here?"

"Back here by the washer, come and hang up these clothes for me."

Whew. She sounded sober and I was delighted to only have wet clothes to contend with. I called out, "Did you remember to buy more clothespins? The last time I hung up clothes, there weren't enough."

"Well, you'll just have to make do with what we have. Double up on the clothes, hang the socks in with the pants and shirts instead of using clothespins for them."

"Mom, I've already thought of that. Why can't you buy some more?"

"What? You think money grows on trees?"

"I wish," I replied, then before I could come back with a smart-aleck answer, I thought better of it, deciding not to argue because I was planning on asking for a favor.

Outside, the wind had picked up a bit. I stood, watching it shiver its way through the mesquite trees, their leaves a quiet shimmy. The cactus watching and hoping for a threat of rain. Just like I was hoping these clothes would dry faster so I wouldn't be out here hanging up clothes until ten o'clock tonight. With the wind's cooperation, I could hang out a second load before supper. Hanging up clothes gave me time to think! I carefully placed a sock in with each shirt, so nothing hung alone.

It would be nice to ask Sassy over for a weekend so I could make up for the horrible thing I did. Pausing, I tried to imagine how Sassy might view my family. I had spent the night at Sassy's house before and felt envy because she had such a sweet mother and father. They were already up in years, Sassy's mother with white hair, and she was plump and jolly. Never had I seen them drinking alcohol.

There was always plenty of food on the table and Sassy's dad laughed and smiled a lot. The only negative thing I did notice was that Sassy's mom was strict on cleaning and chores, but that wasn't a bad thing, was it? After all, I did most of the cooking and the largest share of cleaning. I've always heard that hard work never killed anyone and was counting on it to be true.

With a wooden clothespin in mid-air, a thought hit me, *what if they get drunk while Sassy is here and start fighting?* I tried to shrug off this horrid thought!

Surely, not! Surely, they would behave with a visitor in the house. *But what if they don't?   What if they embarrass me? What if Sassy decides she doesn't want to be my friend anymore? I mean I can't tell her about them because then she'd never want to come. Besides, I could never talk bad about my family to anyone.*

I looked down at the empty clothes basket. Oh well, I smiled, I guess I'll just have to take a chance. If she's really a friend, maybe she'll understand.

That evening, lying across my mattress and writing in my diary, I glanced over at the alarm clock. It sat on a pile of books next to my mattress. My stomach growled, it was nine o'clock and we still hadn't had any supper.

Jumping up, I went into the living room, "Mom, when are we going to eat? I'm hungry."

When she looked at me, I quickly counted the pile of beer cans sitting next to them. They were on their way to a good buzz.

"Okay, why doncha go in and start the gravy? I'll make some hamburger patties."

Going into the kitchen I hunted for the big cast iron skillet. It was sitting in a sink full of dirty dishes. With a heavy sigh, I dug it out to wash thinking how much I hated making gravy! It was at the top of my list of, Things I HATE to do.

Never Amount rounded the corner and skidded to a stop, "Are we going to eat now? His big, brown eyes looked as round as saucers. He was a bottomless pit when it came to food.

"Not yet, but soon! I'm starting the gravy now."

Putting a few tablespoons of Crisco in the pan, I stood there watching till it was hot, then sprinkled flour and quickly added salt and pepper. When the flour started to turn brown, I added ½ cup of milk and 3 cups of water. The gravy was always thin and runny and I stood at the stove stirring forever, it seemed, waiting for it to thicken. It didn't do any good to complain about it because the dad insisted on having gravy with almost every meal. I didn't like it myself, partly because I detest making it all the time.

Mom finally came in stumbling against the counter. I watched her chopping onions to add to the hamburger patties, hoping her finger didn't add to the mixture.

Tonight, she seemed to be in a good mood which would work well with my plans. "Mom, I was wondering if I could ask a favor?"

"What iz it?"

"Well, y'know that friend that I spent the night with a few weeks ago?

"Yeah."

"Well, I'd really like to return the favor and ask her to spend the night."

"Allrighty then, when's ya wanta do it?"

I tried hard to not let her slurring irritate me. "I was thinking this weekend." To my surprise she answered, "Okay."

Wow, I shouldn't waste this moment and her mood, so decided to push my luck one step further.

"I was thinking that since her parents took us to a movie when I stayed at their house, could you drive us to the roller rink?"

"Maybe. Is dat gravy done?"

Maybe was as good as a yes! "No, not yet, but I'm working on it. Thanks Mom!"

The next day was Thursday and soon as I got off the school bus, I scoured the crowd looking for Sassy. Fervently prayed she wasn't still mad and would be willing to come home with me for the weekend.

I didn't see her in the hall that morning, and while sitting in Biology, I began to worry. *What if she didn't come to school today? I don't have a way to get in touch with her since we don't have a phone. What if her cuts were so serious, she was maimed for life?!*

I was nervously chewing the top of my pen cap, sucking it off the pen, then pressing it back with my tongue. A silly, nervous habit I had picked up and was so absorbed in my thoughts, I didn't hear the teacher ask a question. Suddenly I heard the class laughing. They were looking at me, so I suddenly inhaled the pen cap swallowing it hole! *Oh man, now I had a new set of worries! If gum takes seven years to digest, how much longer will a pen cap take?*

The teacher was still staring at me and I felt my face begin to flame. Coughing and wondering what he asked, I hoped no one noticed my missing pen cap.

"Sir, could you repeat the question?"

The class cracked up while I sat there, beet red and confused.

"I was wondering if you would like to hand in your homework with the rest of the class?"

"Oh… sure, sorry," I scrambled in my desk to find my homework. Concentrating in class was hard with my thoughts so scattered. *Was I crazy to ask a friend to come home with me? Them getting drunk was always at the top of my worry list. Was there anything good in the house to eat or just that USDA garbage? What if they got in a fight? What will she think about my bedroom? I don't even have a real bed. What can we do for fun?*

What if they get drunk?

By the time Biology class was over I had just about talked myself out of asking Sassy to come home with me. I decided to just play it by ear and try to catch Sassy coming out of P.E. class. Or I could make an excuse to go to the bathroom right before the bell signals an end to Algebra, race across the lawn and catch her when she leaves class.

My plan worked without a hitch and I stood next to the gym door when Sassy came walking through. She glanced at me and I put on my very best smile, but she turned away and kept on walking.

"Wait," I yelled, "are you still mad at me? I REALLY am sorry. I've been so worried about you that I hardly slept last night."

She stopped. She was standing there with a weird expression on her face, not even looking at me.

When I caught up to her, it was as if she didn't even see me. "Earth calling Sassy! Where were you just then? Are you still mad at me?"

"Oh.... what, no. Just something Mrs. Abby said to me. I should be mad at you, but...." she turned and beamed her beautiful smile straight at me. "Did you really lose sleep worrying about me?"

"I did! And then today when I didn't see you anywhere, my mind was filled with all kinds of worries. Like maybe I maimed you for life!"

She flipped her hair back, giggling with pure pleasure! I heaved a huge sigh of relief, so thrilled to see her smile and hear her laugh. Her positive outlook on life was something I truly treasured in our friendship. Better yet, I knew she had forgiven me.

I took another deep breath and before I changed my mind, I plunged right in, "Hey, I want to ask if you'd like to come spend the weekend at my house? I already asked Mom and she said she'd drive us to the roller rink on Friday. Whaddya think?"

Sassy looked excited, "I think that sounds like a plan. I'm sure Mother will say it's okay and better yet; it will give us the whole weekend to talk about boys!"

"Yeah. Maybe that hunk-a-hunk of burning love will be at the roller rink, too!"

A thoughtful look crossed her face, "Hmmm.... that gives me an idea."

"What?"

"I'll tell you later."

"Okay, tell your mom you can ride the bus home with me on Friday. Oh, and er, uhm.... well maybe we should talk about my parents."

"Sure. Why, what's up? Heh, let's move, the bell's about to ring."

"Oh okay, we'll talk about it on the bus ride home."

"Sounds great, see ya!"

The bus pulled to a stop and we jumped off. There hadn't been any opportunity to talk to Sassy about my parents. What would I say anyway? I just prayed the weekend would go by without a hitch. My stomach was giving me fits worrying about it.

"I'm so glad your parents let you come home with me. They seem like the perfect parents."

"Oh… well, they're okay, I guess. I think they're too strict and man oh'man, you never wanna cross my dad," said Sassy.

"Why? He doesn't hit you, does he? He seems like the sweetest dad ever."

"Well, he is most of the time, but he's really hard to please sometimes. I never feel like I do anything right in his eyes."

I thought about that for a minute. Having never heard Sassy complain about her parents, I was secretly a little relieved. Maybe if her home life wasn't so perfect, then perhaps she wouldn't think my parents were so bad.

"I don't know, but I think I'd trade parents with you in a heartbeat. Your mom and dad seem so mature. Y'know like real adults. Mine act like kids sometimes."

"Really? I'd love to have a younger mom. Seems like she'd be fun to do things with. Y'know, pal around with, not so stuck in the stone ages."

"Yeah, but who wants to pal around with your parents?"

Sassy bust out laughing. "Ya got a point there Sherlock! Hey, what time are we going to the roller rink?"

We walked up the front steps and I held my breath when we walked inside. *Little Bird* was sitting on the couch. "Hey where's Mom? This is my best friend, Sassy."

"Mom and Dad went to town and said they'd be back later."

Whew! A small reprieve before they came home!

I turned and said to Sassy, "C'mon, I'll show you around and let ya meet the other kids." Then we went to my room and I tried to see it though Sassy's eyes, with the mattress on the floor, my record player on an overturned egg crate, and the blanket acting as a door.

"Hey, I've got some great records. Wanna listen to them or would you like to go for a walk in the woods?" I watched her out of the corner of my eye, nervous as I tried to read her thoughts.

She tossed her overnight bag on my mattress and plopped down on it. "I like your room. You have so much light in here!"

I thought my face would split in two my smile was so big. "Thanks, it's kinda small, but y'know how it is, just great to have your own space. Hey, guess what, I bought us some M&M's! I've been saving them for when you came over." I grabbed them from my secret hiding place, "C'mon, let's go for a walk. I'll show you the cows."

"Sounds like a plan, Stan!"

Outside in the dwindling sun, we were walking away from the house, when I turned and saw the kids following two steps behind. Whipping around, a thunderous look in my eye, I said, "Oh no you don't! y'all git on back to the house. We want privacy."

They stopped and looked at me, a mixture of emotions crossing their freckled faces. *Boy Blue* looked defiant and I wondered if he would secretly try to follow us.

"Oh, they're just so cute," said Sassy.

I glanced at Sassy, then tried to soften my tone up a bit. "Look y'all, we never have time to talk at school and I want to tell her a secret, so puleeeese give us some time alone, okay?"

They shuffled their feet a bit, *Never Amount* and *Sky Eyes* already beginning to turn back.

"I'll show you guys a trick when we get back, okay?" piped up Sassy.

"Okay!" they said in unison and quickly ran towards the house.

We continued our way towards a line of mesquite trees, following the cow path to the deep gully I found when walking alone in the woods.

"The cows are usually back here. Are you scared of 'em?"

"Heck no, I've been around cows many times. Why, are you?"

"Sometimes. Once they followed me and Scout," I said watching Scout as he leap-frogged ahead of us.

"They surrounded me then Scout ran off and left me behind. It made me nervous having them crowd me like that." I was walking and talking and suddenly stopped realizing Sassy wasn't beside me. Turning, I saw she had stopped dead still in her tracks. Her face was white as a bed sheet blowing in the breeze and she was staring at the ground.

"Sassy, what's wrong?"

"Sssssnake!" she quivered, her voice barely a whisper pointing to a rattlesnake lying on the path between us.

"OH MY GOSH!

Sass, don't panic, just do as I tell you. Don't run, just very slowly start backing up. Don't make any sudden movements. Ya gotta move really slow. They have poor eyesight y'know, but they can hear real good. I'm gonna try to get around to you and walk backwards with you."

Suddenly Sassy cracked up laughing. That startled me, and I wondered if it was a nervous reaction, like when *Little Bird* always laughed at a scary movie. I looked at the snake, alarmed, just knowing it would leap to strike her at any minute.

Sassy was now laughing so hard she could barely talk, "oh, oh… oh my goodness, it's too funny."

I was totally astonished by her reaction. Would I have to slap her?

"It's just a snake skin!" She finally got enough breath to say, "but you should have seen your face, and you just kept poppin' those M & M's in your mouth giving me instructions. Hah, ha, ha! Oh, oh… oh my stomach hurts from laughing so hard!"

I stood there, feeling the blood rushing back to my face, heaving a sigh of relief. So many emotions ran through me that I barely knew which one to latch on to.

Suddenly, I burst out laughing. It felt so good to laugh with a friend.

When we got back to the house, my parents were already there. Sassy had met Mom before but had never met the dad, so I introduced him.

"So what time are you taking us to the roller rink?" I asked.

"Soon," said Mom, "Are y'all ready to go now? We thought we'd drop you off for a couple of hours. Then if you don't mind coming back to the kids, we want to go out after we bring you home."

Surprised to hear Mom *ask* me to watch the kids, I figured it must be because Sassy was here. *Uh oh, if they were going out, that meant drinking. Maybe we'll be in bed by the time they return.* I just prayed they wouldn't get in a fight.

The roller rink was on the edge of town and was in an old beat-up, round tent. Kind of like a circus tent only made into a skating rink. The place always crawling with kids on Friday and Saturday night. I wasn't very good at skating and hoped Sassy wasn't either. We tied on our skates looking around for familiar faces. "Do you see Mr. Hunka-hunka- burnin' love, Sass?"

"Why, whoever do you mean?" she drawled, a sly look on her face, then laughing said, "Oh, I think he'll show."

"What makes you think that? Sassy, what did you do?"

"Nothing. Much. I just let him know we'd be here."

As soon as the parents drove off, Sassy had pulled out a bright tube of red lipstick and painted her lips. She offered the tube to me, but I shook my head. It wasn't that I didn't like make-up, just not that particular shade. Sassy was wearing a tight, pink sweater that clung to her like a second skin. I noticed the pimply-faced goon behind the counter could hardly keep his eyes off Sassy while handing us our skates. I wondered if I had a sweater like hers, only in blue of course, would he eyeball me like that? I didn't think so.

There was just something different about Sassy, fresh and bursting with life, like a tree in bud. She was always laughing and positive and I was a bit sullen and moody. She often helped bring me out of the *doldrums*, (another vocabulary-building word). I rolled the word over in my mind, liking the sound of it.

Friday night was 50's music night and Elvis' *You Ain't Nothing but a Hound Dog* was blaring from the speakers.

Sassy grabbed my hand. "C'mon girl, let's skate."

We took off around the rink, looking for friends from school, but it seemed to be mainly upper classmen or little kids. We skated to two more Elvis songs when the lights dimmed and Bobby Vinton's, *Mr. Lonely,* came on. Couples paired up and took to the floor, skating hand-in-hand. Skating over to the side, I turned around looking back for Sassy, but didn't see her anywhere. I glanced to the entrance that led outside, and thought I saw a pink sweater pass by the lighted doorway. *Had Sassy gone outside? Uh-oh, we're not supposed to leave the rink.* I skated towards the entrance against the flow of couples. In the darkened room I didn't see the guy who had just twirled his partner. Dodging them was impossible and I went flying into the checkout counter, knocking skates and that pimple-faced goon flat-out cockeyed. The counter tilted and fell against him, and he fell against the curtain of the tent. Thankfully everything came to a stop, but it happened at the same time the music went off and the lights came back up.

I stood there, wearing my usual crimson face, minus the tight blue sweater to help ease my embarrassment. The goon glared while I muttered apologies trying to escape into the crowd.

Once again, I searched faces, looking for a pink sweater. *Where is she?* I guess it serves me right after what I did to her this week. Paybacks are never pleasant, even when delivered by the hand of fate. *That's it! No wonder everything's going wrong. I had forgotten. Today is Friday the 13th!*

I stood patiently waiting for Sassy by the entrance and in the same instant she burst through the door, I caught sight of my parent's car pulling into the driveway. No time to question her about her disappearing act until later.

They drove up to the front of the house and dropped us off. I thought Sassy had to be hungry by now, so we went scrounging around for something to eat. Looking through the cupboards and fridge, I saw nothing befitting two hungry teen-age girls, but finally remembered the popcorn! That was our staple snack in the house.

"Hey Sass, want me to make popcorn? I think we might have some iced tea too."

"Sounds good to me!" Sass turned as the kids ran into the kitchen.

Boy Blue blurted, "Okay, remember what you promised? You said you'd do a trick for us. Can you, can you? Puh-leease!"

"Leave her alone," I said.

"No, it's okay, I don't mind, really." She smiled at their upturned little faces, crowding around her expectantly.

I was standing by the stove, waiting for the popcorn to start popping in the pan, to begin shaking it back and forth. I was happy seeing smiles scattered across the kid's faces. It was high excitement for us to have a visitor, especially an overnight guest. How could I deny them this distraction, even if I did want Sassy all to myself.

She had their complete attention. "Have you ever seen anyone swallow their whole hand?" She asked, her blue eyes big and round, looking into each eager face.

"No, never!" said *Never Amount.*

"No one can do that," scoffed *Boy Blue*.

"I bet SHE can," said *Little Bird*, smiling up at Sassy.

"Do it! Do it!" piped *Sky Eyes*.

With slow and deliberate exaggeration, Sassy began crumpling her fist up tightly, one finger at a time, then with a bit of extra exertion she managed to fit her entire fist into her mouth.

"Wow!" the little ones chimed in unison, clapping loud. Even I stood dumfounded at this amazing feat. I think we were all in awe of our delightful visitor.

"Okay, you twerps, scoot out of here. Go watch TV, and I'll bring you some popcorn."

They stood a moment longer watching Sassy pull her hand back out, making sure she didn't accidentally swallow it.

After they left the room, I laughed, "you know they're going to be trying to do that for the rest of the evening. That was some accomplishment! Maybe it will keep them busy and out of our hair until bedtime."

"Well, it's good to be famous for something!" replied Sassy.

Later when the kids were in bed, I asked Sassy if she wanted to go outside and sit on the porch. It was hot inside the house and knew it would be cooler sitting out under the stars, listening to the call of the coyotes and the trill of the whippoorwills. Occasionally the lonesome sound of a train whistle would compete with the night's celestial symphony.

"Wow," said Sassy. "Look how big and bright the stars look tonight!"

I laughed, "they're always that big, silly."

"I know," she sighed, "but they look better when you live out in the country. I miss that sometimes but living in town is great too!"

"Sassy, you are unquibbically ever an optimist!"

"I'm a what? What was that word you used? Un-quibble what? Sometimes you come up with the weirdest words. Are you sure that's a word?"

"Sure, it is! Or I think so, anyway you're always so upbeat about things and that's one thing I love about you. Hey, listen, about my parents...."

Suddenly, looking down the long driveway, I noticed a car slow down out on the highway. The taillights came on, the car braking in the middle of the highway and backing up towards our driveway. Beside me, Sassy sat up straight, peering into the darkness.

"Now, I wonder who that is?" I said, standing up to get a better look. Two figures got out of the car and the car took off with a squeal of tires, leaving them behind.

"This doesn't look right, Sassy. Cmon, let's go in the house and lock the doors. I don't like the looks of this."

I turned but Sassy kept peering down the road. She reached out and put her hand on my shoulder, "no, wait," she said whispering, "I think I know who it is."

Standing there stunned, thoughts spinning around in my head as I realized the implication of what Sassy just said.

"Sassy, what did you do? Who are they?"

A tremulous smile flit across her face. "Well, I told a couple of guys at the skating rink to come over. That your parents would be away. You're not mad, are you?"

"Sassy, why? You know we can get in so much trouble! What if my parents come home and they're here?"

"I don't know why I do these things. Maybe Mrs. Abby is right about me."

"What are you talking about? What does this have to do with the P.E. teacher?"

Sassy looked up and I could see she was near tears. "Mrs. Abby had a talk with me today. She said I really needed to take a good look at myself, in the mirror. With all the make-up I wear and the way I dress, she asked if this was what I wanted to present to the world? Is this the image I wanted to make for myself for the rest of my life? She said I needed to take a hard look at some of the decisions I make and figure out why I made them. I just don't know why I do some of the things I do." A small sob caught in her throat.

"Do you understand?" Sassy looked at me then towards the boys starting up the path. She continued, hurrying to finish what she was trying to say, "I don't know why I want guys' attention all the time. I just do! Let's just have fun tonight. Then we can make them leave."

Feeling uncomfortable, but also feeling bad about pushing her in the bushes, I hesitated. I was still responsible for protecting the kids, but had to wonder if

I was too much of a fuddy-duddy, not wanting to have fun in the way other girls did?

When the boys walked up on the porch, Sassy introduced them, but all I could think of was protecting the kids and getting the boys out of here before the parents returned. Knowing I probably looked like a square in Sassy's eyes, so trying to relax and have fun, I began to flirt and talk to the boys.

After a little time on the porch, I noticed one of the boys starting to do more than flirt with Sassy, so I invited them in for some iced tea. We sat on the couch and when I got up to go to the kitchen, I saw headlights coming down the driveway.

"JIMINY CRICKETS!" I jumped up, yelling, "It's my parents!"

The boys jumped up and started running in circles, hurrying to the window and back, nervous as rats in a trap.

"Quick," I said, "soon as I tell you they've passed by the house, you need to run out that door and get out of here. Hopefully they'll park in the back driveway."

I stood nervously watching, waiting and hoping they wouldn't pull up in front blocking the boy's escape because if that happened, they would have to run out the back way where my brothers slept. If they woke up, I knew they could never be trusted not to squeal.

The four of us stood, standing back away from the windows watching the car slowly approach. It felt like it took forever, and I was holding my breath. Thankfully, we saw them drive around to the back.

"Go!" I seethed a whisper, "and don't stop!"

The boys ran out the door, and I tried not to laugh when one of them fell headlong into the barbed-wire fence. We heard uttered profanities and could barely see their silhouettes scampering down the driveway.

We had put sleeping bags on the living room floor for our slumber party and dove head first in them, feigning sleep just as we heard footsteps enter the living room. My heart was beating so loud in my chest that I just knew Mom would hear it drumming from the doorway. I was wondering if the boys had been spotted and how severe the punishment would be if they had.

My mother coughed. Neither of us moved. "Are you girls awake?"

My heart ceased its thundering, knowing by her tone we had not been found out. Yawning, I sat up, "I'm awake. y'all sure are back early."

Sassy turned over and sat up too, "I'm awake. Did you have fun?"

"No, not really," replied Mom, " so I was hoping y'all would be awake. Do you want to play some cards? Or Yahtzee?"

Shoot! I didn't want to play games with my mom. I wanted to spend time with Sassy. Now, how am I going to get Sassy aside to tell her not to give in to my mom?

"Well, we're kinda tired," I yawned, "You know, all that skating?" I turned around, rolling my eyes at Sassy, hoping she would get the message and play along with me.

"Well, I know just the thing for you. A big glass of iced tea will wake you up, then we can talk and play games all night." Mom left the room heading for the kitchen.

"Damnit!" I said, "I don't want to play games with her."

"It won't be so bad. Let's just go along, we'll have fun, you'll see. Man, oh man, was that ever close," she giggled.

We burst out laughing and I got up to go to the bathroom. Disappointed again that I would have to share Sassy.

Walking past the kitchen, I noticed Mom smashing something white into a spoon and adding it to our iced tea glasses. I stood there wondering what she was doing. She must have heard me behind her, because she jumped before turning around.

"Mom, what're you doing?"

"Oh, I'm adding a little more sugar to the tea."

"Well, why are you crushing it with a spoon?"

"You know how sugar clumps in lumps sometimes. I had to crush it up."

"But I already sweetened the tea."

"Yeah, well it wasn't sweet enough. Go on, get the Yahtzee game out and I'll be there in a minute."

"Okay, but I'm going to the bathroom first."

The night flew by and before we knew it, morning had sprung a yellow leak across the sky. We had been up the entire night, sprawled across the living room floor, playing cards and laughing hysterically at the silliest things. I had to admit it hadn't been as bad as I thought, but still felt resentful missing time alone with

Sassy. As daylight filtered into the room, Mom got up and went into the bedroom with the dad.

Sassy sat back on her heels, smiling, "Your mom's cool! And really pretty. She's not like a mom at all, more like one of us."

"Yeah, well that's all well and good until she tries to mack on one of your boyfriends," I angrily whispered.

"No way!" she said with a shocked look on her face, "does she really do that?"

Suddenly, I felt guilty for saying anything bad about my mom. After all, she did volunteer to take us skating and got our tea for us all night. Maybe she just wanted to make our sleepover a hit.

"Hey, I bet you're hungry. All you've had to eat is popcorn and tea since you got here. C'mon, let's go in the kitchen see what we can rustle up."

"Okay. Can you believe we stayed up all night? I'm not even tired, but I sure am hungry."

"Me too! Well, it shouldn't take long to fix something." I knew what we had in the kitchen but hoped to find something I'd overlooked. Standing there staring into the fridge, I knew nothing had been added since the last time I looked but was trying to think of something. We didn't even have eggs, and I was thankful Sassy was distracted with the kids trooping into the kitchen, their hair all tousled, still in their t-shirts and underwear.

They marched by to go watch Saturday morning cartoons while I wracked my brain. *We have that USDA spam that tastes like dog food. We still have some USDA Karo syrup. I'll just have to fix us some pancakes using flour and water. We can use that nasty white syrup if Sassy wants syrup for her pancakes. Thankfully, we still have a stick of butter.*

I washed a dirty bowl in the sink and counted plates to make sure there were enough clean ones. Then I mixed flour and water to the right consistency. Maybe if I add a little bit of sugar to sweeten the batter it will taste better. I grabbed the canister and looked inside. The sugar was as smooth as sifted sand, so I shook it around looking for the lumps Mom mentioned. *No lumps.* I puzzled over that.

I poured the batter into the hot skillet, adding a little Crisco now and then. Soon a plate of pancakes was warming in the oven and I called the kids and Sassy, sitting with them in front of the TV.

"Do you want syrup with your pancakes?" I asked once we were seated around the table.

"Sure," she said grabbing the bottle of Karo syrup.

I watched as she poured some over her pancakes, then took a bite. A broad smile lit her face, her blue eyes wide as she looked my way.

"Y'know, I think these are the best pancakes I've ever eaten!"

"Oh Sassy, you're the best friend a girl could ever have!"

No Beer Allowed

Everyone is a moon and has a dark side
which he never shows to anybody.
~ Mark Twain ~

Sad looked up at the blinkin' neon sign. It blocked out the moon's heavenly glow. Nothin heavenly about this night! Took her backpack off and dug around fer her jacket. It would make a blanket fer her and Scout to bed down on. Wonderin what time it was. They had snuck out around midnight and reckened they'd been walkin' fer hours. Funny to be sleepin under the glow of *Buster's Beer Barn*, since she'd been a'hatin all these beer joints! Wouldn't even watch the TV ads for Bud, Coors or Lone Star. Seems to her they's the root of all evil instead of money. She thought about takin a rock to this here beer joint instead of layin down to sleep, but bein dog tired and hopin Scout was too, "no offense to ya, Scout."

Sad whistled fer him and they curled up on her jacket. Thankful he didn't get sprayed by that skunk he played with as we walked down that long, lonely highway in the dark of the night. Skeered her a bit when it came up on them and no amount a callin' that dog would bring him back. Dern if he didn't come back awhile later smellin' the same as when he left.

"Scout, you a strange un' playin' with pole cats under the moon."

He just licked her face and snuggled closer. In no time he was asleep, but Sad's minds a racin'. Rubbin her butt and thinkin about the stripes that were bound to have come up from that belt. Didn't hurt none, but she couldn't get past the fact that he hadn't a right to strike her.

It was her dress after all!

Not her mom's.

Papaw told Nanny to get her a new dress for the dance at the school party. He knew where the parents spent their money. So out of the blue, Papaw tole Nanny. Just like that!

Made Sad believe in the angels.

Then last night mom asked to borry it. They was a goin' out again to that beer joint they loved so much. Leavin' Sad home with the kids. Feed um, clean up after um, watch um. She was sick of it. When she asked, to borry it, Sad knew her dress would come back reekin' of sweat, beer and at least one or two cigarette burns makin it useless.

So, Sad said, "no, she can't borry it. Papaw bought it for me."   That's when he ripped it in two!

Right down the middle.

Sad started yellin' at em both!

He tore off his belt and let her have it good. Ain't never been struck by a belt before. Sad was usually the one swingin' it when the kids git out of hand. Not that she would hit em hard. They was like her own kids. Hadn't she hid em many a time when the dad and mom were havin' one of their drunken brawls?

Sad felt sorry to leave the kids behind and strike out on her own. But maybe she could get a job and send for 'em.   At fourteen, she already had a grown-up job besides babysittin'.

"Caw-caw-caw!"

Woke up and saw the blackbird sittin' on the telephone line.

"Ahh, shut-up, you ain't no rooster."

Cold from the dew wet on her shoulder, Sad sat up. Scout stretched and licked her face then took off to find a place to pee. Lookin' at the sun, she figgered it's early. Best be on our way. But to where?

Sad whistled for Scout.

"C'mon ya ol' yeller dog, we've got to go cross country, get away from this highway."

Scout came right on like a good ol' dog should. She thought back to the day he found her. Closest thing she had to a best friend.

Especially now.

Walkin' cross farmers' fields and climbin' over barb-wire fences, ain't no time before she was hot as all get out and wonderin' how many miles they'd done walked.

Off in the distance she heard men's voices and figgered they were close to the highway agin. Would be nice to get a ride, ceptin Sad was skeered. Skeered to hitchhike, cuz she'd heard stories of teenage girls that were raped, murdered. Besides, she had too many things to do in life to be gettin' murdered. Someday she was gonna be a famous writer. She stood still thinking about the place she'd buy for her and the kids. A place with horses and chickens and a cow for milk. They'd have everythin' they wanted to eat, but <u>NO BEER</u>! Of that she was certain. Thinking of the milk carton in the fridge that she secretly snuck sips from. No one allowed to drink it cuz it was his. If she bought two cows, surely there would be enough milk for all us kids.

"Hold on there bob-a-louie!" Sad's daydreamin' had took her right near the highway and she heard them men a talkin' close like. Keepin' a tree between her and them, she could see it was a construction site. Sad was a wonderin' what kinda men do that kinda work. Family men she was a hopin', who won't hurt teenage girls that run away from home.

Sad put her hand down to warn Scout to be quiet so she could study their faces. Too far away to hear their words. She didn't see no beer cans scattered around, so's maybe they'd be alright. One thing fer sure, she was tired of walkin'.

Takin' a deep breath, Sad jumped right in, "Howdy!" She said, knowin' she startled 'em cuz they get real quiet for a minute, lookin' around for a car or tryin' to tell where she came from.

The cleaner lookin' guy, probably the boss, spoke first.

"Girl, you bout scared us silly appearin' like that. What you doin' all the way out here?"

"Just walkin'," Sad said, figurin' the less said the better.

"You break down somewhere? Where's your car?"

"No, no car. Any of you headin' to town?"

"Which town is that? There's quite a few out there."

"Uh…Wichita," She was hopin' it was the right one.

"Goin that way now, need a ride?" he says.

"If'n my dog can come too."

Goin' down the road, Sad was nervus. Shoulda spoke up when he put Scout in back of his truck. Woulda felt better if Scout was a sittin' here beside me.

"So, tell me," he says outta the side of his face, not quite a' lookin' at me, "what's a pretty, young girl like you doin' out here all alone?"

Sad figgered this question would come up. And feeling that always tellin' the truth was the best, jes not all of it.

"Thought I'd go to Wichita and get me a job."

"Oh, what kinda job ya lookin' for?"

"One that pays the bills." Sad had heard grown-ups talk like this and figgered he'd think she was grown up too.

"Really? What kinda bills you need to pay at this time in yer life?"

"Uhhh…y'know, rent and groceries and the like…"

Suddenly she remembered the tear on the back of her shirt from going under the barb-wire when she had crossed a farmer's field. She didn't wanta show no skin and reached for her backpack to get her jacket. Noticin' him out of the corner of her eye looking over at her.

He a lickin' his lips and actin' all nervus. Like a bolt of lightnin, it hit her that he was skeered of Sad. Wonderin' what she had in that backpack. Maybe ready to pull outta gun.

For a minute Sad sat there amazed.

She had put fear in a grownup!

It was a powerful feelin,' so she sat there awile longer rumagin' in her backpack and enjoyin' the feel of it.

"Uhhh…whatcha lookin' for?"

Sad looked down, hidin' a smile, jest knowin' his fear had finally made him ask.

"Jest this," she said, pullin' out her jacket.

She watched the color come back into his face.

He licked his lips and said, "We're almost to Wichita. Where'd you want me to drop you off?"

"Oh, bout a block from the high school."

He did like Sad tole him, but right before she reached for the door handle, his hand shot out like a dirty ol' snake and rested heavy on her upper thigh.

"Do you really have to go? Why doncha come with me and be my little girl?"

Sad looked at that boss man and realized she wasn't skeered of him. But he did make her empty stomach turn over.

*****

I heard the school bell ring and looked up into Mrs. Rush's face.

"Are you ready to turn in your essay?"

Looking across the aisle at Ashley in her new yellow dress and white patent leather shoes, I noticed that permanent smirk on her face as she sat waiting for me to answer. That smirk made me miss Sassy something terrible. Ever since Sassy had moved away, life seemed so much harder. Having a best friend around made things a bit more bearable even if I didn't tell her everything.

"No ma'am," I replied, crumpling the pages in front of me. "May I please turn in my assignment tomorrow?"

"Certainly, but first thing in the morning, you're already behind because of the days you missed."

In the hallway Ashley said, "Are you going to the school dance?"

I glanced up, wondering what it would be like to trade shoes with Ashley for just one single day.

Finally, I answered her, "Probably not, I have to finish my documented research on the destruction of dolphins caught in tuna nets."

A Dunk in Holy Water

I saw sorrow turning into clarity.
~Yoko Ono~

Sad tossed her clothes into her backpack, glancing out the bedroom window. She knew the school bus had to be careening down the road and just knew it would arrive before they all made it out the door.

"Hurry up y'all, the bus's gonna be here any minute!"

Quickly scanning her side of the room for order, she scowled at the unmade bed on her sister's side. Thank goodness it's Friday and I can leave and babysit my cousin in town. She loved staying at her aunt's house. They only drank Dr. Peppers and Cokes, meals were served on a regular basis, and the house, while big, and rambling, was always tidy. Even now she could picture herself with her aunt, uncle and their cute little boy sitting down in front of the TV, balancing dinner on TV trays to watch the Dick Van Dyke show.

She cocked her head to the side; sure she could hear the air brakes squealing as the bus tumbled down the hill to their stop. "C'mon kids, it's almost here!"

Grabbing her backpack, she ignored the growling of her stomach. At least there would be a warm lunch at school, the black coffee she drank earlier was already forming a tight little knot in her stomach.

The kids trooped up the steps of the bus in front of her and when Sad entered, she heard laughter rumble through the seated crowd. She stepped up and noticed they were all pointing behind her, now shrieking with laughter.

"What now?" she turned, catching a glimpse of a silvery-black face and short stubby horns. Silver, their pet goat, was climbing the steps right behind her. Sad's face flushing crimson, as she flung her things on a vacant seat, turning to push Silver back off the bus. He lowered his head and butted her in the knees. The students roared, some almost rolling out of their seats, they were laughing so hard.

Sad edged her way behind Silver and grabbed his tail and one leg. He was trying to dart past her down the aisle. Tackling him in a full body lunge, she began dragging him backwards, glancing up to catch the impatient glare of the bus driver. His bushy mustache quivering as he drummed a tattoo on the steering wheel.

"Dang it! We're already running late," he muttered.

"I'm sorry, I'll just be a minute," Sad growled back, now a firm grip around Silver's neck as she dragged him off the bus towards the guilty unlatched gate.

She felt sorry for Silver, who had a bit of an identity crisis. He used to think he was a horse because a horse sorta raised him, but since coming to live with them, minus the horse, he thought he was a kid now, only the human kind instead of the billy-goat kind.

Sad shoved him through the gate, patting him fondly between the horns before latching the gate, leaving him safe inside the yard. "Sorry Silver, no book-learning for you today, besides you'd only eat the pages!"

Running back to the bus, she was determined to play it off and not make eye contact with the sulky driver. After all it was kinda funny, and if he failed to see the humor, then she felt sorry for him. Before settling in her seat, she shot a glare at each of her siblings, a stern reminder to whoever failed to latch the gate. She saw *Never Amount* slink down in his seat. Ah Hah! She had found the culprit but settled back in the seat because she didn't really care. Settling back, she smiled, thinking about her absence away from them all this weekend.

Never Amount pushed his glasses up on his nose, his silky eyelashes blinking as he stared at the back of his big sister's long wavy locks. Her glare had hurt him more than he would ever let on. Brushing his shaggy dark hair out of his eyes, he sighed, then turned to stare out the window at the scrubby cedar trees, cradling the foothills around *J.G. Lake*.

He caught a whiff of the piney scent floating through the window that always reminded him of Christmas. He liked Christmas! They always got an apple and an orange in the socks they hung up on Christmas Eve. Fruit was scarce the rest of the time. Thinking of fruit made his stomach growl.

He watched the sun shining through the trees, capturing dust mites that were swirling and shimmering as they drifted lazily in the breeze. They reminded him of some kinda alien fairy-bugs looking for a home. He wished he had a pencil handy to try and draw what he was seeing. He straightened his shoulders hoping to remember just how they looked when he got to school.

School! The thought of it made his stomach hurt and his shoulders tense. There always seemed to be someone poking fun of him, calling him four-eyes or holding their nose and sneering at his clothes, pretending he stunk. He never understood what they wanted from him, how he was supposed to be, how to change, what to do to make them accept him or just leave him alone. If he wasn't being picked on at school, it was at home. He just never seemed to get it right.

The only place he felt truly right or good enough was at church. There, inside those four walls he felt safe, at peace within himself. Loved. Accepted. No one picked on him there. He hoped mom or dad would give them a ride to church Saturday. It was supposed to be a special service. A new speaker was coming from out of town and there was going to be a potluck!

His stomach tumbled over and growled at the thought of all that homemade food! Wishing that lunch was the first subject at school instead of History. Who could concentrate on History with smells from the cafeteria drifting through the open windows? He wondered what was on the menu today. It didn't really matter; it was all good. A full meal with milk and dessert too!

A familiar guffaw and a cute little giggle startled him out of his reverie. He looked across the aisle at his brother, the *blue-eyed wonder*, making time with the cute little redhead girl sitting in front of him. He watched her blushing prettily at whatever his brother said to make her giggle. She was so beautiful that it made *Never Amount's* heart ache with a pain-flashed jolt like lightning. Her bouncy red curls and sparkling hazel eyes made him want to be a famous painter with her as his model.

Sighing, he turned his eyes back to the window, knowing the *blue-eyed wonder* never had his underwear pulled all the way up his butt crack at school.

****

The school bus grumbled its way into the parking lot, and Sad grabbed her books and made a beeline for the door. Just as she reached the front steps, she heard the bell ring. Praying it wasn't the tardy bell, she breathed a sigh of relief when she saw students milling around in front of their lockers. Fumbling with her lock, she noticed Lucy coming down the hall towards her.

"Heh Luce!" yelled Sad.

"Looks like you're running late as usual," replied Lucy, stopping next to Sad's locker.

"Yeah well… you wouldn't believe the reason even if I told you."

"Sounds like the beginning of another great short story," answered Lucy.

"Could be! I wish our Reluctant Writer Class were next instead of Algebra. I hate trying to deal with *Algebra* on an empty stomach."

"Better than what I had to deal with first thing," answered Lucy.

Sad glanced over realizing she hadn't noticed that her friend's normal sunny disposition was cloudier than usual.

Lucy, inappropriately named because she reminded Sad of Peppermint Patty with her round, freckled face and chestnut brown hair. She seemed so laid back and cool that Sad always looked down at Lucy's feet, expecting her to be clad in the sandals that Peppermint Patty was famous for.

"Why, Pep, I mean Lucy, what's up?"

"I just spent 15 minutes in the Principal's office all because Benny dropped out of school last year."

"What's that got to do with you? You're not Benny."

"Yeah, well tell that to Dowdy Mr. Rowdy. He seems to think because I got a C in Biology that I'm heading down the same path as my brother, so decided to lecture me first thing this morning. Cheez, they just don't get it!"

"I know what you mean," replied Sad, "Mrs. Freaking' Home EC hates my guts because she caught my mother smoking in the bathroom when she was in school, can you believe that? She actually mentioned it in front of class. These small-town people have minuscule minds. They need to get a life! So Lucy, what are you doing this weekend? Maybe we can get together?"

"Well… I have several yard sales lined up that I have to go to."

Sad looked at Lucy and shook her head in puzzlement. "Did you say you *HAVE TO* go to yard sales?"

"Yeah, I always go to see if there are any Bibles that need rescuing."

"Rescuing? You mean, is this something you're doing for church?"

"No, I just don't want them out there without a good home. They shouldn't be sold at garage sales anyway. They're too valuable!"

"Okay Luce, well good luck with that! I'll see you later."

Sad smiled, waving goodbye to Lucy before walking into class. She shook her head, *hmmm…* there's a lot more to that girl than meets the eye.

****

Both the Junior and High School students shared the lunchroom. *Never Amount* carefully carried his cherished tray of food to a lonely table in the far corner. He kept his head down, steering between tables filled with students, peering intently for feet that would jump out to trip him on his way. He could feel his stomach grumble as the aroma drifting up from the chicken strips and mashed potatoes were teasing and tantalizing his nostrils. His mouth began watering just thinking about putting each lovely bite into his open mouth.

Safe at last, he reached the table and set his tray down, once again smiling at the meal, imaging the cool, velvety chocolate milk as it tickled his tongue with that heavenly first sip. He knew this would probably be the only meal he had until nine or ten o'clock that night. With his big sister leaving for the weekend, home-cooked meals were often forgotten, drifting away while the stack of beer cans grew taller.

He remembered the time he and the other kids stole potatoes from the potato sack in the middle of the night. All of them running helter-skelter like four freaky hooligans out into the middle of the dark highway, munching on their crunchy treasures under the light of the sly ol' moon.

Daring a glance at the other tables, he furtively watched the other students sitting there, all casual-like and talking, ignoring their meal or throwing food away without even tasting it. He never could understand how they could be so wasteful, wishing he could secretly round up their discards and take it home for later. He knew his brothers and sisters would appreciate this contribution also.

He lifted a bite of the mashed potatoes to his lips remembering again the taste of moon-struck potatoes, his eyes closed in anticipation.

THUNK!

Jumping at the sound of a heavy fist crashing on the table! His fork clanked to the floor, and the mashed potatoes landed on top of his holey ol' tennis-shoes.

Never Amount peered into the steely blue, pinprick eyes of Frank, with black stubble littering his chin just below his gooney, grinning face.

Frank's swaggering shadow hovered over him like a vulture swooping down for a gluttonous meal.

Memories of being shoved into the locker, underwear pulled up between his butt cheeks and countless ruined lunches flashed before *Never Amount's* eyes. He knew what was coming.

Not saying a word, he sat there silent, watching while Frank poured the carton of chocolate milk over the rest of his mashed potatoes, chicken strips and green beans. A volcanic river of chocolate lava destruction spread through his tray of food, spilling off the table and staining his last pair of clean blue jeans. He glanced at the untouched banana pudding and Frank followed his gaze; then, as if in slow motion, smashed the empty milk carton into the pudding.

The room erupted in nervous laughter, trickling behind like a tyrant's tinkle as Frank and his goons began prowling the lunchroom canvassing for their next victim.

Never Amount sat still, his shoulders slumped, peering at his plate. The smell of chocolate now obscuring the appetizing aroma from before.

He thought about eating it anyway but felt the eyes of the room focusing on him, watching and waiting to see what he would do.

He didn't really know what to do, so he just sat there staring at the chocolate stain on his pants, wishing the bell would ring and signal an end to lunch.

****

Saturday morning sunshine trickled in through the ruffled curtains, a tender caress on Sad's face. She yawned and stretched, a huge smile breaking out like the sun.

What was it about Saturday morning sunshine that seemed so special? No school, no books, no teachers and NO Parents! Great reasons to hop out of bed.

She looked around at the little guestroom, her room when she stayed at her Aunt's house. It was wonderful waking up here. Just like being in a regular family. The room was clean, carpeted and WARM.

She thought about this past winter at the house where they now lived remembering the snow they had tracked into the bedroom she shared with her sisters. They had been astonished when the snow stayed on the floor for a whole week, never melting. Making jokes about building a miniature snowman and betting on when it would melt.

Here she had a room all to herself, cozy and warm, a bed to sleep in with TWO sheets. There would be a balanced meal at a proper time, pleasant conversation, and best of all 'no worries' of drunken brawls. No hiding guns or kids.

In the bathroom she tried to shrug off the bothersome thoughts the same way she shrugged out of her T-shirt and panties. Climbing into the shower, a sliver of guilt slipped under the door. Why was it that when she was away from the kids, she still worried? She picked up the bar of soap, inhaled the fresh scent of Irish Spring and lathered up. Wishing she could wash away her worries and watch them swirl down the drain.

Surely, they would be all right. Right? Besides, they needed to start looking out for themselves. She couldn't be there every minute. She had a right to a life of her own. RIGHT???

****

Never Amount strained to carry the bucket of water across the yard without spilling a drop. Since his big sister was in town, he had cheerfully volunteered to feed and water the rabbits in her place. Hoping his actions would help persuade his parents into giving them a ride to church.

It was a beautiful day, the sun lukewarm, instead of busily branding everything in sight. Delicate drops of dew still clinging to each tiny blade of grass.

Suddenly, he was hit hard behind the knees! He pitched headlong, laid out flat on the grass, spilling the bucket of water and drowning the tiny patch of ground he had just been observing. He flipped over and saw Silver pawing the ground, head lowered, his little goat-goatee shaking. Was that damn goat laughing?

"Silver! Look what you did! Now I gotta start all over." Silver ambled over and lowered his head for a scratch between the ears.

"You ain't gettin' nothin' till I get this bucket of water over to the rabbits."

This time he walked crab-like, keeping a wary eye on Silver until he made it to the rabbit cages. He reached inside for the water dishes filling each one carefully. Glancing quickly over his shoulder making sure no one saw him reach inside to stroke the soft spot between the silky rabbit ears.

"Hey Rascal," he said softly, "how ya doin today?" He glanced around again making sure no one was watching as he talked to the rabbits.

None of the rabbits were supposed to have names since they were for breeding and eating, but *Never Amount* didn't care, naming each rabbit, always dreading the day he would have to help kill and skin them. His stomach turned over at the thought.

"Rascal, look what I got for ya!" Reaching inside his pocket, he pulled out the nub of a carrot. He took a little bite before turning the rest over to the eager bunny.

Watching him take the carrot between his paws and start gnawing, he remembered his worry for his favorite rabbit. Since Rascal was the primary breeder, maybe he would be spared from the skillet. If not, there was always the possibility of a cage being left unlatched on *accident*.

He heard the back door to the house slam and looked up to see his parents heading towards the driveway. He tossed the bucket down and sprinted over to catch them before they reached the pick-up.

They looked up at his approach. He was wishing anyone else could ask the question. He already knew before he asked what they would say to him. Maybe if his big sister had been there to ask, or the *blue-eyed wonder*, the answer would be different.

"I was wondering if I could ask you something?" He could hear the hesitation in his voice, so clearing his throat, hoping to make it sound stronger.

"What is it?" asked his dad, barely turning around.

"Well, er… there's this church thing today that we wanted to go to. We were wondering if you'd give us a ride into town?"

His dad turned and looked behind *Never Amount* as if to question, "we?"

Self-conscious now, *Never Amount* turned around and looked behind him even though he knew he was alone.

"We're not going to town. Takes too much gas and we don't want to wait around in town for church to be over."

"But… we really wanted to go."

His dad looked at *Never Amount* and laughed, "So go," he said climbing in the truck. Without a backward glance he started the engine, backed out of the driveway, and headed down the road.

Never Amount stood for a few minutes watching them drive in the opposite direction of town. He knew they were going to the liquor store. Town was quite a few miles in the opposite direction.

He sighed, thinking about those four walls where he really felt at peace. He could picture it in his mind: the solemn quiet, the altar where the preacher stood, the chairs behind him for the choir, and behind the choir, the baptismal.

He really, *really* wanted to go to church today. He needed to be there. He knew the other kids wanted to go too. Feeling like he had let them all down, he looked around at the sun shining soft and gentle on the grass, feeling the silence surround him.

A huge weight descended on his shoulders. He just had to get to church today. It wasn't about the food or the special speaker. It wasn't about the friends or the singing. He just needed to be there today, within those four sacred walls.

Straightening up, he turned to go inside and face the other kids. He hated to tell them their parent's answer, but after all it was his own fault for bungling the request. He might as well get it over with.

****

Sad stepped out of the shower, dressing quickly in her favorite jeans and a fresh T-shirt. Walking into the living room, she saw her little cousin playing with his trucks and cars. He was so cute with his brown hair, blue eyes and a sprinkle of freckles across his nose like tiny, sea shells scattered on a beach.

Looking up at Sad he smiled, and she felt her heart melt at the sight of him. Sad's mother often said he was spoiled because he was an only child, but Sad didn't think so, at least not when he was around her or happily playing amongst her brothers and sisters. He seemed to fit right in, never turning up his nose when they offered him potted meat sandwiches and water for lunch.

Her aunt walked into the room, smiling at them both. Sad loved her round face and curly red hair. She had freckles all over her face, arms and back too! The angels must really love her to have kissed her in so many places. That's what people said whenever someone complained about having freckles. Those freckles were angel's kisses. Sad didn't think it was true, but she was happy to pass the rumor around.

"Well good morning you two! Want to go for a drive so I can get a Dr. Pepper?"

"I want one too!" chimed her cousin.

"Sure, I'll go along," answered Sad.

It was their morning routine. Sad thought it strange that they always drove to the store to get a Dr. Pepper for her aunt and a coke for her uncle at breakfast time. In Sad's family everyone drank coffee first thing in the morning and usually that was all.

They trooped out the back door, and into the waiting car joining her uncle. Sad sat in the backseat with her cousin. They pulled up to the little 7-11, and Sad's uncle asked if she wanted a coke? In Texas, if someone asked you if you wanted a coke, it just meant what type of soda. *Coke* covered everything.

"No, thank-you." answered Sad.

Her aunt turned around, a question in her eyes when she looked at Sad, "Would you like something else? You can have anything you want."

"Okay then, how about a grape Nehi?"

Her uncle nodded, "I'm sure you want peanuts to put in it, right?"

"Yes please!" Sad was so excited that he thought of the peanuts and she sat there trying to remember the last time she had had peanuts poured into her grape Nehi. She thought maybe back when she was a kid in the 4th grade. It was kind of like drinking a peanut butter sandwich!

"I want peanuts too," piped her cousin.

"Sure! Let's all have peanuts and coke for breakfast!"

They started laughing, chanting "peanuts and coke, peanuts and coke" while Sad's uncle disappeared into the store.

"I'm so happy you agreed to baby sit tonight," said her aunt from the front seat.

"Me too!" replied Sad, "You know I love coming to your house. Where are you two going?"

"We're going to go see Charley Pride in concert. I'm so excited!"

"Oh, I don't think I've heard of him. Is he new?"

"Yes, he's a new country-western singer and wait till you hear him. He's black, but he sings like he's white."

"Oh." Sad didn't really know what else to say and sat trying to puzzle that one out. Did a black man's singing sound different than a white man's singing? She started to ask her aunt to clarify, but didn't want to appear stupid.

"Do you have any records by him?" she asked instead.

Her aunt had a great record collection! Sad's parents only listened to country and western, but her aunt had records of Elvis Presley, Bobby Darin, Roy Orbison, Johnnie Cash and many others. Sad got a kick out of listening to Elvis records while she and her cousin went waltzing around the room.

"Not yet, but maybe we'll get one after tonight. Listen, we're going to leave early so we can go out to eat."

"Are you going to eat at Liverwurst's?" That was Sad's nickname for the restaurant called *Underwoods*. It made perfect sense to Sad, but her aunt just gave her a funny look as she turned to get her Dr. Pepper from her husband.

Sad accepted her grape Nehi and peanuts with a polite 'thank you,' then settled back, cupping her hand carefully over the neck of her bottle to pour the peanuts in the purple fizzing soda. Heavenly!!!

"Let's do a few drags through town," suggested her uncle, reversing the car and pulling out of the parking lot.

Sad sighed happily. She was so lucky to have a 'cool' aunt and uncle. What a perfect Saturday morning!

Later that afternoon, they stood in the driveway, waving to her aunt and uncle as they drove away. They sat on the porch for a moment until they could no longer see them. Jumping to her feet, she turned to her cousin, "Want to go play some records and dance?"

"Sure," he nodded, following her inside. They had just started dancing to "Jailhouse Rock" when Sad heard a car pull up in the driveway.

Probably her aunt returning. She quickly scanned the room to see what they might have left behind. Seeing nothing she hurried to the front door, then took a step backwards, shocked to see her mother walking up the steps. Sad wondered what she was doing here. Didn't she know her sister was going out of town? She forced a smile on her face, but felt it slip and slide right off, looking at the frown confronting her now.

"What's wrong?" asked Sad.

"Do you know where they are?" asked her mother.

"Yes. They just left to go out to eat, then they're going to see Charlie Pride in concert."

"Not them!" Answered her mother, looking even more angry. "I'm talking about your brothers and sisters! Do you know where they are?"

"What are you talking about?"

Sad's throat felt all clogged up and she could feel that hard knot forming in her stomach. She began to tremble. What was wrong? Why didn't her mother know where the kids where? What could have happened?

"Well apparently, they have run away from home. They aren't at the house. Did they come here? Did they tell you they were going to do this?"

"No, no… of course not! But, where could they be? You've got to find them. Did you check at Nanny's?"

"No, not yet. We're heading that way now." She turned to leave.

"Wait! Is someone going to let me know when they find them?"

Sad's mother didn't reply as she joined the dad in the car. Without a backward glance they drove out of sight.

Sad stood in the driveway, clutching and un-clutching her fists. What had the parents done to cause the kids to run away? Where could they be? She felt so helpless and alone. They were her kids too! And now she felt she had failed them. Somehow, she had let them down when they needed her most. "Please God," she prayed, "keep them safe and bring them back home."

****

It had been a long, long, hard walk, but a brilliant plan. They had left a note, but not in an obvious spot. They didn't have a ride, but after all….

They did have permission!

Never Amount left the laughter, the food, the fun and fellowship and slid into the quiet sanctuary. Slowly, he approached the altar. He knelt and bowed his head.

Peace flooded his limbs. In here he was accepted, just as he was. In here he was everything he was ever meant to be. Asking for forgiveness, he felt the pardon flow into his heart.

There was only one thing left to do. He looked around and saw he was still alone. Smiling, he thought, *not really alone*. He walked to the baptismal and in reverence looked down into the quiet, still water.

The Holy Water.

One quick dunk and he would be changed forever.

Quietly he slipped into the pool and slowly slipped beneath the water. He closed his eyes and waited. He just needed one dunk in Holy water to make his life worth living.

**But Jesus said, "Let the little children
come to Me, and do not forbid them;
for of such is the kingdom of heaven."
Matthew 19:14 NKJV**

A Dance in the Emerald Forest

*If your face is swollen from the severe beatings of life,
smile and pretend to be a fat man.*
~ Nigerian Proverb ~
Chris Cleave, *Little Bee*

Have you ever tried to fry an egg in Texas on a sidewalk in July? Well I'm telling you it can be done! Not that I've tried, (I'd rather eat my eggs with runny yellow yolk, no tar intended) but whenever I skip barefoot across the street from my aunt's house and run to the Quick Mart, the tar sticks to my feet.

A person would think I'd have enough sense to put on shoes, but I love my feet being free, not stuffed inside my smelly ol' tennis shoes. Besides, I'm rebelling against Mom.

I mean, really, none of us wear shoes in the summer. Yet, she acts like it's my fault that I stepped on a rusty nail and my foot swole up the size of a chunk of Papaw's petrified wood. It looked like a chunk of wood too, all brown and green and hard. So, Mom got mad because she had to spend her cigarette money on a tetanus shot. No compassion, no words of sympathy, just "ya shoulda been wearing shoes."

Thank Goodness that I'm now living at my aunt's and uncle's house. I mean, the parents know I can barely stand the sight of them.

They were thrilled to be rid of me as well, with our constant arguing and me giving dirty looks to their drinking buddies. Besides, I had my job at the Diamond

Dairy Diner in town, so it made sense for me to live with them. Plus, now they have a built-in babysitter.

Lately everything is going my way. Yay-heh-heh! Next month, I could start taking Drivers ED and then with license in hand, I can save up for a car. Only two more years of school left! I can hardly wait to be eighteen and do as I please.

The icing on the cake is that just last month I met a very handsome soldier and am hoping he will come back to see me.

It all started on a Friday night while I was at work. I had agreed to go to a dance with this guy from school. I didn't really like him very much, but figured it was something to do.

So that evening, two soldiers walked in with my *So-called date,* and they took a seat in the booth. I walked on over to take their order and when I looked into the eyes of one of the soldiers, I felt like I was falling into a rain-stroked forest. Eyes shaped like almonds that sparkled with shimmers of green, like two emeralds hidden in the trees. I felt my hands shake when I looked into his eyes, so quickly turned away.

Flirting came natural to me, I can't deny it, but in that moment, I felt clumsy and childish. Too much *Little Miss Muffet* and not enough *Marilyn Monroe*! I tried my best to be charming and calmly clever but felt like I was swimming underwater.

Did he notice?

While preparing their order, I kept turning at weird angles to peer around the milkshake maker and ice bin, trying to catch a glimpse of him.

The cook kept giving me funny looks, so I stuck out my tongue to let him know to mind his own business. I peeked through the handle of the coffee machine.

He had wavy, black hair and his skin was that perfect shade of a little too much cream in your coffee. I figure that somewhere down the line he had Latino or Italian or Indian blood flowing through his veins.

Whoo-Boy! I had to get a grip.

When I walked back to their table, I beckoned *Marilyn* to walk for me and stuffed *Little Miss Muffet* in the cooler.

"So, what're you guys up to tonight?" I put on my best smile, trying hard to not sink into that emerald forest, commanding *Marilyn* to behave herself.

"Well, we're out on furlough for a couple of days." This from Rodney, a local guy, but I barely knew him since he was older than I was.

"I bet it feels great to be back in your hometown. Aren't you both excited to travel to new places? Where are you guys stationed?"

"Virginia for now, but we'll probably get shipped overseas next month." This came from *Emerald Eyes*.

I held his voice in my head, twirling it around for a few moments trying to feel his tone. It was almost like tasting a new piece of fruit for the first time, slowly you place it between your lips, then it settles on your tongue, begins to tingle your taste buds, until a startling burst of flavor erupts in your mouth! Finally letting it slide slowly down your throat.

Unfortunately, this caused a delayed reaction in my brain and I looked up realizing the conversation had stopped and all eyes were on me.

Deliberately ignoring *Emerald Eyes*, I turned back to my *So-called date*. "What, I'm sorry, what did you say?"

"I said, we're still on for the dance tomorrow, right?"

"Oh yeah, sure."

"Well, I asked these two block-heads to come along. Is that okay with you?"

"Uh…" I was having so much trouble thinking, and desperately wanted to hear *Emerald Eyes* voice again. Plus, me in the car with three guys would never fly with my aunt. It made me feel a bit queasy as well.

"Well, uhhmmm… I'm not sure. Are there any other girls going?"

"Sure, I asked Deanna to come with us," said Rodney, "you know her from school, right?"

I nodded. "Okay, so what time are you picking me up?"

"Probably around seven at night because the dance is out of town," said my *So-called date*.

"Sounds great!" I replied, inviting *Marilyn* to transform my walk as I went back to the counter. I didn't even turn around to see if he was watching. I mean who could turn away from *Marilyn*, right?

Up until that moment, I had not worried about what I was going to wear. Now it mattered! I drove my aunt crazy trying to find something that I thought was good enough.

"Why don't you wear a dress?" she suggested.

"I'm not going to wear a dress! Nobody wears a dress to a Country and Western dance. How come I don't own any Cowboy boots? I mean, I don't even have a decent shirt to wear! And look at these old blue jeans! Arrrrgggghhhhh!"

"Did you go through my closet? I know I'm bigger than you, but I have a few things that are too tight for me that might fit."

She was trying so hard to help and I loved her for it.

"I did. I've already gone through it three times! I mean you should see this dreamboat's eyes." I looked at her feeling desperate, tossing clothes this way and that like a crazed mongoose, not that a mongoose had clothes, but I had heard they were a bit crazy.

"Okay, okay, I get it. Let's run over to Nancy's house, she's more your size and maybe she has something you can wear.

"What size shoes does she wear? Do you think she has any cowboy boots?"

It was a quarter after six on Saturday night, and I had already changed shirts three times, brushed my teeth three times and felt like screaming at least 42 times.

Taking a deep breath, I tried to calm down! Where was *Marilyn* when I needed her? Probably out dancing with someone tall, dark and handsome.

Every time I looked in the mirror all I could see was *Little Miss Muffet* staring back at me. "Go away!" I seethed, "didn't I put you on ice? You're going to ruin everything."

Finally, I could see my own reflection. Was my hair wavy enough? Having long giving up on ironing my hair to make it straight like Sassy's', I had slept in those prickly rollers that punched holes in my head all night long!

Guys have it so easy! Just put on pants and a shirt, toss on some aftershave and they're out the door. I carefully examined my make-up, just a hint of eye shadow and mascara, and a glossy pink lipstick. Brown eyes stared solemnly back questioning my sanity. Oh, what's the use, I'll never be *Marilyn.* So, I might as well just be myself and if he doesn't like me, then he's the loser.

"A car jest pulled up in da driveway."

I looked up to see my little cousin standing in the doorway of my bedroom.

"Mama said ta tell ya."

"Okay. Thanks Sweetie, come give me a big hug." I stooped down to let him put his little arms around my neck. Had I mentioned how cute and adorable he was? "Thanks," I whispered in his ear.

"Why you tank me? I no give you nufen."

"Oh no? Well, I guess I'm gonna hafta tickle you until you do!" He ran off squealing with delight.

Turning once more for a final look in the mirror, I winked at my reflection. *C'mon gal, it's show time!*

My *So-called date* was waiting with my aunt and uncle in the living room. He stood tall and nervous under their scrutiny. We said our goodbyes with their emphasis on me being back by midnight.

"Yeah," I quipped, low enough so he would only hear, "or I'll turn into a pumpkin."

He just stared at me with a blank look and we turned to leave. He opened the back door of the car. I rolled my eyes, annoyed he hadn't gotten my joke, and hopped in the back seat, greeting Rodney, Deanna and *Emerald Eyes* who were all sitting in the front.

The conversation in the car was lively, everyone talking at once. Deanna and I were discussing the upcoming Drivers ED, while the guys talked about basic training. Deanna was sitting between the two men and kept turning around to talk to me. My eyes kept straying to the back of *Emerald Eye's* head, noticing he had one tuft of hair that wasn't quite combed down with the rest. For some reason I wanted to reach up and smooth it down. I sat on my hands and tried to focus on what Deanna was saying.

"Can you believe she did that?"

Whoops, lost again. Maybe I can play it off, "No, go figure, why would she do that?"

Deanna rattled on and I finally caught up with the conversation just as we pulled into the parking lot at the dance hall.

Inside, the room was smoky and dark, but the music was loud and lively. There were several couples already out on the floor. I stood mesmerized watching them dip and sway to a lively version of *Cotton-eyed Joe*. When the song came to an end, the guys led us to a table, then left to go get coca-colas for everyone.

"Deanna, have you and Rodney been dating long?" I asked.

"No, not really. He just called me up this morning and wanted to know if I'd like to go to a dance with y'all."

"Oh really? Just this morning?"

"Yeah, I was totally surprised to hear from him. I think we're like third or fourth cousins or something, but I wasn't doing anything so said sure, why not."

I filed that little piece of information away. Rodney had lied to me about having a date.

"So, are you any good at dancing? I asked, "This is the first time I've ever been to a Country and Western dance."

The guys were returning so I quickly said, "shhh, please don't let them know that, okay?"

Nodding, she jumped up to go dance with Rodney.

Emerald Eyes glanced at me and I smiled back. Then my *So-called date* held out his hand for me to join him on the dance floor. I gulped, then stood up. My legs were a bit unsteady. I hoped I wouldn't get out there and look like a fool. Once out on the floor, I said, "Look, I'm new at this, so you'll have to teach me."

"Really? Well, can ya believe my luck? You never told me that."

"Well, you never asked me." We started doing a weird hands on my shoulders swaying deal. He towered over me, and I really didn't even know where to put my hands. He was stepping on my foot, and I yelped in pain.

Abruptly he stopped, dropped his hands from my shoulders and turned to walk back to the table, leaving me standing there, staring after his ape-like back. I was furious, so embarrassed and grateful for the dark room to hide my scarlet face.

When I sat down next to him, he turned his head sideways and said, "I'm going outside for a while."

Nodding, I just sat there, feeling humiliated and stupid. I was so glad no one else was sitting at the table. After a bit, *Emerald Eyes* walked over and sat down next to me.

"Are you having a good time?" he asked.

"Sure, this band is terrific!"

"Where's your date?"

"Ummmm… he went outside for some air," I nodded towards the door.

"Well, if you were my date, I wouldn't leave you alone for a minute."

I felt myself blush again and looked down at the table, not knowing what to say.

"Look, don't go anywhere, I'll be right back," he said, standing and walking towards the outside entrance.

I sat there thinking about the way one lock of his hair had swooped down over his eyes while he talked to me. In less than five minutes he was back.

"Would you honor me with a dance?" he asked, holding out his hand.

I shook my head, "I'm really not any good at it."

He leaned over and whispered in my ear, "Neither am I, so let's not be *good at it* together."

I felt like I was floating on air and took his hand. Out on the dance floor, he led us to the middle of the room. Other couples were twirling and spinning around, and I felt them fade from view when he turned to look into my eyes.

"Put your other hand on my shoulder," he said, "now just follow me, it's a two-step and pretty easy to learn. I'm not trying to be fresh but if you lean in a little closer, you'll be able to follow my lead."

Like magic, my body seemed to fit just right against him, and my feet seemed to know what to do on their own. I was still nervous, and felt my stomach doing all sorts of flip-flops, but he just kept smiling and leading me across the floor. I felt I barely had time to breathe before the song was over and he was guiding me back to the table.

"You were terrific," he bent down and whispered in my ear.

"Well, I had a great teacher," I smiled back.

"Do you know you have the most darling dimples?"

"I do?" I felt my face turning hot. I quickly looked down.

"Ahh, you're blushing again." he teased.

"No, I'm not!" I said and turned away. Suddenly I saw my *So-called date* in the doorway and guiltily glanced away.

"It's okay," he said.

"What?"

"It's okay with him," he nodded at the door, "I asked him if I could keep you company."

"You did?"

"Sure, c'mon let's dance again, now that you're such an expert."

Giggling like a schoolgirl, I stood up to follow him. Oh well, I thought, I am a schoolgirl!

We stayed on the dance floor for three more songs and by the time we returned to the table, our group was seated.

Sitting down next to my *So-called date*, I was relieved when *Emerald Eyes* sat down on the other side of me.

"I thought you said you couldn't dance," whispered my *So-called date* in a hateful tone.

"I just can't dance with *you*," I retorted, staring straight-ahead trying to hear what Deanna and Rodney were talking about. My hands were lying under the table tightly clenched against my thighs.

Suddenly I felt a warm sensation began to grow in the pit of my stomach and a smile spread across my face when *he* reached over and took my right hand in his own. My heart was beating a pitter-patter like a startled bunny, but my fingers quickly warmed nestling inside his hand.

Trying to join in the conversation at the table, I was so relieved when my *So-called date* got up to go talk to a group leaning against the wall. The band called for an intermission and *Emerald Eyes* went to talk to the singer in the band.

Deanna raised her eyebrows. Laughing, I whispered, "Can you believe I agreed to go out with him," nodding towards the wall.

"Yeah, I'd say you two aren't a very good match. Now, Mr. Dreamy over there...," she began, then stopped when he returned to sit next to me.

"I hope you two aren't talking about me," *Emerald Eyes* said, laughing, when we both started giggling guiltily.

Rodney and Deanna jumped up to go talk to another couple seated across the room and I was delighted to have *him* all to myself once more.

"I hope I'm not causing a problem with your boyfriend."

"Him," I sneered, "he's not my boyfriend. We just had a class together in school last year."

"Well, that's a relief. I was hoping it was something like that."

"You know, I'm embarrassed to admit this, but I don't even know your name."

"My family and friends call me Rusty."

"Rusty. I like that!" And then we couldn't stop talking. He told me about his life in the Army, his family up north. I told him about my job, my friends, my life, my family. We were talking so much and I was laughing hysterically at his jokes. He was so funny. We barely noticed who came or went around us. We sat with our chairs turned slightly towards each other and he never let go of my hand.

The band returned and announced over the loudspeaker, "This next song is a special request," and they began to play *Silver Wings* by Merle Haggard.

Rusty leaned over and whispered, "This is my favorite song. Please honor me with this dance."

Our bodies felt like they had melted together, as we moved to the sway and rhythm of the song. I wanted this moment to last forever. His head was resting right above my ear. The spicy scent of his aftershave and the feeling of him holding me in his arms was driving me crazy. Once, he leaned down and his lips grazed my neck. A delicious tingling, like an electric shock went from where his lips brushed my neck all the way down to my toes.

When we finally returned to the table, Rodney and my *So-called date* were there.

"Deanna wants to stay longer and is riding home with her friends," said Rodney, "but we need to leave now so we can get you home by midnight."

I could hardly believe that the evening had slipped away as swift as a waterfall cascading over a mountain. I felt my heart plunge as well, down into the deepest depths, swirling around at the bottom like a lonely piece of debris.

When we got to the car, my *So-called date* opened the back door for me to get inside. Reluctantly I crawled in and scrunched over so I wouldn't be sitting right next to him.

Rusty and Rodney got in front.

Once we were underway, my *So-called date* tried to maneuver an arm around me and I pulled away, holding a hand to my head as if I had a headache. Thankfully, he chose to ignore me and scooted up close to the front seat to talk with the guys. I leaned my head against the seat, just wishing to be back home, alone with my thoughts.

The men had been talking for about five minutes, when alarmed I heard my *So-called date* say loudly, "Stop the car!"

I sat upright, wondering what had transpired that would make him say that. He had sounded a bit irritated and I hadn't been paying any attention to the conversation in front. What had been said? Why were we stopping? What had I missed? Oh no! Was there going to be a fight between them? I certainly didn't want that!

Rodney pulled the car over to the side of the road. Rusty opened the door and got out. My *So-called date* opened the door and got out. I held my breath waiting to see what would happen next.

My *so-called date* got in the front seat. Rusty got in the back seat with me. My imaginary headache vanished, flying away like a tropical bird in paradise.

When the car started up again and we were well underway, Rusty put his arm around me and drew me close, "are you happy now?"

"Yes, so very happy," I whispered and felt the breath catch in my throat when he put his lips on mine in a gentle, tender kiss. One kiss, and soon another, and then another... until I was floating free, nothing at all like lonely debris.

Rusty walked me up to the door of my aunt's house and patiently waited until I was safe inside, standing in the doorway. I didn't know what to say. We stood staring into each other's eyes a moment longer.

"When do you go back to Basic Training?" I asked.

"Well, that's over already. Tomorrow we head out to specialized training, and then we get a permanent assignment."

"Oh. Well I wish you all the best."

"Thanks." He looked past me and saw my aunt and uncle sitting in the living room watching TV.

"Good night then," he said, "I really enjoyed the evening."

"So did I. Thank you for teaching me to dance."

"Oh, believe me, it was my pleasure!"

I started blushing again and studied my feet. He reached out, and with one finger touched my face to tip my chin up. Then quickly gave me one last kiss."

"Good night and God bless you on your journey." I said, watching him disappear into the dark towards the waiting car. I touched my fingers to my lips, then blew a kiss into the night, hoping the stars lit a path from me to him.

The evening was over. I was turning back into a pumpkin and wasn't very happy about it! Heading to my room, I heard my aunt call out, "that wasn't the same guy who picked you up!"

"No. No, it definitely was not." Smiling, I said my good nights. I wanted to be alone with my thoughts.

Wanting to be a Princess reliving the ball for just a moment longer.

Enchanted!

That's how I was feeling. I had never felt this way about anyone I had dated before. There was something so very special about him. I loved the way he made me laugh, and somehow, he made me feel like a precious jewel hidden in the forest, that he had just discovered.

I knew I would never forget this night.

O is for Oregon and P is for Pot

I felt like a pumpkin sitting in for Humpty-Dumpty for at least two weeks after Rusty left. Then a pleasant distraction came along when my aunt, uncle, and cousins arrived from Oregon for a visit.

Apparently, it just wasn't in my cards to remain a Princess, or go for a ride in a handsome carriage with six white stallions prancing down the road. Instead my ride would be in the back of a flatbed truck with homemade side-walls, snuggled next to two gigantic barrels of natural gas stolen from the oil fields, a few belongings tossed in, and a bunch of rambunctious kids.

Since meeting Prince Charming, I was trying hard to keep *Sad* in the closet…

I long to be happy,

I wish to be free,

I'm trying to become,

who God wants me to be!

…. *however*, a girl can only take so much.

MUCH arrived one morning in the form of my mother! She drove into the driveway at my aunt's house and hurried inside.

Wednesday morning. Wasn't Wednesday the day babies are born, *'full of woe'*? Hmmm…I should

265

remember to ask her which day of the week I had been born.

Walking into the house, I could tell by the look on her face, she was expecting a confrontation. Her shoulders thrust forward, her face with that hard, steely look that meant she was determined to have her way.

Immediately feeling tense, I prepared for battle.

She was sober.

"I've come by to tell you something important," she began.

"Do you want some coffee?" I countered.

"Is there any made?" She knew her sister and husband preferred cokes to coffee, but I still drank coffee.

"No, but I can make some."

"Don't bother, I really just came by to let you know."

"Know what?"

"That we're moving to Oregon!" She paused for effect, then continued, "We're leaving with my sister and their family when they leave to go back."

That took me a moment to digest. This was sudden, but then look who I was talking to. We had moved in haste so many times, that long ago I stopped counting. But we had been here, in one place now, for the past four years. The longest time ever!

Well, I would certainly miss them when they left, especially the kids, and maybe even in time miss my parents, but I loved my life here with my aunt and uncle.

With Junior High behind me now, I had two more years left in High School. I had made quite a few friends.

Also received a letter award in Writing! Finally, I was looking forward to graduating with my classmates. Having a steady job and my driver's license, looming on the horizon...I could buy a car. Maybe in a couple of years, I could drive to Oregon to visit them.

Then, I realized she was still talking.

"…. so, I've already packed up some of your things at the house."

"Oh thanks, are you bringing them over here?" I asked.

"What? What do you mean bring them over here? I can just put them in the truck."

"The truck?"

"Yes, we're taking that flatbed truck. Your dad and Uncle are building sides around it so it will be safe. It should be fun, don't you think? You always enjoy spending time with your cousins, so some of them can ride in back with you."

"Wait a minute! What are you talking about? I can't go! You'll just have to go without me. I thought you were here to say good-bye."

"No, she snorted. "You can't stay behind."

"But I have my whole life here! I'm supposed to start Drivers ED soon! All my friends are here and my job…" I was trying so hard not to cry or beg or cry. Tears never moved her.

"Well, you'll just have to make friends in a new place, take Drivers ED in Oregon."

"NO! I refuse to go! Why do you always have to destroy my life?"

"Oh please, don't be so dramatic! No one is spoiling your life."

"Why can't I live here? It's not fair! I just won't go!"

"Oh, you'll go all right. You're underage and don't have a choice." She sneered, "Besides, who ever told you life is fair?"

I stood staring in her face, determined to put my foot down and take my stand, but she dealt the final blow, "We're leaving Saturday. There's only room for you to take one small box. I expect you to be ready by Friday evening. Your aunt will drive you to Nanny's house and we'll leave from there." She turned and left.

I ran to my room and flung myself on my bed. My room! My bed! My friends! Family that I love left behind. All the stability I had grown to count on lay in shambles at my feet. I was too distraught to even cry and just lay there wishing death would come now.

Then suddenly I had another horrible thought. *Rusty!* He wouldn't know where to find me! He would come back to Texas and I'd be gone.

Oh Wednesday, you are full of woe.

Farewell to Prince Charming and my happily ever after.

#*@&# !!!

So, what can one say about a trip to Oregon in a flatbed truck, with two barrels of stolen fuel, and a bunch of rowdy kids?

I mean one can only stand *99 Bottles of Beer on the Wall* for so long. I hate that song! One can only spend so much time wishing to look like my cousin, with her dark skin, black hair and exotic eyes. One can only imagine to be anywhere else for so long, but reality keeps prodding ONE with a toe, finger, or elbow in the side.

The truck broke down in Idaho and we were stuck admiring fields of potatoes for so long, that I contemplated running off to join a band named *Tater Tots*.

Farmers driving by suddenly veered off to the opposite side of the highway when they came abreast of us, never stopping to ask why we sat unmoving for such a long time beside their fields. Who could blame them? We looked like a horde of hillbillies in that truck. All we needed was a rocking chair strapped to the roof.

Finally, we made it to Oregon! I had forgotten the beauty of the mountains surrounding Oregon and the graceful sway of sky-scraping pines crowding the landscape.

Peering out through the slits of the sideboards, I was so thankful when we pulled into a roadside park. I stood there, stretching my cramped limbs and inhaling deep gulps of the sweet, tangy scent of pine. Certainly smelt better than gasoline or sweaty kids!

Deliberately ignoring stares of fellow roadside dwellers, I went inside the restroom.

Wow! Even the restrooms were beautiful in Oregon.

I could happily live right here inside this park. It felt wonderful to not be cramped inside that truck for any length of time, and I meant to take advantage of this stop.

Splashing water on my face, I combed my hair and took my toothpaste and toothbrush out of my purse to brush my teeth. The water was cold and delicious. I had a vague memory of how fresh and tasty the water had been when we lived here before. Always optimistic! When life grabbed you by the butt, I was determined to make the best of things, in spite of my parent's evil intentions to ruin all things light and lovely.

I glanced in the mirror but didn't see my reflection. Instead, I saw the pillow left behind lying on my bed. I imagined the round, freckled face of my aunt, with her red curly hair standing in the doorway, looking around the room that once was mine. Her hand gently stroking the hair of her little boy as they stood together in silence, looking around the room emptied of my belongings.

I could see the long, black braid of Nanny's, cradled down her back, now slightly stooped with age. She sits alone at the kitchen table drying her tears, replaying our memories together, praying her prayers for our safety.

I see my Pa-Paw sitting in the shade of his shed, next to the riding lawn mower with the little wagon he made to pull his grandchildren around his immaculate grounds. Slowly he stands and unhitches the wagon from the mower and strums a hollow note from his steel guitar.

I see the purple martins swoop and sway against the sky, snatching mosquitoes in midflight, returning with confidence to the grand hotels my grandfather created for them.

I see the giant tarantula cross his garden, gobbling up the wrong kind of bugs. I see the little horny toads with their thorny heads, skitter around the big red ant bed that we never disturb, because everything has a purpose, a reason for living, a job to do.

I see the wide Texas sky filled with white, cottony clouds and children sitting below studying the shape of them and finding rabbits or dragons aloft.

I see the bonny Bluebonnets swaying in spring, their own rhythmic dance with the Indian blankets, paintbrushes and sunflowers. And then there are the stars at night, that are big and bright, deep in the heart of Texas.

Also, in the heart of me.

"Hey… hey!"

Startled out of my reverie, I look down and see my little, red-haired cousin tugging at my pants leg, her solemn brown eyes underlined by freckles. She is peering up into my face. "They said to tell you to come on, we're leaving now."

I nod and smile watching her run out the door. Glancing back in the mirror, I lift my hand in a silent salute to Texas.

Can you remember the nursery rhyme *'there was an old woman who lived in a shoe, she had so many children, she didn't know what to do'?* Well, that's what it was like living with our kinfolk that summer. Four adults and thirteen kids! Four of those thirteen were teens. Can you imagine this month of mayhem!!!

My uncle was a chef at a fancy restaurant, so I knew we wouldn't starve.

We ate a lot of eggs.

I think my hair grew three inches that month! After the usual pairing off and taking of sides, we settled into the carefree routine that all kids enjoy in the summer.

I spent a lot of time hanging out with my beautiful dark-haired, dark-eyed cousin, but I did worry that if Rusty ever found me, would he choose her over me?

Like vapor, all my worries vanished when one day a letter came addressed to me. From Rusty! Shrieking with joy, I danced a little jig, clutching the letter to my heart, I ran off to ferret myself away to read what he wrote. Trembling with excitement, I was struck by a horrid thought! What if he's writing to say he's found another girl?

Now I stared at the letter, wishing to be one of those mind-readers who could tell what was written through a folded piece of paper.

Like ripping off a Band-Aid, I opened it quick and scanned the contents. His handwriting was a little scribbly but easy enough to read. He said my aunt had given him our address. OH! How romantic, he had been beside himself with grief when he returned to Texas and I was gone. He wanted to come see me in Oregon!

The summer now sweet and bearable once again! I had my handsome soldier boy wanting to come see me!!! Did it really matter where I lived as long as he could find me? I stood, staring out the window when I heard someone behind me. Turning, I saw my cousin enter the room we shared.

"You sure look happy! So, what did he say?" she asked.

"Can you believe it? He wants to come see me! Here! In Oregon!"

"That's terrific!" she said. "Then we can all have a chance to meet him."

"Yes…. uhhh, sure." I said, but that niggling doubt played through my head. Looking again at her exotic beauty, I remembered watching her flirt with boys on the street and seeing them reduced to babbling beasts. I couldn't help but wonder. How could Prince Charming resist such an enchanting creature?

The next morning when I woke up, I left my room to go downstairs and stopped, sniffing the air. An unusual sweet scent wafted through the hallway. I had never smelled anything like it before. I sniffed my way downstairs and saw that the kids (all nine of them) were already up and spilling in and out of doorways like bees in a bonnet. There were so many of them, I often felt like I was trying to make my way through a herd of buffalo.

Most of the time, I just ignored them and hung out with the teens. I was the eldest girl with two male cousins a few years older. These were the same cousins I once played Tarzan and Jane, black Knight, white Knight and damsels in distress with when we were little kids. Sometimes I felt we were still playing these roles. My cousins were as different as night from day and often

I preferred the company of my sweet-tempered cousin with his red birthmark to his dark-haired brother.

We were quite a conglomeration (*I was still working on my vocabulary again to sharpen my writing skills, especially now that I had someone to write to*) of skin, eye and hair color among thirteen kids. Black hair, black eyes, brown hair, brown eyes, blond hair, blue eyes and red hair, brown eyes. We were like a living rainbow!

Suddenly a loud shriek split my eardrums and I rushed to find out what new trauma was unfolding this time.

"It's a flying saucer!" shouted one of the youngest blond-haired boys.

"Don't be silly," I said, "do you want to frighten everyone?"

Little Bird flew in the door right behind him, her eyes wide with fear, "it's true! Come see!"

The parents had already left for the day, so I hurried outside to see what nonsense had scared them. Looking up where they pointed, I felt the blood drain from my face. It truly was a flying saucer!

"Quick," I said, "go get your big brothers."

I didn't know what to make of the shiny silver saucer high in the sky and my trembling was making it hard to think. Turning, I told them to go back inside.

"But we want to see!" They were all protesting as I shooed them back towards the door, their little faces now looking upwards as they crowded against the doorway.

"Then stay on the porch! Don't go out in the street." I envisioned one of them being beamed up or struck dead by a laser!

People were spilling out of their houses into the street, staring up into the sky. This only made me more nervous. By now the house was empty of kids and everyone stood on the porch silently gazing up at the saucer.

When my oldest cousin arrived, I turned to him, "What do you think we should do?"

"I'm not sure. It really does look like a flying saucer."

"I know! I wonder if the police have been called?"

"Good idea, I'm going to go inside and call them," he said.

"All right, I'll stand watch and keep the kids on the porch."

The saucer still hovered above us, shiny and silver.

A pulsating orb, high in the sky.

More people had gathered out on the street now, standing in front of their houses, gesturing and talking. I could see they were nervous as well.

My cousin quickly returned, laughing his head off.

"What? Why are you laughing? What did they say?"

"It's a blimp," he said.

"A blimp? What is that?" I was confused. I had never heard of a blimp before.

"It's like a big balloon that companies use to advertise," he explained.

"Oh my gosh, don't they know they frightened us all out of our wits?"

"Yeah," he laughed, "they said they were overrun with frantic calls."

"Well, I don't think it's funny," I said, storming inside, "I mean there are children around who were terrified!"

"Ah, don't be so uptight. Come upstairs with me and I'll give you something to help you relax."

"What?" His words made me feel even more uptight and suspicious to boot. Curious to see what the *Dark Knight* was up to, I raced up the stairs behind him. Once in his room, he closed the door. Reaching inside a little tin box, he pulled out a rolled-up cigarette.

"What's that? I prefer Marlboros to rolled cigarettes." I could smoke with the best of them when I felt like it, but I didn't feel like smoking now.

"It's not a cigarette," he said calmly and lit up. Catching a whiff of it, I flashed back to that morning and the unidentified sweet scent I had noticed in the air.

"I can't believe this!" I was furious now. "Is that pot?"

"Yep, wanta try it?"

"No! I do not! Are you crazy? Do your parents know you have drugs in this house?"

"They don't care what I do. After all, I am eighteen. A lazy grin spread across his face. "Besides, your parents sure don't care."

"What are you talking about? What does this have to do with them?"

He just laughed, raised his eyebrows and smiled. Inhaling once more, he blew the smoke right in my face.

"YOU!" I punched a finger directly in his face, "YOU better not be giving my parents pot! Don't you know I have enough trouble dealing with them now? Every. Single. Time. They drink!!!" I punched the words out, but I wanted to punch him!

"Don't be so judgmental," he shrugged, turning away.

Storming out of the door, I slammed it as hard as I could. I felt like a cement cloak weighing a thousand pounds was draped across my shoulders. Not willing to admit his words had stung. Was I judgmental?

It wasn't the first time I had heard that word in connection with myself. My mother called me that once before, with the dad nodding in agreement. Was I the one in the wrong here? Was I an uptight, stick in the mud, self-righteous prig who didn't know how to have fun?

Sighing, I shrugged. Two more years. Just two more years and then I would be eighteen and could put all of this behind me.

That summer should have been called *the Summer of Sinner and Saint!* It was an initiation of sorts. My coming of age, realizing that life seemed to be a series of 'good vs. evil, saint vs. sinner,' just like in Mad Magazine. This was the way of life. Always.

There was *always* a battle going on somewhere. Most often inside myself. Some battles I could clearly see where the lines were drawn, but most often, they were fuzzy and hard to recognize.

I was reading my Bible almost every day and could see that it seemed to work that way back in biblical times as well. Even Job, who in God's eyes was a good and righteous man, had to suffer. Even King David, beloved by God and others, didn't always choose right over wrong. Why should I be any different from famous people in the Bible?

I so longed to be good and often entertained thoughts of becoming a missionary when I finished High School. That is, if I decided against settling down, getting married and raising a family. Either choice was fine as long as I could write!

Sometimes I still resented being born a girl. It always seemed like men had more choices in life. Men had less fear and more freedom of movement. I was often jealous of my older male cousins and the fact that no one seemed to care about their coming and going, but if one of us teenage girls were out of sight for long, *wooboy*, there would be some kinda reckoning.

Perhaps that's why one night my beautiful cousin and I decided to sneak out and run the streets at two in the morning.

It was just a wild and crazy impulse and I think I was needing to prove to myself that I wasn't some kinda prig.

It must have been a full moon that night, because we ran laughing and giggling, like a couple of moon-crazed hounds. That's when the hounds found us. We were approaching a park, when out of the darkness, we heard a baying bark and heavy panting.

We stopped dead in out tracks, peering into the trees.

"It sounds like wolves! I'm scared," said my cousin, clutching my arm.

"It can't be wolves in the city."

"What if it's werewolves?" she said shivering.

"Just stand still, I think they're coming our way."

"Let's run! C'mon, we have to get out of here now!"

Out of the dark, three barking, slobbering and growling Dobermans came charging from the trees straight towards us.

She screamed and started to turn and run.

"Stop!" I grabbed her arm. "Don't move. If you run, they will attack you."

They ran right up to us and we stood still as statues while they sniffed and slobbered and growled all around us. Then, as if of one mind, they turned and raced off into the dark of night.

"Oh my gosh, that was so scary. How did you know what to do?" she asked.

"It seems to be my specialty," I laughed. "Knowing what to do in emergencies. I'm a smooth operator!"

Giggling and laughing, hysterical now, we ran all the way back home, sneaking in just as the last finger of night relinquished its pinch on the light. We never tried that again.

★★★

The summer was coming to a swift, merciful end and I was delighted when it came time to move out of my cousin's house.

We moved a few miles away, right next door to a house of Jesus Freaks! It was called *The House of No More Shadows*.

The day we moved in, I raced to the top of the third floor and claimed my room. It reminded me of a Writer's Turret, with sloped ceilings and a small window to gaze out over the rooftops of the smaller houses below.

I loved it! My writer's retreat.

After the summer of living with so many, it felt luxurious to be high above the noise and complications of life. The only restriction was that we weren't allowed to go into any of the rooms in the basement. The dad said the house belonged to his new employer and the owner's stuff was stored down there.

Naturally that piqued all of us kids' curiosity.

However, I put that thought aside because my focus was on the ever-growing pile of letters from Rusty, stashed away in my treasure box, and thinking about checking out my new school. The High School wasn't too far away, and I could walk to school once again.

The morning after we settled in, I went to register for school and pick out my classes. When I got back home the dad was standing in the living room with his back to the fireplace.

"You do realize that without a fire, you aren't going to get warm," I teased. He was currently *in favour* after finding us this house.

He guffawed, "yeah, just a habit I guess. I'm kinda looking forward to cooler temps so we can fire it up."

"That will be fun! Having a fireplace with a snowstorm swirling outside."

"So where did you run off to so early this morning?" he asked.

"Well, I decided to go talk with the school counselor and set my schedule."

"Did you pick anything exciting?"

I think this was the longest conversation we had had over the past four years and I was beginning to enjoy it. We really didn't have much of a relationship.

"Yes, they had quite a few more selections. Nothing like in Texas. Plus, I'm a couple of credits ahead so I can graduate six months ahead of my class. Anyway, I picked French II and Shakespeare's World."

"Shakespeare's World? How will that help you get a job?

"Well I believe it will help me along in my writing career. After all, I need to be well read and Shakespeare was a great writer!"

"I think French is a waste of time as well," he countered. "You should have picked Spanish instead. You'll never have the chance to use French in your lifetime!"

The bubble popped!   How dare he!

Feeling indignant, I snapped, "You have no clue where I will go or what I will do, in my life! Or even what countries I will visit!" Turning, I stormed up the stairs to my Writer's Turret and soundly slammed the door.

The House of No More Shadows

I have decided to stick with love.
Hate is too great a burden to bear.
~ Martin Luther King Jr. ~

I watched them like a hawk, or maybe a mourning dove. Nestled high above the ground in my infamous Writer's Turret, my fascination remained constant on the house next door.

Young people of all size, shape and color went to and fro (*I didn't know what 'fro' actually meant*) but, I was determined to find out more about the people next door.

Most of them seemed to be about the age of college students, with a few sprinkled in looking older. There were some I thought might be around my age.

The most remarkable thing was that they all seemed to be so peaceful, with big smiles on their faces. Happiness was a feat within itself as far as I was concerned! So, I made plans to make my move.

The day dawned bright and sunny without the gloomy curtains of rain we had been experiencing lately. It was the last Friday before school would begin, so I went outside and sat down on the front porch steps. When a friendly-faced lady walked from around the back of their house to go inside, I jumped up and sauntered over to stand next to the fence separating our properties.

"Hello," I called out, "we just moved in next door." Smiling, I put on my most award-winning grin.

She stood by the foot of their steps smiling back at me. Her hair was golden blond, long and straight, (*the kind I wished for*) and her eyes were a soft tawny brown. Kind of like a cat's eyes. She wore a simple summer dress. I thought she must be in her early twenties.

"Well, hello back! Welcome to the neighborhood!" Her teeth were straight, and brilliant white. She walked over towards me. "I'm Ruth."

"Hi Ruth. This seems to be a terrific neighborhood. And these big ol' houses sure are roomy."

I wasn't one for beating around the bush, so I got straight to the point. "I've been wondering exactly what your place is all about, y' know because of the name plate on the door that says, *'The House of No More Shadows,'* which makes me full up curious!"

"Ahhh, I'm sure you've heard what they say about curiosity."

I laughed, "yes, 'curiosity killed the cat, but you know what they say after that, doncha?"

She glanced up at the house, and for the first time I noticed a bright orange, red, and brown basket tucked over her arm. It was filled with fruits and vegetables.

"I'm about to go make a salad for our folks. Would you care to join us? Then I can tell you all about this house."

I didn't want to intrude, but curiosity had grabbed me by the seat of the pants and seemed to be in control of my legs as well. "I'd love to join you, but you have to let me help."

"You've got a deal," she said.

I quickly joined her and we both headed up the stairs into the house. Inside I caught a glimpse of a small living room and noticed a few closed doors as we headed down the hall to the kitchen in the back of the house. Everything was spit-shiny clean and when we entered the large kitchen, I noticed pots and pans of all shapes and sizes hanging from the ceiling on long hooks.

Ruth paused beside a long table placed in the center of the kitchen. It looked like a worktable with shelves below stashed with all kinds of canned goods, spices and kitchen supplies.

"Jessica usually helps me with lunch, but since you're here, she can keep working in the garden. I'm going to wash these veggies and let you chop them up for our salad."

"Everything is so shiny, clean and tidy in here. Are you the one who keeps it that way?" I asked.

"Oh no, there's about ten other girls that help out. Occasionally, some of the brothers lend a hand when they aren't out on assignment."

I wondered if they were Baptist because there was that word '*brother*' again. "Assignment?" I asked.

"Yes, the men go out on work assignments which helps to bring in funds in order to keep us in operation. The women run the garden, laundry, cooking and cleaning. It seems to work out perfectly this way."

"So, tell me more about the name, how did you come up with it?"

"Well, when we first established the house, we asked everyone what they thought we should name it and this name was what suited us best."

She glanced over, handed me some lettuce and tomatoes to chop, then laughed at my expression. "Your face is an open book," she said, "I see questions leaping out of your eyes and I keep teasing you. I'm sorry."

I didn't know what to say so just laughed along with her. I wondered how she could see what was on my face and perhaps even read my mind. No one had ever said that to me before, so I wasn't sure if it was a good thing or a bad thing having a *face like an open book.*

"So, what do all of you do here?" I finally asked, feeling awkward and unsure of how to express myself better.

Just then a man about the same age as Ruth entered the kitchen. He was tall with shoulder-length sandy hair, a well-kept goatee and he wore a loose-fitting white shirt and jeans. He also wore sandals on his feet. He kinda reminded me of what Jesus or one of his disciples might look like in modern day.

He walked over, snatched a carrot and then jumped out of the way when Ruth tried to pop him with a kitchen towel.

He turned to me offering the carrot, "want a bite?"

Laughing, I shook my head, suddenly blushing under his gaze.

"This is Josiah," said Ruth, "Our incorrigible and fearless leader."

"You know you should have more manners when we have a guest," she scolded. "For your punishment you can tell her all about our house. She has a million questions so please put her out of her misery."

Looking back and forth between the two, I examined their faces to see if they were irritated or annoyed with me, but they both just beamed sunny smiles my way. Josiah winked and then asked me point blank, "do you know the Lord?"

That took me back a minute. Talk about being direct.

"Well, uhhh… yes, as a matter of fact I do! I was baptized when I was thirteen."

I felt my face flush again and felt like a microscope specimen. It was only fair though; I had come here with my own questions and perhaps they had a few of their own.

"But," Josiah persisted, "do you know *Him*?" emphasizing the Him.

Maybe he was looking for a deeper answer, so I searched my heart, took a deep breath and said, "ever since I was a little girl, I wanted to know *Him*," I said, emphasizing *Him* the way Josiah had done.

"I remember asking my grandmother if God was stronger than Superman. She assured me that God was omnipotent, omnipresent and yes even stronger than Superman. That's really when I decided *Who* I wanted to put my trust in but, I didn't know about asking Jesus into my heart until I was thirteen."

I could hear that old mantra playing in my head, the one I used to console myself with as a child when scared, '*faster than a speeding bullet, more powerful than a locomotive, able to leap a tall building with a single bound.*' It brought me so much comfort knowing the Lord was out there to protect and care for me. But I couldn't tell them that or they would think me loco as a locomotive.

My answer seemed to satisfy him and they both smiled in agreement. I felt like I had won a prize at bingo! "*Now* will you tell me about this house?"

"Well this house is a place of worship, a place of welcome, a place for seekers needing comfort. A home away from home. We don't discriminate against anyone; we believe we are all equal in the eyes of the Lord. We have simple rules and simple needs. Working together, we try to live in harmony with our Lord and with each other," explained Josiah.

"I'm a bit of a seeker myself!" I exclaimed.

"So, are you a certain *type* of religion?", I asked, liking what I heard so far, deep down hoping they held the answer to some of the mysteries surrounding Christianity that were constantly bothering me. Especially that one particular commandment that I was having trouble obeying.

"Nope. We're just a body of believers," answered Ruth. "We don't feel like there has to be one set religion. Many of us come from different religious backgrounds. There are people here from the Jewish faith, Catholics, Baptists and I came from a Pentecostal background myself. What about yourself? Where do you fit in?"

"Well, I was raised Heathen," I said, knowing that would get a laugh, "but then I was baptized by the Baptists, went to a Seventh Day Adventist Church for a while, even went to the Jehovah Witness retreat one summer. I've been trying for at least three years to find out what the right denomination is and where I should go," I said, leaning in hoping they held the key and would put it in my hand.

"Many of us have been down that same road," continued Josiah, "each of us looking for the right way. What we've found is that Jesus is the answer. His message of love expressed throughout the gospel. We continually read our Bible to look for answers to our questions. We feel that by putting our hand in His, and trying to do our very best to trust Him, then the questions in our lives will be answered."

"It's really quite simple, yet profound! He continued, "So easy, but also very hard at times."

Ruth glanced up at the clock on the wall. It was twelve o'clock. "Lunch is ready, so let's take our conversation into the dining room and join the others. I am so glad you're here, sharing a meal with us."

When we walked into the dining room, I was surprised to see six other people, setting silverware and dishes around a long wooden table. I hadn't heard anyone enter the house because I was so wrapped up in our conversation.

Josiah and Ruth introduced me to the others, and we bowed our heads as Josiah said a simple prayer and thanked God for bringing them a special guest to share their meal with.

"Normally we have about twenty or more for dinner," explained Ruth, "but lunches are light because most of the brothers are gone for the day. Some of the sisters sell fruit and vegetables at a little stand in the city as well."

I took a bite of the delicious salad and noticed how everyone broke off a piece of crusty French bread, passed around the table. The salad was delicious with chopped ham, cheese and boiled eggs, so it really was a complete meal.

We passed around a pitcher of water and everyone chattered away about this and that. My mind was filled with all we had talked about in the kitchen.

I felt like an honored guest at their table. Studying the peaceful smiles on their faces and listening to the lively conversation sprinkled with laughter, I was thinking, *'this seems too good to be true. Living next door to these folks was FANTASTIC!!!*

After lunch I helped with the dishes wishing I could stay all day, but I didn't want to wear out my welcome, so made my good-byes.

Walking with me to the door, Ruth turned and said, "We have a Bible Study on Tuesday and Thursday around seven in the evening, and play games and have a Sing-along on Wednesdays. You're welcome to join us anytime."

"Thanks, I would love to!" To my surprise she leaned over and gave me a warm hug.

Feeling like I was floating on air, I went back home. So thankful and filled with such peace that I didn't even notice my mother standing near the doorway when I entered.

"Where have you been?" she asked, her voice a bit cross, "I've been looking for you for over an hour."

"Oh, I was meeting the people next door. They invited me to lunch."

"Well, you shouldn't be bothering them."

"Mom, I wasn't bothering them. They're wonderful Christians and I want to go back for a Bible study with them during the week."

"Hmmm… I don't know about that. They look like a cult."

"Well, they're not! Cheez, I can't believe you sometimes." So much for peace, I thought, storming up the stairs to lock myself away.

The next morning, I woke up later than usual. After all, it was the last free weekend before I began my junior year at the new High School. I was all sorts of nervous about Monday, because I was used to being in a small school with my friends. Now I would be attending a big city school with strangers.

When I went downstairs, I noticed *Never Amount* and *Boy Blue* in a furtive huddle by the basement door in the kitchen. They were startled when I came in, so I knew something was up. "Okay, you two, what did you do?"

"Nothing," answered *Boy Blue*, turning his most innocent look my way. He could be a bit of a con acting all innocent when he wasn't, so I looked at *Never Amount* instead, drilling him with my eyes. He began to squirm.

"Ah Ha! I thought so, you two can't lie to me! Now fess up." *Boy Blue* sighed, "oh, all right but you can't tell Dad."

"Have you guys been in the basement?" (*I was trying to get used to using the Oregon term 'you guys' as opposed to the Texas 'y'all' before school started*). Teasing about the accent was bad enough, and I didn't want to stick out like some kinda hillbilly.

"….and so, we thought…"

Realizing I had drifted out of their conversation, I said, "wait, back up, start over."

Never Amount rolled his eyes and *Boy Blue* sighed, then continued, "Well you know how Dad said never go into the basement?"

"Yes. And so why did you?"

"Wait, how do you know?" asked *Boy Blue* eyeing me suspiciously.

"I've told you before, I have eyes in the back of my head. So, did you go into any of the rooms down there?" I didn't want to admit it, but I was as curious as they were.

"That's just the thing," said *Never Amount*, "we got scared. We heard noises coming from one of the rooms and ran back upstairs."

"What kinda noises?"

"Just weird scratching noises."

"Well it was probably just a mouse. You boys need to stay outta there."

"It sounded a lot bigger than a mouse," muttered *Boy Blue* under his breath.

Just then *Little Bird* and *Sky Eyes* ran into the kitchen. "y'all gotta come to the park with us," said *Little Bird*.

"Yep, you'll never believe it. It's a wonderful surprise!" added *Sky Eyes*.

I glanced at the clock and noticed it was already approaching noon. "Oh okay, let me put my tennis shoes on and we'll come see your surprise."

The park was only a few blocks away and the kids and I had already visited it earlier to check it out and try the swings. Besides, it would be a good distraction to keep the boys away from the basement.

When we got to the edge of the park, *Sky Eyes* couldn't keep still, she was so excited, hopping from one foot to the next. *Little Bird* started giggling. "Look!" they said in unison.

I looked to where they were pointing, and over by the picnic tables was a big van with lots of people milling around. Many kids, large and small were milling around beginning to form lines in front of the van.

"What's that all about?" I asked.

"Free FOOD!" yelled *Sky Eyes,* and *Little Bird* nodded, "yep for kids like us. The other kids told us this van comes here three times a week to feed kids who don't have food when school is out. Today is their last day."

"Wow," said *Never Amount*, "that's terrific! I wish we knew about it before. Can we go get some?" he turned towards me, his hungry, big brown eyes focused on me.

Shoot, I thought, why not? These kids miss meals all the time, sometimes we only get one meal a day. Secretly I was too embarrassed to take a handout and felt that pride thing well up inside me, but I wasn't going to stop them. My stomach started growling.

"Go on," I said, "I think that's a grand idea. They should be proud of what they're doing, feeding hungry, little kids. Make sure you thank them. I'll see you guys later."

"Don't leave," pleaded *Little Bird*.

"Yeah, come with us puh-leeease," added *Sky Eyes* stretching out her hand.

Shrugging, I relented. It was only one meal after all. Walking over to join the line, I looked around for others my age and noticed kids of every age, race and size. We might be different in many ways, but we had one thing in common. We were all hungry.

Grateful, I accepted the sandwich, apple and milk, sincerely thanking the adults who smiled, generously handing out food. When everyone had been served, they even invited everyone back for seconds. This would never happen in the small town we had just left. Perhaps living in a big city wasn't all bad.

*****

The first few days of school were frightening, exhilarating, challenging and confusing. All kinds of crazy emotions rolled into one big fast and furious, tumultuous ball. I couldn't help but be constantly comparing this school with my last one. There were so many differences, mostly good, but some that disturbed me.

The good things were that there were so many more options for classes in which to choose. I thought they had more opportunities for a student to become a productive member of society with job counseling and placement available. Student counseling was offered as well.

So many choices.

Even the cafeteria had several choices. I stood in the middle of the dining room overwhelmed by indecision. There was a section for those wanting fast food like burgers, pizza and such. And a section for a larger meal with hot food. There was even a fruit and salad bar! In the halls were vending machines in case you needed a between class snack.

By chance, I noticed students dropping trash on the floor and not bothering to pick it up, and some students were throwing food across the room at each other. I looked around for a teacher to establish order and realized there weren't any, nor would there ever be anyone to bring order in the lunchroom. Insanity ran amuck and I was astonished that people in High School could be so irresponsible, wasteful and disrespectful of property.

I did enjoy the fact that we didn't have a dress code like my school back home but sometimes I couldn't tell the teachers from the kids. We all seemed to dress the same! Jeans and T-shirts with tennis shoes or sandals were the norm for everybody.

Once when entering a hallway, I smelled that familiar, sweet odor and wasn't sure if it was teachers or students, or a combination of both, smoking pot under the stairwell.

After only a few days I began to realize that I seemed to prefer order over chaos. However, I was good at adapting. Hadn't I been practicing it since birth? But, in order to survive I would have to find a pocket of peace and sanity within myself.

Wednesday evening after the parents had left to go to a local bar, I went next door to join the sing-along at *The House of No More Shadows*. They welcomed me in like a long-lost friend and I realized that truly, they were my only friends in this city.

Josiah and Ruth introduced me around and I took a seat on the floor with some of the others. All the chairs, sofas, and beanbags were filled and singing was underway.

A girl with long black hair strummed a guitar and another bounced a set of cymbals against her knees. A very handsome black man with long braids beat a rhythm on a bongo. Everyone joined in the singing and some of the songs were familiar to me but, some I just hummed along with.

In between songs, Josiah would ask a particular person if they had anything to share, a prayer request or praise.   Whenever someone had a particularly troublesome event to share, Ruth wrote it down for everyone to pray about later.

I had never seen such tender, loving care and concern as what I saw displayed in this house. They truly were a family united. With so many differences among them, different dialect, different social and religious backgrounds, they just seemed to have the answer to deal with every situation. If someone didn't have the answer, they prayed about it.

In the next few weeks, I divided my time between writing letters to Rusty, trying to adapt to my new school and, going to visit my new friends next door.

I attended their Bible studies, saw people baptized in the shower and once even shared my own concern about not having any friends at school. Their prayers to God for me to find a friend soon really touched my heart.

I tried to dodge my parents who were constantly bombarding me with unfair remarks about the house next door.

One evening, after returning from a particularly poignant Bible study about trying to love the Lord with your whole heart, mind and spirit and also to love your neighbor as yourself, I walked back home filled with such joy and peace, that I felt like I was floating.

My mother called me in from the living room.

"You're spending an awful lot of time over there," she said, peering suspiciously into my face.

"I love being with them. We just had a fantastic Bible Study, it was about…"

She interrupted, "well I just don't think it's right that you're with those people so much. They're older than you. And why does your face look like that every time you come home?"

"Like what?" I had no clue what she was talking about but felt frantic for her to not deny me this sanctuary. It was my only peace of mind.

"I don't know, you just look funny. Like too happy. Are you sure you're not smoking something with them or trying out drugs?"

"MOM," I was aghast. "How can you say something like that? These are good decent, people! They don't do drugs! And I *am* just so happy when I'm with them. I feel so peaceful after I come back from being there. They are teaching me more about loving others through the Lord. Why can't you understand that?"

She just stared at me, and I could tell by the look on her face she didn't believe me.

I wanted to say, *'just because you do drugs doesn't mean everyone does,'* but bit my tongue. I knew it wouldn't be a very loving thing to say.

All my life I had been so quick to attack when someone lashed out at me, especially with words and on occasion even my fists. What had it got me? Only more pain and heartache. If loving people more, even my parents, would help me feel more at peace, then I was willing to give it a try.

"Well, don't get too attached," she said, "your father's job isn't working out like he expected and he's looking for something else. If he gets a different job, we can't stay in the boss' house."

With a heavy heart, I turned and started upstairs to bed.

"Oh, I forgot to tell you," she called after me, "there's a letter from Rusty. It went to your aunt's house before you sent him your new address. It's on your bed."

Upstairs, I picked up the letter, but my mind was still replaying the conversation between my mother and me.

Same ol' song, never for long, in any place. Always, always on the move. This time, I would just run away and move in with my friends next door. How could I leave behind my only peace of mind?

With that thought for comfort I opened Rusty's letter. It was postmarked behind his most recent letter. And I couldn't believe my eyes! He was coming for a visit! Next week!

*****

I was enjoying school in spite of not knowing a soul or having any friends. Occasionally, I searched the faces of my teachers thinking that perhaps, I could befriend one of them.

Feeling much older than my peers, even scoffing at the immaturity I saw around me, I often had doubts whether I could even like someone my age.

In an Economics class we were told to choose stock options to follow for a year. This was the first time I had heard about stocks and bonds. I chose Campbell Soup and Kodak Film. Surely there was safety in these two corporations.

The entire school was all abuzz about the scandals happening with President Nixon and our teachers used the headlines to focus our attention on politics and World Events. My focus, however, was not on the President, Campbell Soup or the price of tea in China. My head was in a cloud drifting to a tune in a moonlit dance, lips ever so soft on mine. Thinking of emerald eyes that sparkled in an enchanted forest.

I always completed my homework on time, so my grades remained high, but in class I really wasn't there.

Envisioning Rusty's upcoming visit, I thought how excited he would be to meet my new friends, feeling he was sure to be sympathetic about my impending dilemma of having to leave them. Surely, he would stand beside me and help me to plead my case against my parents so I could stay with Ruth and Josiah if the decision came to move again.

I mean really! How many times must I pull my tender roots out of the ground to be replanted?

*****

OH, splendid day! Oregon was spectacular in all her glory of red, yellow, brown and green! Surely the leaves were shivering with excitement just as excited as me! The temperature was perfect and the sky a sea of blue, dotted with puffy, white clouds skimming overhead like sailboats in a race.

Shifting nervously from foot to foot, I waited for the Greyhound bus to pull into the station. Thankful that the dad decided to wait in the car so at least we could have one breathtaking and perfect kiss before dealing with parents.

And then he was here, standing before me handsome and perfect in every way. We stood looking into each other's eyes, and when I went to go into his arms, he glanced around and said, "Uh, where are your parents?"

Hmmm, it wasn't the reaction I was hoping for and I felt my smile slide right off my face plopping to rest on my tennis shoes.

"In the car, well… Mom's at home."

"It's great to finally see you again," he said. "Your letters have been terrific."

"Yours as well. Are you ready to go or do you need to wait for a bag?"

"No. I'm ready, everything is here," he said, indicating a small gym bag thrown over his shoulder.

He crooked his arm for me to take and my smile returned with this familiar gesture of his. It was old-fashioned and quite gentlemanly; something that always tickled me inside.

We headed to the car and kept up the small talk. He must be nervous about meeting my parents and that's why we're acting like strangers with each other.

I introduced him to the dad and soon they were chatting like old friends. Actually, I felt a bit left out, but was relieved he wasn't nervous anymore. When we pulled up in front of the house, he said, "Nice house. It's really big."

"Yeah, too bad we have to move out next week," said the dad.

My heart took a sudden plunge. How dare he spring the news on me like this! When I gave him a dirty look, he looked confused and said, "what? Didn't your mother tell you?"

Instead of answering, I took Rusty's bag and said, "C'mon, I'll show you where you're sleeping."

Inside I was seething, but knew I had to get a grip on myself. It wasn't fair to drag Rusty into family drama. This was his last vacation before he headed overseas, and I didn't want to ruin it for him. It was hard enough meeting so many people at one time.

"I hope you don't mind bunking with my brothers. They'll share a bed and you can have this one to yourself."

"I don't mind at all. I can sleep on a couch or the floor. I don't want to put anyone out."

"No, they'll be delighted to have company."

When we returned downstairs, I took Rusty in to meet the family. They were gathered in the living room. The boys immediately began to drill him with questions about the military and the girls nodded and shyly ducking their heads. I knew that was a ruse. They would talk his ear off before the night was over.

In between the chatter, my mother was looking him up and down and starting the twenty questions game. After about the fourth question, I decided to come to his rescue.

"Would you like to go for a walk?"

He searched the faces of my parents trying to see if they objected and for some reason this irritated me. Finally, he nodded and we headed out the door.

"Your parents seem really nice," he began, "especially your dad."

"Hmmm… well I'm sure you're feeling overwhelmed having to meet everyone at once like that…"

"No, it's okay. I'm used to a big family."

I realized there were still so many things we didn't know about each other. I had about twenty or fifty questions of my own.

We walked to the park and on the way I told him about *The House of No More Shadows* and how wonderful the people were who lived there. "I can't wait to take you next door to meet them. Would you like to go over tonight for a Bible Study?"

"Uh no, I don't really think so. Don't you think we should spend some time with your parents?"

"Oh well, I guess so. Maybe another night, then?"

"Maybe. So how's school so far?"

And then I told him how different everything was here than from Texas. How I was enjoying my classes, but how lonely it was without any friends.

He reached over and pulled me close. "You don't have to feel lonely. You have me!"

"Yes, but you're going overseas soon."

"Well, you'll still be writing me. Do you think your parents would let you come for a visit?"

"Shoot no!" I said. "I'm just now allowed to go out on a date."

"Sometimes I forget how young you are. You seem so mature for your age. It's one of the things I like about you," he smiled.

Uh oh, I felt myself slipping away into the Emerald Forest. "Really? And what are some of the other things you like about me?"

Under one of the trees he finally pulled me into his arms for a long and satisfying kiss. The kiss I missed at the bus station. His spicy scented aftershave, tickling my senses, and my arms reached up to wrap around his neck. Now this was more like it!

When we walked back to the house, I noticed a couple of the brothers from the house next door milling about. Looking at their shoulder-length hair, I wondered what Rusty would look like with long, curly hair.

I stopped to introduce Rusty to them and felt him stiffen. His greeting to them was short and curt. When we walked away, I said, "you know they're really nice people."

"I didn't say they weren't," he replied.

*****

The next couple of days did not bode well for our budding relationship. We seemed to argue about everything.

The final straw came a few hours before he had to catch a bus to a small town in the mountains up north. He was headed there to visit his family. We were sitting outside on the porch.

When Josiah came out of the house next door, I jumped up and waved.

"I don't see why you're so fascinated with those people," said Rusty.

"I have tried. To Explain. This to you. Before." I punched the words out like nails from a nail gun. "They're my friends. My only friends here and they're beautiful Christian people who genuinely care about me."

"Oh, and I don't?"

"Well, if you did, it would seem to me, that you would take an interest in what interests me!"

"And those guys over there apparently have your interest, is that it?"

"You really don't have a clue. Do you have a relationship with Jesus Christ?"

"I don't see what that has to do with it!" His eyes had a hard glint to them, like a light sparking off a stone. I had never seen this look from him before.

"If you don't have a real relationship with God, then our relationship can never work," I said softly, feeling as if a chunk of coal had settled cold and hard inside my stomach.

"Well I guess when I leave, then this will be good-bye," he said.

Looking at him, I searched his eyes for the person I had met in Texas. This visit had not been anything like I expected.

Deep down, I was miserable, but knew we were not suitably matched. Our house would be a house divided if we ever decided to marry. But, was I really ready to let him go?

"I think your father is right," he said, "those people next door are not a good influence on you."

"What time does your bus leave again?"

*****

It should have been Wednesday, Wednesday full of woe, but it wasn't. It was a Saturday. Watching from my Writer's Turret, I saw the big truck pull up outside to take our belongings to a house outside of the city. I just couldn't leave my newfound friends! When I knew I wasn't being watched, I went down the back way, through the kitchen and slipped out the basement door.

Ruth answered my knock and immediately could tell how upset I was when she saw my swollen eyes and tear stained cheeks.

"Come inside. What is it? What has happened?"

"I really need to talk to you and Josiah," I said struggling to not lose control. I wanted to be clear-headed when I made my appeal to them.

"Come on, let's go somewhere we can talk in private. Josiah, can you join us," she said as Josiah started to walk by.

Once we were seated in a small office, they both smiled, waiting for me to begin.

"Well, I've been having trouble with one of the Ten Commandments. I think that sometimes it shouldn't apply for certain situations."

"Which commandment are you having trouble with?" asked Josiah.

"The *Honor Your Father and Mother* one. I mean what if they don't deserve to be honored?" I looked them both straight in the eyes. Surely, they would understand my dilemma.

"Doesn't matter," said Josiah, returning my look.

"But they want me to move away from here and I want to come live with you guys. They don't understand the way I feel."

"Doesn't matter," said Ruth, turning a sympathetic look my way.

"But they think I'm over here doing drugs when I come back feeling all peaceful!"

"Doesn't matter," they both said in unison.

"Are you saying my feelings don't matter?" I could feel tears filling my eyes again.

"Oh, my dear, no!" they said. "What we are saying," continued Josiah, "is that you still have to obey and trust the Lord to take care of you in these situations. We would never allow you to come here and disobey your parents. While you are underage, you have to abide by your parents' rules."

"Yes, and we know how hard it can be to live with parents that don't know the Lord the same way you do," continued Ruth, "but you still have to honor, love and do your best to respect them while living under their roof."

By now I was sobbing, I couldn't believe what they were saying. How could they turn me away like this?

Ruth came over, sat down, and put her arms around me. "I know it's hard for you to understand now, but God put that commandment in the Bible for a reason. It is a very important commandment and the first that comes with a promise. Remember how we talked about how important love is, more important than all the other gifts?"

I nodded.

"Well, try to love your parents the way God loves you. Try to understand that He loves them too! It will make a huge difference in your life."

"But it just seems so hard! Sometimes, I feel I haven't any love left for them."

"Josiah and I will be praying for you every day, and we'll ask the others to pray as well. You're always welcome in this house, but you have to live with your parents."

I nodded once more, but my head and heart felt as heavy as the tablets of stone on which the commandments had been written.

Josiah and Ruth stood and put their hands on my shoulders and prayed a beautiful prayer over me, asking for God's protection and peace and that He would fill my heart with love for my parents.

Life would be so much harder not having them next door. Once again, I was waving good-bye to people I had grown to love and trust.

Returning by way of the basement I said to the Lord, "Well Lord, if I can survive the next two years and obey this commandment of Yours, You might get another missionary for Your team!"

I stood wiping my tears and heard a small shuffling sound. Peering around in the gloomy basement at all the closed doors, I tried to pinpoint where the sound came from. I heard it again and my heart thudded in my chest. "Who's there?" I cried out. Silence. I walked over and put my hand on the doorknob of the room I thought the sound came from. One of the doors we weren't allowed to open.

God's commandment flitted through my mind soft as angel wings. I released the knob and quickly ran up the stairs. Some doors were better left unopened!

Doodle Rock Island

You have brains in your head. You have feet in your shoes.
You can steer yourself in any direction you choose.
You're on your own and you know what you know.
And you are the guy who'll decide where to go.
~ Dr. Seuss ~

The ashes on the cigarette stood high. Stacked, but bent slightly like an old man wearing a wrinkled, gray accordion suit. Poised to take the plunge to the floor. That old man was the least of my worries.

Suddenly lyrics leapt into my head spiraling like a sprite dancing with shadows in the snow,

'A winter's day.

In a deep and dark December.

I am alone...

twirling inside me like a waterspout rising in rhythm from the ocean floor,

Up in walls.

A fortress deep and mighty.

That none may penetrate.

I have no need of friendship, for friendship causes pain...

I am a rock, I am an island....

twisting like a tornado hungrily grazing through an empty prairie,

Don't talk of love, well I've heard the word before.

It's sleeping in my memory.

I have my books and my poetry to protect me.
I am shielded in my armor.
Hiding in my room, safe within my womb.
I touch no one and no one touches me.
I am a rock, I am an island.
For a rock feels no pain and an island never
cries. '

Simon and Garfunkel really knew what they were singing about. That's exactly how I feel.

Come to think of it, do they really know what it is to feel so totally lost and alone? After all Simon had Garfunkel, and Garfunkel had Simon.

How can they relate to someone like me?

Someone who feels like the only grown-up in her family. Someone who feels like an island among seven. An island where everyone visits her shore daily in search of shelter, food, comfort and safety.

Once again, I glance at the cigarette between Mom's fingers.

How can she do that? Her head had fallen slightly forward, chin resting on chest, yet her fingers remained tight, holding her cigarette upright?

The ashes, now having taken the plunge, lay sleeping on the floor. Ashes dead, but the clean fiery head still burned bright, alive and red.

At the age of sixteen, I had learned a few things about life and decided it was about time to have a theme song. Besides, I am sick to death of feeling pain and crying my eyes out with no results. I will just have to toughen up. Become a fortress. A rock! An island! I had already learned:

Promises- Were made only to be broken.

Friendships-Were made only to be left behind.

Love-Well, love has a hollow sound and is way too loosely translated. Somewhere along the way, love must've got swallowed up by reality. And reality, well reality left teeth prints not only on my butt, but on my soul as well.

So, like the song says, *'don't talk of love,'* for love it seems to me, should be forbidden to come out of anyone's mouth until it was proven.

Love certainly wasn't sitting beside me, a parent with the nods, while I waited to catch a lit cigarette before it fell, hitting the couch and burning us all up in our beds.

Funny, but that kinda reminds me of that old childhood riddle where you put your finger in a little spiral of dirt in the ground where a doodle-bug lives, and sing *'doodle-bug, doodle-bug, come out of your home, for your house is on fire and your children will burn.'* Then the little doodle-bug scurries to the surface.

Hmmm, I wonder how rich folks amused themselves when they were little kids. Probably don't even know about houses where doodle-bugs live. Man, I must really be tired.

So, what does that make me? An island? A rock? Or a doodle-bug.

Whoops! Almost too late. Just in the nick of time, I snatched up the falling cigarette as it fell from

Mom's fingers. Unfortunately, by moving so fast, I knocked over a glass, which made a noise that woke her up!

Dammit! After trying so hard to let her pass out for the night.

"Wha.. wha…whersit at?"

Turning a bleary eye, she looked over at me, then down at her hand. Almost falling off the couch, she reached for her cigarettes lying on the coffee table, took one out, lit it, and inhaled. Then she glanced over at me, "Whaz you doin' up?"

"Just sitting here, reading," I nodded towards the book in my hands.

"Wal gaw-on ta bed."

"I will in a minute," I looked down at the pages, I hadn't a clue what the book was that I held in my hands, hadn't even looked at it. So I sat still, hoping that she would nod off again soon.

This time I'll hide her cigarettes so I can go to bed. The bottle of gin had already been poured down the sink. I knew she would think she had drunk it all. I had no clue where the pills were or even what she had taken.

"Wars ma drink?" She looked down and noticed the overturned glass. Then she looked at the wall and hissed under her breath, calling me over. "Ya see em?"

I glanced in the direction she was looking. "What? There's nothing there."

"Sssssnakes! Canya see um, snnnaakees," her voice trembled.

"Mom, there's no snakes."

"Yesss dar iss! Get da gun. Ya gotta ssshoot um."

The rifle was hidden, and the kids were asleep. I had no clue where *he* had gone after they started fighting. "Mom, I'm telling you, you're just seeing things. Close your eyes. Or why don't you go to bed?"

She struggled to look at me again, then finally closed her eyes. Her heavy slump back into the couch made me want to sigh with relief, but I kept quiet.

Then after a time, I very slowly stood and stretched, trying to loosen the tension in my neck and shoulders. It was going to be a long night. Sitting back down, I tried to beckon the words into my head once again.

My new theme song. I need those words to help me drift through the night. The music would give me strength.

Suddenly, I knew what I would do when I finally turned eighteen!

I would find an island to live on.

I would live there, writing my books and poetry.

I would name it Doodle Rock Island!!!

Way cool!

Looking over, I noticed the old, gray man in accordion suit was back, inching his way up, waiting to take the plunge.

Things that go Cold in the Night

Sorrow seems sent for our instruction, as we darken the cages of birds when we teach them to sing.
~ Jean Paul ~

The snow.

Again.

Quiet, peaceful, simple.

Unlike their lives.

The Oregon mountainous foothills surrounding Portland had a simplistic beauty that Sad wished could reflect the inside dynamics of her family life.

Raising the axe over her head, she brought it down hard into the chunk of wood in front of her. The stillness of the early morn splintered and lay in two pieces beside the chopping block. The chopping block smiled up at her. The pine-scented morning air blew a congratulatory kiss! Sad took an imaginary bow. She deserved it after all, it took a lot of muscle to be able to split a chunk of wood in two like that.

She was not a little girl anymore. But the snow always rekindled that 'little beggar' taunt. Following her through the years, burning her memory like fiery fingers of sizzling orbs. The humiliation fresh in her mind. Then.

And now.

A new humiliation.

Sad gritted her teeth and swung the axe again. The chunk of wood split in two and lay dead at her feet. One chunk reminded her of Dina, the girl who lived just down the road. The one she thought was a friend.

She swung the axe again, this time at the piece of dead wood at her feet. The axe swung wide and stuck in the earth beneath the fallen snow.

Straightening up, Sad tossed back her hair, getting the long strands away from her face. Glaring up the road towards the house on the hill, she had half a mind to stomp through the snow and fling a few venomous words at the hateful girl! Silence that smug look on her face. The look burned into her memory.

It had happened when Sad stepped on the bus yesterday morning. Dina looked right at her, pointing a finger in Sad's direction, causing everyone on the bus to look at her and then with a self-satisfied smirk, Dina had blurted out. "Oh, I see you're wearing my dress!"

Sad stood confused.

Who was she talking to? What did she mean?

She glanced down at the skirt and blouse she had put on that morning. Remembering how delighted she had been to see something new in the bag of clothes left lying in the living room floor. Sad plucked them out, ironed them, never questioning where the outfit came from. People gave their family old clothes all the time.

Horror painted a red flag across Sad's face! She muttered something and sat down. She would not cry in front of them. And she would never, ever, wear something she didn't know from whence it came.

She had learned a valuable lesson that day.

Sad lifted her head and sat up straight and proud in the bus. She would not be the little beggar girl a third time!

Sad bent over and picked up the axe. Brushed the snow off. Glanced at the small stack of wood and resolved to finish the chore before lunchtime.

She was glad the little shack where she and her sisters slept had a wood-burning stove, but continually worried about the dilapidated bus where her brothers slept. The doorway and a window or two were missing, and old rugs and the duct tape that covered them surely wouldn't keep out the cold. The worry was a gnawing gnat on her mind every shivery night. She had told the boys to come inside the shack with them if they got too cold, but they insisted they were fine.

She saw *Little Bird* fly from the outhouse. The door-less outhouse. It sat facing the woods. In the winter, they scraped snow off the seat and in the summer fought bees. Sad smiled. It was actually kinda funny! Surely the makings of a poem or a song.

"Want to come over here and stack this wood for me?" She called out before *Little Bird* could fly away.

"Okay."

Sad smiled at the upturned freckled nose, the big brown eyes and dimpled smile. *Little Bird* was a beloved child. She didn't talk much, worked hard, and was always the first to laugh. Sad relied on her a lot, sometimes too much. Even though *Little Bird* was second to the youngest, Sad often thought her to be more mature than her two brothers.

She reached out tousling her straight, bowl-cut chestnut hair, then turned back to the job at hand.

The morning sun melted into the day. Twilight teased the afternoon and Sad realized with a start that her

Saturday had almost escaped. After chopping the wood, she had gone through her clothes with a fine-tooth comb, ensuring there would not be a repeat of the bus fiasco. Then she ironed a batch of shirts for the lady down the hill. The extra money would buy her shampoo and orange juice if her parents didn't borrow it first. She had learned long ago that beer, cigarettes and coffee were first priorities in this household.

Now she stood cooking fried potatoes in the one-bedroom main house, where her parents slept, wondering when they would return. She didn't really care, less drama when they were away. But always in the back of her mind the question of how they would be upon returning. A worrisome thread, always pecking at her brain.

Sad called the kids into the house for fried potato sandwiches. They swarmed in, smiling with cherry red noses from being out in the cold. She added more logs to the wood burning stove, standing in the center of the living room. They all crowded around trying to stay warm while munching on supper.

"Want to watch TV?" she asked.

They nodded their heads and settled on the floor and couch. Sad began changing the channels one at a time, trying to adjust the antenna so they could see what the choices were. The dad had hooked up a line to get reception and some cable networks. She knew that he had done it after they couldn't pay the bill. Sometimes they got electricity that way too, after the electric company shut them off. She didn't know how he did it, but was glad he was smart that way. It was hard to do homework without lights at night.

"That one!" hollered *Never Amount*.

Sad stopped turning the knob, startled out of her reverie. "What?"

"Go back a channel," he said, "it looked like a scary movie."

"I don't know," replied Sad, looking into the faces of the two younger girls. She turned the knob one click back to see what was on. It didn't look too scary, she thought.

The movie was, *"Wait Until Dark"* starring Audrey Hepburn. Perhaps it wouldn't be too unsettling. "This one?"

They nodded; eyes glued to the screen. How quick they were to enter another reality, unlike her when it came to television. The only time she was lost from reality was reading stories or writing them.

She tried to concentrate on the movie but kept getting distracted. Her ear cocked to listen for a car in the driveway, her shoulders tensing, the potatoes forming a cold, greasy knot in her belly. With the dark now putting on his pajamas and settling in for the night, she just knew they would come home crocked. She turned back to watch the movie.

Suspense filled the small two-room cabin. The blind woman couldn't see the killers stalking her inside her own house! Suddenly *Little Bird* started giggling. Sad looked over at her.

"What's so funny?"

"Nothing." she said.

"Then why are you laughing?"

Little Bird just shook her head, eyes glued to the TV. Then Sad remembered. This not so chatty little girl always laughed when she was scared or unhappy. Sad smiled and went to sit between the two little ones, lending her presence to help their unease.

The movie ended and they all stood up, everyone talking at once to shake the scary scene from their minds. There was nothing else to do but send them to bed. She hoped they wouldn't have nightmares. Sad watched the boy's troop to their bus, told the little girls to run to their shack.

"But…I'm scared," objected *Sky Eyes*.

"Go on, I'll be there in just a minute. I need to wash up these dishes."

They stood there looking towards the darkened shack, their eyes big in their face, begging a silent plea.

"C'mon, I'll walk with you and turn on the light."

Three sets of feet crushed a path through the new-fallen snow. Sad shivered inside the darkened shack and turned on the light.

"Brrrr… it's cold in here. Jump under the covers and I'll start us a fire."

Sad twisted some newspaper, put in some kindling and lit the small fire. She added more kindling until it was burning strong, then added larger pieces of wood.

The crunch of tires sounded a warning in the driveway. Quickly, she turned off the light inside the shack, peering out into the darkened night towards her brothers' bus, glad to see it dark.

Only the light of the moon was left for her, to study if the two figures leaving the car were stumbling. Holding her breath to listen for angry words or laughter.

"Is Mama home?" asked *Little Bird.*

"Shhh…" said Sad into the hushed room, "go to sleep."

She turned back to the window, peering out, then heard an angry male voice and the main cabin door slam.

She peeled off her shoes, jeans, slipped out of her bra and crawled into bed. Dishes could wait. She was going to sleep, too.

Hoping for the sun to come up soon. In the morning everything would be all right.

She listened to the hush, rush, crush of the fire eating wood and fell fast asleep.

Sad was dreaming a woodpecker was tapping on a tall pine tree.

Tap, tap, tap.

Now, it was pecking at her sleeve…

"Wake-up! Please wake-up," came a whisper in the night.

Sad was startled awake by a little hand tugging at her sleeve. By the light of the dying embers glowing from the woodstove, Sad could make out *Little Bird,* standing next to her bed.

"What are you doing? Why are you out of bed?"

"She's at the window." Her big brown eyes glowed large and frightened in her pale face.

"No one's at the window. You're just dreaming. Go on back to bed."

Little Bird shook her head and turned towards the window, pulling harder at Sad's sleeve.

"No, I heard her. Mama's at the window. She's crying."

"Why would she be at the window? She can come in the door."

"I dunno," said *Little Bird*, a sob trapped in her throat.

Sad climbed out of the bed, irritated, but knowing she would have to look.

She went to the window, the two little girls both up now and following close behind her.

The moon had settled high in the sky, etching the snow with the blackened shadows of dancing branches from the wind-spooked trees.

Sad peered out the window, then gasped when her mother's tear-blotched face peered back. She stood shivering in the snow. Barefoot, wearing only a thin, sleeveless negligee to protect her from the whipping wind.

Shaking fingers stretching out to Sad then grasped at the window frame. Blue lips trembling as she tried to call her name.

"Come to the door!" yelled Sad.

"No....no.... I can't," she quivered.

"Come around to the door," demanded Sad, "we'll open it for you."

She seemed to melt into the snow as she shivered at the window. Sad pushed the window open. Said it louder into the terrified night. "Come to the door, Mom."

"I can't," she whispered, scared creeping vines inside her voice, "he'll see me. He locked me out."

The hushed words reverberated loud, bounced around the room, banged against the heads of the two little girls peering out the window who pressed close against Sad.

Sad turned, looked at the horrified expression on *Little Bird's* face. Tears were running a river down her little cheeks, trembling when she turned, and looking terrified at the bolted door of their shack. As if she expected the devil himself to break down their door.

Together they turned, pulling their shivering frostbitten mother through the window into the room. She could barely talk, her teeth were chattering like skeleton-bones rattling on Halloween. All hands pulling blankets off their beds to wrap around their crying mother.

"Ddddd   uuuu   oooo   nnn't...   let   ... hhhhiiiimmmm ...innnnn." she chattered.

Sad stoked up the fire, tossing on more logs.

"Don't worry, he's not coming," she said, resolute, somehow knowing it to be true.

Sky Eyes jumped back into the bed, pulling a blanket over her head. Sad looked around for *Little Bird*.

She saw her then, standing resolute by the door facing out into the room, moonlight painting molten steel across her masked face of iron.

Her arms were stretched wide, back braced to barricade the door. Terror toes digging hard into the wood floor, her bare feet firmly anchored.

A tiny bird transformed into an Iron Angel.

Sad watched her. Heaving a heavy sign into the darkened room.

The distance between them grew heavy.

Wishing.

Wishing for the sun and the sound of an angel laughing.

The Alcove of Angst

Sometimes...
...when I write the stories about our lives,
I worry that I am not telling the story right.
I want to get it right.

I know it is wrong to talk bad
about my family.
I have held on to our dark secrets
my whole life long.

I have nursed my wounds alone,
during the darkest hours of the night,
with only **God's song** like a hummingbird
buzzing in my ear for comfort.
I often ask are His songs enough?

I don't want folks to think
that I don't love my mother, because I do.
Very much!

She makes me potato soup
when I'm sick with tonsillitis.
Even when the fever gives me strange dreams,

I know she will be somewhere in the house,
perhaps saying a prayer for my recovery.
I think about the songs she sang when I was a
little girl, and the time she made us
schnickerdoodle cookies for Christmas.
She taught us the beauty in
lightning and thunder.
We are never afraid of storms.

I know she loves us with a jealous love.
She tells me that I'm beautiful.

With all these wonderful things to remember,
on top of the sad,
I am often filled with questions,
left feeling confused.

An
Alcove of Angst
deep within my soul.

Soldier Boy, oh my little soldier boy…

Truly, it is in darkness that one finds the light,
so when we are in sorrow,
then this light is nearest of all to us.
~ Meister Eckhart ~

Slowly releasing the clutch, I sped around the yard on the Yamaha dirt bike, then speeding up, took the hill as fast as I could! Now I was flying high through the air like a bird, or a plane, or an angel with clipped wings. Landing with a jarring jolt, I turned to look back, "how far that time?"

Never Amount quickly measured the distance, "well it's better than last time, but not as far as the first jump. NOW, will you let me ride behind you?"

"Oh, okay. Jump on, but don't hang on too tight. I need to use my body for the jump." I gathered up speed racing around the yard again and when we hit the hill for the jump, he leaned back, instead of against me, and I felt the bike trying to get away from me to flip. *Don't panic, don't panic*, I was praying hard and steadily brought it back under control. We landed hard and a bit bouncy, but safe.

Whew! All I could think of was almost injuring my brother and me. Anger welled up inside of me like a boiling cauldron and I turned into a witch, "DON'T YOU realize that you almost threw us?   NEVER, NEVER lean away from the driver on a jump like that!"

He looked down at his shoes and muttered an apology. "I'm sorry, I didn't know."

Feeling bad about getting so mad, I tried to make it up to him, "it's all right, I should have told you before. I was just scared that we were going to wreck."

"Yeah," he said sheepishly, "me too! You almost popped a wheelie and it wouldn't have been a good one."

"I know! Look, I'm going to run up the road to see Grace, so if Mom asks where I am when they return, tell her I'll be back soon."

"Will do! Watch out for cops so you don't get caught riding a dirt bike on the street."

I took off down the road. Grace only lived a couple of miles away, and on the drive to her house, I thought back to when I first met her.

It was a few weeks after we had moved into the *scrambled eggs house*, (a nickname I came up with) because with the two separate cabins and big, ugly bus, we were all scrambled about.

Stepping on the bus that day, I sighed when I saw crazy Eddie, the bus driver who believed he could get down the mountain without using brakes.

Looking around for an empty seat, I noticed an unfamiliar face. She had long wavy hair, the color of honey, almost the same color as mine. Glancing up at me, kinda timid like, I noticed she had blue eyes, round as saucers. She nodded her head towards the empty seat beside her and mumbled something under her breath. I figured that was an invitation to sit next to her and when the bus suddenly lurched forward, I almost fell on top of her.

Glaring at Eddie, I sat down and thanked her. Then, I wedged my books between my legs so I could grip the seat in front of me. It would be a white-knuckle ride all the way! "I guess it's pray our way to school today," I said, hoping she would get the joke.

She ducked her head and looked sideways at me. Soft laughter bubbled out like gently falling rain and just under her breath, she whispered, "I always do it too!"

"Do what?" I was intrigued by her manner. So obvious that she was extremely shy. She had a way of ducking her head when she talked in a barely audible voice, and she never looked you straight in the eye. It left me wondering who had bruised her spirit. Did she have abusive parents? I felt an overwhelming desire to protect her, which I thought strange. Even for me!

"Pray," she said, "I always pray when I get on this bus."

"Well, now there are two of us, and you know what the Bible says about two or more praying! I introduced myself and asked for her name.

"Grace," she answered quietly.

"Jiminy Crickets!" I exclaimed, "if ever a name fit more perfectly, then I don't know when it was. You look like a Grace. I mean you kinda even remind me of an angel! Besides that, I know God must have sent you to me because I have been so lonely for a Christian friend!"

She laughed very softly, and now it reminded me of the sound a dove makes, cooing. She finally lifted her eyes to meet mine, searching to see if I was serious or making fun of her.

Of course, after that we became fast and faithful friends.

When I pulled up in the driveway in front of her house, she came outside to meet me. "Hello" she said, "Are you still going to the community gathering at church tonight?"

That was another blessing I received when I met Grace. She went to a fantastic little church in the woods and now we both attended. The Pastor had put us to work right away, teaching children and even leading the singing in front of church. He said it would help build our confidence, but I really think he wanted to help Grace overcome her shyness, because I knew that I couldn't carry a tune in a bucket.

I had come to realize that her parents weren't abusing her. The poor dear just suffered from a triple dose of bashfulness, which I would call downright painful.

"I sure hope I can make it. I told Mom about it. Now, if they will just get home in time to bring me."

"Well, why don't you just ride with us? I'm sure my mom won't mind running down to pick you up. What are you bringing to eat? I'm making brownies."

"Yum!" I said, "are you putting nuts in them?" I asked.

"I was going to put some pee-cans in them."

I rolled my eyes and glared at her. "Some what? Girl, how many times must I tell you to pronounce them correctly? It's puh-kahns. I swear you Yankees just don't know how to talk." We both laughed. I was always teasing her, hoping to help her relax, and not drift back into her shell like a turtle pulling its head inside.

"And to answer your question, I have decided to bring gravel sandwiches to eat!"

"GRAVEL sandwiches? Isn't that going to break some teeth?" she laughed.

"No it's not, and if you promise to put some *puh-kahns* in the brownies I'll tell you what's in them." After she agreed, I went on, "gravel sandwiches is something I learned how to make when we lived next door to the Jesus Freaks I told you about."

She laughed, knowing I was teasing when I called them Jesus Freaks, because I had already told her about my dear friends at *The House of No More Shadows*.

"All you do is chop up green olives and mix it into cream cheese, then you spread it on white bread, cut off the crusts and make little finger sandwiches." I didn't tell her that the kids and I always ate the crusts after I cut them off. Never waste food!

"And it's really good?" she asked.

"Oh, my yes! Just wait till you try them. Scrump-dilly-ishous!"

We were sitting on her bed in her lovely, pink and purple bedroom. I looked around wondering what it would be like to have such a cute set-up. It had taken a lot of courage for me to bring Grace to our *scrambled-egg house*, but she took it in stride and never seemed to be shocked at the differences. Mainly, we got together at her house, because she only had one brother and he stayed out of the way, most of the time.

She glanced over, "So when does your boyfriend come to visit again?"

"Well the last letter I got said he'd be here in October."

"Are you excited?"

"I don't know, really. Things were a bit awkward with us before. I don't think he's a Christian, so that's a big problem."

We sat there quiet for a few minutes. My mind had been playing over and over something our Pastor said last week. "Y'know Grace, I've been thinking a lot about what Pastor Pete said last Sunday. All my life I've been so critical of my parent's drinking and when he said what he did, well it just clicked inside of me."

"What did he say?"

"Y' know how he said that everyone has a do and don't list?" She nodded so I continued, "he said it's okay to have a do and don't list. The problem comes when you apply your own do and don't list to other people!"

Grace looked thoughtful, then nodded her head.

"That's what I've been doing wrong. I have to concentrate on my own list and leave them to theirs."

*****

Kneeling alongside the road, my fingers clutching strands of my hair, I doubled over, weeping. Pleading with God, sobbing, as I struck the ground with my fist.

"Please God, please, please, just take me now." Tears ran rivers down my face, dropping on my Beatles sweatshirt and dripping into the hard, cold ground. My faith was being tested once again and I was so tired of the battle. So very tired.

I tried my best to love them. No more judgment calls. No dirty looks. No angry words. Praying for the Lord to fill me with His love for them, always hoping they would see a difference between love and hate. Wishing that things would change; our lives would be different. Better somehow.

But here we were being evicted. Another move. And I was so close to realizing one of my two goals. Why was life always so hard?

Lord, You're the only one I can turn to for help. How in the world can I be expected to leave school and go live in a tent in February with them? But if I don't, won't I be turning my back on them? What do you expect from me?

On top of that, I had also set my Soldier Boy free. Again!

After all, why should he be saddled with such a dysfunctional family for relatives? Didn't he deserve better?

*****

It all started with a letter. After moving from the big three-story house into this *scrambled-eggs place*, I began to wonder if I had given Rusty a fair chance. I didn't have a clue how to reach him. I missed him terribly, but if we weren't really meant for each other, then should I even try to contact him?

So, I said a prayer and sent a letter to the little town where his family lived. I addressed it to him and wrote on the envelope for the postmaster to deliver it to his family if he knew the address. If fate and God meant for us to get together, then I thought that perhaps the letter would find its way.

It did! God and destiny must've meant for us to meet once again.

I'll never forget the beautiful necklace that he brought back to give me when he returned to visit. It was a cross encircled within the Christian fish symbol. Such a thoughtful gift. A symbol of the faith I cherished.

We sat on the front porch, one board of the rickety porch almost giving in when we stepped outside for a moment of privacy.

Fingering the necklace around my neck, I began to giggle when I noticed my little pinky toe sticking out of my ratty ol' tennis shoes. But deep down I felt embarrassed.

Rusty jumped up, pulling me to stand next to him.

"Look, I want to take care of you. Don't you understand?"

I felt myself sinking into those green eyes and posted danger signs in my head warning myself to stay out of the Emerald Forest. I had come to learn it to be treacherous territory at times, but the pull to step inside, allowing the jungle to envelop me was powerful.

"Where does your dad keep his tools?" he asked.

I looked at him, perplexed. "What?"

"Where does he keep his tools? I can fix that board on the porch."

What? Wait a minute! What had he said before the tools part?

"What are you talking about? Let's just sit down and talk," I pulled him down beside me, willing him to forget the porch, my shoes, everything. Well, everything except me.

He had come to see me after being overseas. With him on furlough, I wanted us to spend this time getting to know each other better.

Quality time! Time not divided by siblings or drunken parents or any other drama that always seemed to push its way into our lives.

Sitting there, I subconsciously wiggled my little toe. It felt odd sticking out of my tennis shoes.

Big mistake!

Rusty looked down. "I want to take care of you! Like that…" he pointed to my shoe and reached behind to pull out his wallet. "Here, let me give you some money. You can buy a new pair of tennis shoes."

The breath suddenly whooshed out of my body. Feeling like a rag doll, left lying in the road, waiting to be run over by a bulldozer, it took me a moment to catch my breath.

I stood and pointed a shaky finger into his face. "I don't need your money! This is NOT your problem! I can take care of myself!!!" I felt dizzy from the rage I suddenly felt towards him. "I am NOT your child!!! And you ARE NOT my dad!!!"

His emerald eyes turned into a murky pool of brackish green. He looked at me, agonized, and I mirrored his confusion. How could I explain what I didn't understand myself? I held my ground, glaring back. Angry! Too tired to deal with him any longer I ran away from him to my shack in the back. Slamming the door, HARD, to emphasize my point!

My heart pounding like a caged, wild-bird! Standing just inside the door, I had to have time to think, praying he wouldn't try to follow me.

Was it only yesterday I thought I might actually be in love with him? Hadn't he proved it to me? I remembered the incident and what I had felt afterwards. The memory still burning in my brain!

We had been sitting in the back seat of the car, Rusty's arm protective and warm around me while the dad careened drunkenly down the mountainside; Mom swaying in and out of consciousness in the front seat. My brother acting as barricade, *this time*, to prevent her from jumping out the passenger door.

"Jump out NOW! Please jump!" Mom whispered loud enough for us to hear. *Never Amount* sat clutching the dashboard with one hand and gripping the back of the seat with the other, steeling himself against her, trying to ignore her constant begging and pushing.

My brothers both stood taller than me, and thankfully stronger.

The flashback of a similar ride had left me feeling dizzy and nauseous. I could almost smell the mixture of blood and alcohol. I began to pray that nothing bad would happen.

Nothing that would further humiliate or cause even worse trauma.

Sitting next to him I thought if we survived this episode, then surely, I should love him. But why would anyone ever want to deal with drama to this extent? If he turned and ran, fleeing back to his barracks overseas, I wouldn't blame him.

When I awoke the next morning, he was still there. Not one word about the night's incident. Didn't a man like this deserve my love?

So, then why am I here inside this shack? Maybe I'm just angry at the cards fate dealt me. But, really, who gets mad over a pair of tennis shoes?

Feeling calmer, I went back out to return to the main cabin. The supper meal needed to be prepared. Hungry little eyes following me as I made my way to the sink to peel potatoes. This, a familiar role. A role in which no questions needed answering.

Rusty kept his distance, feeling more comfortable in the presence of the dad than my sullen silence.

I finally realized how uncomfortable I must make him feel. Trying to lighten the atmosphere, I flashed him my dimply smile, the one he said he loved. I knew my brown eyes would turn hazel, (*brown in storms and hazel in calm seas*) and was hoping that would help to soften his mood.

I laughed at his jokes, an ear cocked to listen to the tales he told my siblings, and I felt the room suddenly exhale. A comfortable breeze blew through, while an unspoken truce sang a song.

Bellies were finally full, and the huge harvest moon beckoned me outside to sit on our rickety porch. I patted the unruly board, smiling fondly at the earlier memory. *Poor man, all he wanted to do was fix the porch and buy me some shoes.* The magic cast by the moon and her attentive stars settled soft as a whisper inside me.

I sensed his presence before I heard him and inhaled deeply, hoping to catch his scent, hoping to find my way to answers. Answers to questions I didn't begin to know how to ask.

The moon smiled secretively, as always, withholding her knowledge.

I pulled the image of his face into my mind. It held a simple beauty that captured my heart from the very moment I met him. He also had a charming way of making me laugh as no one had ever done before.

"Y'know, I would never have survived without God's presence in my life." I finally said, wanting to be direct and get straight to the point.

"I really don't know what that's like," he said quietly. I could tell by his tone that he was sincere, and I was grateful he didn't avoid the subject; that he chose to follow me down this path.

"I can't imagine a life without God. He's the One I turn to when there's no answers to be found."

Turning, he looked deep into my eyes. What he saw seemed to be hard for him, because he turned away to stare up at the moon instead. Was he looking to find some clue written across her surface?

He pulled me into his arms and kissed me deeply, with a passion that drove the questions straight out of my head until I couldn't even remember if I had asked one.

"I need to take a walk," he said abruptly and turned to go up the hill in the direction of the rising moon. I wondered what the moon thought of his solitary march.

Waiting in the dark on the front porch steps, I said a prayer asking God to help him find his way. He needed answers and I needed a man who walked with the Lord if we were to continue this relationship. Finally, I saw it clearly: this was the reason we fought so much.

I don't know how long I sat there waiting for him to return, but needing action, I went inside to wash the dishes. The parents had already gone to bed in the next room and I looked around the cabin trying to see it through his eyes.

The main room held only a bench from an old Volkswagen van to sit on, a kitchen table with only two chairs, the pot-bellied stove where we gathered to get warm, a sink to wash dishes and a small closet that held a bathtub. How did he feel about having to use an outhouse? Or sleeping in a broken-down bus on a mattress?

Did he pity me? Is that why he wanted to be with me? Did he look at me like a broken doll that needed to be fixed like the porch step? Was that why I had gotten so angry? I wanted to know he loved me for me. He wasn't the only one needing answers tonight.

Quite unexpectedly, he appeared next to me, drying dishes while I washed them. I glanced at him and noticed something different in his face. He looked peaceful and content within himself, as if answers had come to rest inside him. He caught me staring and said, "Would you come outside with me? I want to talk to you."

Nodding, I followed him outside, quietly waiting for him to begin.

"Y'know that old, broken down church on the hill? Well, I walked up there and stood on that hill and looked at the stars and moon all around me. I was really angry with you. I couldn't seem to figure out what you wanted from me. And I was angry with God."

"So, I shook my fist and yelled into the night that if God was real, if He had really created all the things around me, then to show Himself to me, prove His existence."

I nodded, urging him to continue. I could see he was gripped by a strong emotion, it showed in his face and he swallowed a few times and went on. "Somehow, someway, God made His presence known to me. I know now that what you have been trying to tell me is true. I felt Him inside me, washing over me with a powerful wave of peace! As if love was filling me up, inside out! I don't understand everything, but I want to know more. I want to continue my life with my hand and heart in His."

I was smiling with my whole being and felt God's peace flow through me at his words. "I know it is hard to understand," I said, "but once you invite Him to come into your life, you immediately know it is the right decision. It's a new birth, a new beginning. All your past sins have been washed away. You are like a brand-new creation! Have you ever heard of David Wilkerson?"

He shook his head no, so I continued. "He wrote *'The Cross and the Switchblade,'* and I have another book by him that explains things better than I can."

I ran to find a book that was more geared for people our age and gave it to him. Sitting side by side, we read through some of the pages. I pointed out some helpful chapters for him to read.

"I am so excited for you! You aren't just my boyfriend now, but a brother in Christ as well!"

"I want to be even more than that to you. I love you and I want you to be my wife," he said, getting down on one knee and reaching to take my hand.

I felt the breath catch in my throat. Was he about to do what I thought he was going to do?

"Will you marry me?" He asked.

How could I refuse? I loved him so much! This was the happiest day of my life. Wasn't it?

"Yes, I will marry you."

Late that night, alone in my bed, whispers of doubt flew into my room and buzzed around my head like little, annoying, gnawing gnats. I tried to swat them, but they wouldn't go away.

I would soon be graduating from High School.

He was starting a new journey with the Lord.

Did I really want to jump right out of High School into marriage?

What about my idea to become a Missionary and a famous writer?

Did he really love me?

Did I really love him?

So, for the second time, I sent him away. Explaining the next morning, that we were both too young, and I needed more time to decide which direction I wanted to go after graduation, and he needed more time to get to know the Lord as his personal Savior. I wasn't saying we couldn't marry at a later date, just that we should have more time to grow up a bit.

He seemed to understand, and our parting was on a happier note than before. He left with no strings attached.

But, oh how that dangling string taunted me!

If Only and Alligator Bites

There are times in every young person's life when a decision has to be made. It can be a lonely place. Perhaps that's why they call it *'being stuck between a rock and a hard place.'*

If you find yourself stuck between a rock and a hard place, what do you become? If you sit still, you would probably become part of the rock, or perhaps moss growing on a rock. But if you put even one toe out to take a step, in any direction, then you begin breaking stone. You become part of a JOURNEY!!!

Sometimes the direction will alter your course, completely change where you thought you were going, or entirely screw up your life.

I really hate decision times. I mean they really SUCK the life out of you! No matter how much or how long you try to examine each fork in the road, no one can predict or see into the future. So sometimes you are left forever wondering, *'if only'*…, and is that really fair?

Why can't we have a map laid out for our lives? Oh yeah, I forgot. That's only for the privileged few.

So why do *they* just toss it out like so much garbage? A paid-for college education: well heh, let's just get high, get drunk, screw around, skip class and throw away the hard-earned money that dear, old dad put down. After all, he has plenty more. That brand-new car: well, let's race it into the night sharing drinks with my buddies and crash into trees. And heh, if we survive, he'll just buy me a new car, bail me out of jail, and pay off the judge.

That's life for the privileged few.

If I had been born one of them, would I do the very same thing? I mean here I stand on the precipice of the rest of my life, with two of my goals almost accomplished and I think, does anyone really care besides me? I mean if I even told my goals to someone else, they would probably laugh. The privileged few would certainly laugh! Laugh hard and long with heads thrown back, wink slyly, then buy another round of drinks for the table.

But I know my heavenly Father wouldn't laugh.

He would be proud of me. Because He is the only one who knows what a tough and rocky road it has been for me to get here. And if I can accomplish these two goals after the bumpy road left behind, there's no telling what else I can do.

I may not be wealthy, have designer clothes or a car, and I may not have much going for me, but I know that God has my back. He will always have my back!

Actually, I feel quite sorry for the privileged few who don't have Him to catch them when they fall. What a sad existence they must face each day. It would make me want to crash into trees, too! Instead I feel like going out and hugging one of His trees today. Although trees have rough and scratchy bark, inside they are soft and warm and lovely. Maybe that's why He loves them and me. After all, I can often be scratchy on the outside.

I was sitting on the thin mattress thrown on the floor at my uncle's house, reading over this diary entry. Trying to decide what kinda poem to write for my American Literature class. Going over in my head the last few decisions I had made, hoping with all my heart that they had been the right ones.

I wanted to write a poem about life. What is life? Well life for me seemed to be a bumpy road, often filled with deep potholes and occasionally an alligator to bite your butt. But if that were all I focused on, then life would be a terrible place.

I mean take a moment to look around when walking down life's road. There are beautiful sunsets filled with amazing colors of crimson, burgundy, orange and yellow, brilliant hues.

There are trees that sway in the breeze with branches that almost beckon you to come over for a closer look. If you do, then you may find little flowers blossoming between tender blades of grass in places you'd never imagine. Sometimes even between, *'a rock and a hard place.'* If you stand in the forest, fill your lungs with the clean, sweet air and remain quite still, you might even hear what the trees are trying to say, or experience a timid doe tiptoeing out to see who has invaded her home.

There are so many amazing things to see along the road.

Never focus on the potholes or alligator bites!

Looking back over the past several months, crying alongside the road that one day was fresh in my memory, I had been in anguish wondering how to finish High School, how to decide what to do with the rest of my life.

The first decision had been really hard; making a stand to separate from my parents. Letting the kids go on to face life without me to protect them. Constantly I replayed the scene over in my head. Telling them I had to choose my schooling over their decision.

I spent so many sleepless nights wondering how they were, living in the Oregon woods in a tent in February. I worried if they had enough food, so guilt often clogged my throat whenever I had a meal to eat. I worried if they were warm enough, so ran around without a jacket in freezing temperatures, just to know how they felt.

I went to school carrying my sleeping bag and books, living sometimes with my aunt in the city, sometimes with my uncle in the hills and sometimes staying with Grace.

Thankfully, it wasn't too long before my parents found another house just down the road from where we had lived before. The problem was that it was still out of my school district. Now I drove my aunt's street bike, a snazzy little Kawasaki to Grace's house, so I could catch the bus with her. Sometimes, I drove from my uncle's house to spend the weekends with my parents and the kids. Being a gypsy somehow suited me.

I was a senior in school and would graduate in January, six months ahead of my peers. School was a breeze this year because all my classes involved my favorite subjects, reading and writing. In the afternoons

I worked my job in the school cafeteria, and Job Corp at school was trying to help me find work in the city.

The Bible says: *'all things work together for good for those who love God and are called according to His purpose.'* *Romans 8:28*

I know this is true because that's how I got my job at school. It happened after a big fight with Mom. We were yelling at each other in the snow (*why do we have so many bad snow days?*) and she knocked the glasses off my face and stepped on them! I don't think she meant to, it just happened in the scuffle. I can't even remember what we were fighting about, but everything worked out for me later on.

Without telling anyone how they got broke, I went to the school guidance counselor and told her I didn't have money to buy glasses and could she ask my teachers to let me sit closer to the chalkboard. The counselor said they could buy me a pair of eyeglasses.

I knew I couldn't, *wouldn't* accept charity. Instead, they found me a job in the school cafeteria. Now I could pay for my glasses and was delighted to have money for orange juice and shampoo! However, trying to avoid the parents who were always borrowing from me for their cigarettes became something of an issue.

The parents were thrilled about the house they lived in now, for a couple of reasons. One, it was much nicer than the *scrambled-eggs place*. And number two was the icing on their cake. They discovered a huge field of cultivated marijuana growing in the woods behind the house. They were in a good mood almost every time I visited, and since I had been keeping my *'do and don't list'* to myself, what could I say?

Startled out of my reverie by a knock at the laundry room door, (*I slept in here for a bit of privacy*), I hid my diary under the sleeping bag and yelled "Come in."

My rock-star handsome uncle was at the door. "Hey, supper's ready. Do you want to eat tonight?"

I loved this uncle and his young wife. My uncle really *'got me'*, perhaps because he used to write when he was younger. They didn't seem to mind my strange eating habits or the weird things I came up with sometimes.

"Sure," I replied, "I think I've written up an appetite!"

Once he closed the door, I looked over the poem I wrote for class, then glanced at the letter I had just written to Rusty.

The poem I felt good about, but the letter…well that's another story!

What is Life

An old gray man stood in a field
and looked at the beauty around him
but he did not see.

With trembling arms, he raised his fist
and in a strangled voice whispered,
What is life?

He stood there silently, listening
as the wind played with his beard
and lifted his pale, thin hair.
Then with a shrug he wearily turned
and trudged down the hill.

As the meadow again grew silent
a soft whisper echoed through the grass,
'You fool, you fool, you fool.'
Don't you know? Oh can't you see?

Why life is right under your nose.

Life is the stillness before sunset
and the noise when it's past.
And the kiss of the dew
on the fresh morning grass.

Life is the rippling of a brook
and the roar of the sea
and the fall's golden leaves
as they drift from the tree.

Life is a child's merry laughter
or his heartbreaking sob.
And a young man's dreams
when he's found his first job.

Life is the twinkle in an old man's eye
And his face when it gets that knowing smile
as he looks at the picture of his beloved wife
and knows that, yes, it has all been
worthwhile.

Life is the look that passes between two in
love
as they walk hand in hand
then run laughing and jumping
in the soft golden sand.

Life is many things
even the fluttering of a sparrow's wings.

Life is hate and pain and sorrow
and waking up to a new tomorrow.

Life is the soft yesterdays
and all that has past
the knowledge of knowing
that life will last.

Oh if you'd only look and see
there's life enough for you and for me

But friend, if you walk
with your nose pointed down
your life, I'm sorry
will never be found.

A Sister that Cries and a Suitcase that Flies

Sadness flies away on the wings of time.
~ Jean de la Fontaine ~

I believe when one is writing a story where bits and pieces of it are particularly brutal and mostly true, you have to become the starring actress on a Broadway stage and give the performance of a lifetime. You have to search for the best of yourself and also admit the worst in order to show your audience *you are not afraid.*

Not afraid of them, and not afraid to **be** the truth. I knew I would never receive an Emmy for this performance, but actually would receive something better. I could set my story free and in doing so, set myself free as well.

I was no longer the Sad little girl sitting like a ladybug on the wall with a notepad in hand, jotting down the stories of my life. Instead, I am now a young woman, very much in love with my handsome, emerald-eyed man. My darling soldier boy. All too eager for happily ever after, babes of my own, and someday, a rocking chair on the porch to sit and wait for visits from my grandchildren.

Perhaps it's silly to think of grandchildren before one is even married, but I hope to be the best grandma ever! That way I could honor my dear Nanny for being such a loving role model and for all the comfort she gave me along my way.

I was thinking about my grandmother and the last conversation we had right before I wrote that last letter to Rusty. Nanny and I were sitting side by side on a porch swing, pushing it lazily on a perfect, soft summer day. You know the kind that brings to mind butterflies and buttery breezes? A *Walt Disney* kinda day.

"Nanny, I don't know how I could have made it without you in my life," I said, nuzzling up next to her and laying my head on her shoulder. "You have been an inspiration to me all these years. Your kindness, understanding, and the way you never say anything harsh about anyone or to anyone."

"Honey, I'm not perfect. Only God, His Son and the Holy Spirit are perfect. They are the ones you should look up to."

"I know you're not perfect Nanny, which brings me to the question I want to ask you. You are the most loving person I know in life. So, I was wondering how would you feel if I decide to marry outside my race? Would you still love me the same?"

"Honey, nothing you could ever do would change the way I love you. I hate to admit it, but it would be hard for me to love someone of a different race, but I would try my best for you."

And there it was. Even my dearest Nanny had things she struggled with inside. Deep down I had always known, but I had to ask anyway to make sure she wasn't wearing wings under her clothes. She was still the most perfect person I knew.

The letter I had written to Rusty was to tell him that I would marry him. We set the date for soon after my graduation. Graduating High School was my accomplishment of goal number one.

As my wedding day approached, I was the typical 'head in the clouds bride-to-be,' with daisy chains swirling in fields of clover, imagining a barefoot walk beside a beautiful, rocky stream. Total flower child that I imagined myself to be.

I thought nothing about reality, my wedding in winter, cold, soaking rain showers and all that rot. Mom said people wouldn't want to tromp around in a muddy field, so I compromised, insisting on daisies laced with blue forget-me-nots sewn around the waistband of my wedding dress. That was about all I got from my cloudy head.

I determined our marriage would be *oh so* different from the life I grew up with, because having been raised by alcoholics, we didn't want the same problem following us into our marriage. We were Christians! If God is for us, who can be against us?

However, I wasn't so foolish to believe my kids should have or would have everything I didn't, but at least we could provide them with happy memories. That was better than a fancy house, expensive cars, and designer clothes.

A happy childhood filled with memories of wonderful times around the Christmas tree, birthday blessings, and best of all, a mother and father who didn't fight or drink to get drunk. That was my deepest desire for my children.

Looking in the mirror I saw a lovely young woman, full of hope. Feeling so positive that our future held only bright horizons for us. Love for God, each other and our children could overcome every obstacle in our path. I was not so foolish to think that we wouldn't have obstacles. Everyone does. But I did believe in the power of love.

♥♥♥

For my last days at home, I wanted one good memory to put in my suitcase and take away with me. One that would shine bright when I unpacked it in my new home.

I had already filled one suitcase with gifts from my bridal shower. My friends at my school cafeteria job had thrown me a surprise shower! Such a sweet gesture. And now my suitcase was packed with their treasures. A beautiful crystal vase and the most perfect blue glassware that I had ever seen. Little things with memories already attached to start our new life together.

So, I decided the one memory I wanted to pack was a marvelous Thanksgiving dinner, with all our family gathered together one last time! After all, it would be my last as an unmarried woman. I felt that once I left home, when I returned nothing would be quite the same.

Thanksgiving morning, I stood at the stove, stirring the pudding for lemon pie in the *Grass Hut* (that's what I had nicknamed my parent's house). I always love to make the pudding for the chocolate and lemon pies. Everyone else who tried got frustrated and ended up with lumpy pies. This must be another *'all things working together'* lesson, because how many hours, days, years had I spent making gravy?

Little Bird tried to fly through the kitchen, but I called out, "Can you grab those pie crusts out of the oven for me?"

Just then, *Never Amount* and *Boy Blue* ran down the stairs and tried to hurry past, but I scooped them up as well, "hey, take out that trash over by the door and run feed the dogs so we don't have to worry about them while we're away." They nodded and kept on running but grabbed the trash on the way out.

Sky Eyes sidled up next to me and stood quietly, watching me stir the yellow-gold mixture around and around. She seemed to be mesmerized, and I found it odd to see her so quiet. Finally, she looked up at me. "Is it true?"

I looked down at her curly brown hair and her doll-baby blue eyes over a cute little upturned nose that was sprinkled with angel kisses. Her freckles reminded me of leaves scattered over a bridge crossing.

"Is what true?" I asked, looking at her serious expression.

"Is it true you're going to get married and go away from us?"

She wasn't smiling and I felt sadness spread through me at her words.

Hearing a creak from the stairs, I noticed Mom stumble down, clutching a glass in her hand. My antenna meter jumped out like elephant ears and I studied her walk across the floor to the living room. Was it steady?

What was in that glass? She usually had coffee in the morning. She should have a cup in her hand. Was she already drinking on this very important day?

Looking at *Sky Eyes*, I thought about her question. "Yes, Sweetie Pie, I'm getting married. Aren't you excited to get to go to a wedding?"

Mom entered the room and I called out, "Heh, do you think two pies will be enough? I could make up a pecan pie as well."

"Sure, that would be good," she said.

Hmmm…I couldn't tell by her voice but would have to watch her a little closer.

"I can't believe it," said *Sky Eyes*.

"What?" I peered down at her and noticed her cheeks were wet. She was looking down at the floor now. "What? What is it that you can't believe?"

She looked up at me and her big blue eyes were drowning in a river of tears. "I can't believe you are leaving us to *them*," she sobbed, running from the room.

And there it was. Punched in the heart by a ten-year old. I felt like a dangling participle. *Turning the corner, a handsome modifier appeared. Thus I was knocked into an Emerald Forest.* It should read, *turning the corner into the Emerald Forest, I was saved by a handsome modifier and we lived happily ever after.*

But corners were sometimes hard to go around. And I knew that those little blue eyes would follow me forever.

By the time we drove over to my uncle and aunt's place, I knew what was in the glass. Although the

Oregon woods were resplendent in all their glory with Autumn's beautiful colors, the sky a perfect shade of blue with cotton ball clouds, and the air held a perfect crispness which makes life and food and fun just right....

I just couldn't relax. Instead of enjoying this day, I felt like a thundercloud that was building and churning, gathering up speed on a dark and stormy day.

My aunt, uncle and eight kids from the city had already arrived. I walked inside carrying two of the three pies, with *Little Bird* right behind with the pecan pie. She set it down and flew out to play. I noticed *Sky Eyes* happily playing with the two youngest boys. Looking out the window, I saw my mother stumble out of the car and make her way to the house.

Avoiding the very air she breathed, I waltzed around greeting everyone, stopping to visit with cousins, aunts and uncles who were all waiting for the Dallas Cowboy game to begin. This was part of our family tradition. In this family you were born a Dallas Cowboy fan and living in Oregon didn't change your lineage.

My city aunt didn't realize I was standing at the couch behind her, so I heard her whisper to her husband, "how much do you think she's had to drink? It's only one o'clock!"

I turned away, infuriated with my mother. How could she ruin this? Not just for me, but for everyone?

Running outside, I filled my lungs with the cold, crisp air hoping to clean out the poisonous fumes building up inside me. How dare she ruin this last memory for me? The question followed me everywhere, nipping at my heart, even when talking with my cousins.

I watched the little ones skipping rope and taking turns with a hoola-hoop. Why couldn't I feel carefree and happy as them?

Finally, it was time to eat, and we were called inside. I helped fill plates for the little kids and noticed every adult kept switching their eyes from the television to my mother. She stood, leaning at the sink, not joining in, not bothering to get anything to eat. Was the sink holding her up? How soon would she fall?

We all sat around watching the game and my mother stumbled past to the bathroom. When she came out, my city aunt called out to her, "Your dressing is delicious! Why don't you get a plate?"

My mother whipped around and snarled, "I'll damn well eaaast whan I'm gooood an fredthy." Then slamming the door behind her, she stumbled outside to the car.

I followed.

My heart burning with all the words, all the emotions, all the feelings of anger, hurt, despair, and rejection that I had been pushing back for years.

"JUST WHO DO YOU THINK YOU ARE?" I screamed at her.

She whipped around, astonished to see me following her. "Waaashh did ya say?"

"I SAID, JUST WHO DO YOU THINK YOU ARE? Why do you have to ruin everything for everyone with your drinking?" Angry tears laced my words, and now she started stumbling towards me.

"Youshh better shuttsh up. I canns shtill whup youshh."

"Oh really," I replied, raising my eyebrows and almost laughing out loud. But I kept the car in between us. "You can barely stand up, you're so drunk! This was my one last memory to have before leaving and now you've ruined it! Just like you ruin everything!"

She clamored around the car, trying to get to me. I was still a little afraid of her, but also knew that if she got a hold of me, we would be tumbling around in the dirt, which would only make things worse, no matter how much I might enjoy trying to slap the crap out of her. I had never said things like this to her before, and it felt good! My mouth now as fluid as Multnomah Falls.

"All my life, I've had to watch you ruin our lives. Drinking all the time, so much that as a kid, I've always waited to hear your voice before entering a room, just to know how far gone you were. Promising us all your life that you'd quit drinking, that you would quit fighting with him, that things would be better. Well they aren't, and you didn't, and we still have to keep wallowing behind in your pitiful wake!"

She had stopped following me around the car. I took a deep breath, not able to control what I needed to say until it was done.

"It doesn't even matter what I say to you because you won't remember a damn thing! You never do! You just destroy us and you never remember." I said, sad, my voice almost a whisper now. Turning away, I ran up the road away from the house knowing she wouldn't follow.

*****

The booze, the pills, and the pot. Sleeping around with men she wasn't married to. They say as you grow older you become more like your mother. I was determined I would NOT!

And my mother, well she remembered every word I said that Thanksgiving Day. I guess I had shocked her sober!

Needless to say, the next few weeks were a bit strained between us.

I wish I could say that what I said to her in anger made an impact, and she changed that very day to become the mother I always wished for. The mother who would never leave her children alone in a house or drive drunk and reckless down mountain roads trying to kill us all.

I wish I could say that, but I can't. Because now I knew that I was the only one who could change. It was up to me to decide how the little girl named Sad would affect my life. I knew Sad would always be a part of me, but the life she lived could be used for a higher purpose. The lessons she learned could be used to help others along the way.

For now, I had one more memory to pack into my suitcase.

On a very windy January night, two weeks before my wedding, I decided it didn't matter anymore whether I had any good memories to take with me, because with a bucket full of bad ones, it was probably unlucky to wish for anything different.

I had just left Grace's house where we were deciding on the final touches to my wedding. I had asked her to be my maid of honor. She loaned me a sapphire necklace to wear for my *'something borrowed, something blue.'* Now I was flying down the road to the *Grass Hut* just before dusk. The wind whipped my hair around and into my eyes, so I pulled to the side of the road so I could put on my helmet.

Over the years, I had come to realize that outside forces sometimes drove my mother to drink: *Willie Nelson* records (which I loved, so I couldn't blame Willie) and the wind. The wind made her bat-ape crazy (*my made-up words to keep from cussin'*).

I sat there, feeling the wind gently fingering my hair and thought there's another difference between my mother and me. I love the wind! I couldn't help but think of my last journal entry. I had grown up, no longer using a diary, but a journal.

I'm a child of God

There came a day....
My heart was heavy.
Weary as a threadbare rug,
lying dusty and dirty on the floor.

The phone rang and I picked it up, not knowing that my life would change dramatically from what I was about to hear.

The person on the end of the line was my mother...

"I just called to tell you something I thought you should know," she began.

"Yes?" I felt my heart begin to thud in my chest. I knew this was something important.

I had an overwhelming need to sit down.

"Go on," I said, my voice barely a whisper.

"Well, I've been meaning to tell you this. The man, uh...your dad...er.... uh... Well, he's not your dad!"

I sat silent.
My mind a whirlwind.
A tornado.
A tumbleweed rolling in the wind.

Then a feeling of peace came over me. This explained so much. I should have had a clue when she cried listening to, 'Blue Eyes Crying in the Rain.'

But suddenly, I was angry!!!
Angry that she had waited so long denying me the truth for so many years.

"So that's why he never loved me."

"Yes," she replied.

I hung up the phone.

So many emotions racing through my veins.

So many questions, so many answers.

Finally knowing the reason why I felt different, was different, and had never really connected with the dad or he with me.

I struggled to find the peace I had felt initially.

It came...

The little girl named Sad

may not have a dad...

       ...but

       I'm a child of God!

       Yes I am!

II Corinthians 6:18

*****

It was the weekend of *Sky Eye's* birthday and I didn't want to miss the celebration, but as I approached the house, I could hear their angry words flying around like, well… bat-apes!

So, I went in through the back door instead and hurried upstairs to my room. Maybe keeping out of sight would be a good idea. I wasn't exactly on her *happy to see you* list these days.

Suddenly, I heard them screaming at each other, moving the battle out into the yard. I crept close to the window to listen. I thought they were arguing about money and alcohol, but that wasn't what caught my attention. What caught my attention were the words, "you son-of-a *biscuit eater, (not her exact words.)* I WILL SHOOT YOU DEAD!!!"

I ran out of my room and almost into the kids, standing petrified just outside my door.

Leaving them, I raced down the stairs, frantically searching for the rifle! Knowing I didn't have much time before she entered the house.

Whew! Thankfully, I found it one second before hearing her come through the front door.

Stealthily sneaking up the stairs, I quickly motioned the kids into a closet. "Stay in here," I said, and they nodded, silent and shaking like leaves in a winter storm.

Quickly searching, I finally found a safe hiding place for the gun but heard her screaming my name at the foot of the stairs.

"Where's that damn gun?" she yelled.

Knowing the kids were safe in the closet, I went to stand in front of the bedroom door. She would not get past me.

I heard her coming up the stairs walked quickly forward to face her. A strange peace came over me.

This was a familiar role.

I knew it well.

I was not afraid, but suddenly saddened at the thought that this would be the last time I would be able to protect them.

She reached the top of the stairs. "Where is it?"

"I haven't a clue what you're talking about." I had long ago decided that there were times it was okay to lie. Especially when dealing with drunks and guns.

"OH, YES YOU DO!" she shrieked. "You know exactly what I'm talking about."

She wasn't slurring much and that did concern me because if she could talk, she could probably shoot.

"Look, you need to just go on back downstairs because you're not getting the gun. Shooting him will only land you in prison. Is that what you want?"

She looked me in the eye, then quickly snatched up my suitcase, the one filled with all my wedding treasures. "You give me that gun now or I'll break everything in this suitcase."

I stood there staring at my suitcase. Picturing each and every treasure packed inside.

"Go ahead," I said, "break them. I don't care. But you're not getting the gun." And I turned my back and walked away from her.

She held my heavy suitcase over her head then threw it crashing down the stairs. I heard it hit the steps, bouncing the rest of the way down.

"I hope you're happy now!" she said following my suitcase down the stairs.

The funny thing about it, I was HAPPY.
Happy to be here to help the kids one last time.
Happy to stand up to my mother.

Happy there wouldn't be bloodshed on my sister's birthday weekend. And, truth to be told, happy to be leaving.

"God," I whispered, "You'll have to protect the kids after I'm gone."

Opening the closet door, I motioned them all out. "Go sit in my room and I'll tell you a story." They quickly filed into my room and I told them, "I'll be right back."

Quietly, I listened at the top of the stairs. All was quiet. I ran down to fetch my suitcase and brought it back to my room. Their eyes followed mine, as I put it down on the mattress next to them. I opened it up. Looking inside, I suddenly saw them! There, stowed safe inside my suitcase, tenderly tucked between the UN-broken glasses, the UN-broken crystal, and the UN-broken *'welcome home'* plaque were all my GOOD memories!

I saw *Never Amount's* eyes standing beside a huge plate of food anticipating that first bite and his concentration when he hovered over his sketch pad.

I saw *Boy Blue* whiz past me pulling my hair, and our smiles over his ingenious methods to try and con us with his elaborate schemes.

Hearing *Little Bird's* joyful laughter warming us all up inside, or her eager face expressing her desire for everyone to be happy.

I could see *Sky Eye's* freckled nose and watch her braid thumping merrily against her back as she skipped joyfully down the road, the sun tickling her neck.

I could hear the soft melodic spell cast by the beauty of my mother's voice, singing to the dad's guitar strums. I caught the fragrance of her perfume on the breeze and felt her peace watching a late, summer storm.

I could see the dad's eyes crinkling and his guffaw as he sat watching the *Road Runner* outwit *the Coyote* one more time. His eagerness to teach us something new with a pen and pad to illustrate his latest idea.

I could feel the breeze sweeping over the tall Oregon pines and the gurgle of crystal-clear streams where we fished for crawdads.

I saw Texas with her wide-open skies beckoning and beautiful like my Nanny's arms welcoming me home, her enchanting eyes following me around the room. Her long fingers, tenderly stroking my hair.

There was Papa's *Woody-the-Woodpecker* twanging out on a steel guitar, tarantulas with their hairy legs tickling his palm as he carried them to his garden. The grandkids laughing merrily on another ride in the wagon around the yard.

I could see my aunts and uncles gathering around to play another round of croquet with mallets painted and named accordingly. I could hear the clackity-clack of dominoes shuffled for another round of 42, my loved one's faces' sitting around the kitchen table.

And how could I ever forget the sound of the soft, soughing of the wind whipping along the long, lonesome highways unfurling Spring's bonny bluebonnets in fields of purple grama grass, the Texas longhorns grazing alongside.

So many treasures tenderly tucked inside, that I was surprised they could fit in one tiny suitcase.

I smiled at the kids with their beautiful freckled faces, two sets of blue eyes, two sets of brown, cherishing the memory of all our expeditions as we roamed across this land, their attentive faces patiently waiting for me to give them the 'right' signal.

They sat there waiting expectantly, each one lined up on my mattress smiling back at me, watching as I carefully closed my suitcase

.

"You said you were going to tell us a story," they said.

I laughed, and they snuggled close as we sat nestled together on my mattress on the floor...

"There once was a little girl named Sad. She was born into a topsy-turvy, twisty-turny, upsy-downsy kind of a world."

✳✳✳✳✳

Standing nervously outside the church door of the little country church, I strained to hear the opening strands of the *Wedding March*. Grace had just walked inside with my Rock-Star Uncle, who Rusty chose to be his best man.

Glancing down at my silver high heels, my 'something new,' I examined them for any mud specks, thinking how my 'something old' would be my final two goals accomplished. The first, my high school diploma, and second, my gift to my husband on our wedding night, my vows to God, kept.

Finally, I turned to *the dad* standing next to me, as he waited to walk me down the aisle. *Would my real dad wish he could have been here?*

"Nervous?" he asked.

I nodded.

He reached inside the suit he had just bought that day at *The Salvation Army* for this very special occasion and pulled out a silver flask. He held it out to me, "want a swig? It'll take the edge off."

Laughing, I smiled and shook my head no. He took a drink, and I heard the piano begin to play.

"Ready?" he asked, "I think they're playing your song."

I put one shiny, silver toe forward.

Backward

(I thought it would be fun to put a 'backward' in a book since so many books have forewords)

The past is not dead. In fact, it is not even past.
~ William Faulkner ~

Looking back and examining my ghosts has not always been easy or pleasant, but it has been necessary.

They say not to speak ill of the dead, but often writers have to tackle this grizzly task in hopes of dissolving our ghosts. Perhaps it helps release the stranglehold they have over our lives. When we turn and look inside, deep within that shadowy mirror that was and remains our life, our hope is to receive inspiration, enabling us to smile. Perhaps it will help us to give our ghosts the boot or better understand their nature.

Growing up the way I did often left me with a feeling of overwhelming responsibility. A need to always try and make things right in my world. For myself and for those around me. I have learned that sometimes the world is beyond our control, and when that is the case, all one can do is to let go of the reins and allow God to take control.

During those overwhelming moments I often ran to my Bible, seeking solace and instruction from above. I have never left His Word without having His truth and encouragement warming my heart.

I am thankful for my past and would not give up my siblings for all the gold in the world. I love them dearly and can still see their little eyes following my footsteps, little hands pulling my ponytail and always their love pulling my heartstrings.

The little girl named Sad is so entangled within me that sometimes we just sit down together and have a shot of tequila and a good cry. Then, we embrace the wind and dance in the rain. (*She is of drinking age now and since she is of no religious affiliation, she is allowed to do these things.*)

I love her very much, for she has become a courageous woman, overcoming obstacles, triumphing tragedies, and able to leap over footstools with a single bound. I do not know why God chose for her to go through the hardships in her life, but I am filled with peace that He did, because it made her strong and resilient. It instilled within her joy over sorrow, laughter over tears and always the knowledge that her heavenly Father, always and forever has her back!

Even in my darkest moments, I knew always that I was not alone, that my God, stronger than Superman, would be standing right beside me and would carry me in His arms when I could not walk. I feel confident knowing that He knows the number of tears I have shed, just as He knows the number of hairs on my head.

Just as He was there when I was created in my mother's womb or as I like to call it, in *the baby room.*

PSALM 139

May you never feel alone,

pk potts

ACKNOWLEDGEMENTS

Thank You Father God, my Savior Jesus Christ and the Holy Spirit
for giving me grace in writing this book

I believe this is the section that every author loves to write, but often fears as well. We love it because there are so many special people who play such an important role in our lives, and sincerely want to thank them, reward them, and honor them in some small way. Our fear comes because we don't want to leave anyone out knowing there's never enough recognition when thanking those who are so very, very valuable.

**A SHOUT OUT to all MY READERS,
including my faithful family and friends, THANK
YOU, THANK YOU, THANK YOU!!!**

I would like to acknowledge the people who played an active role in this book. You know who you are and I hope that you see yourselves through eyes of love in which I tried to portray your role in this story. In keeping with anonymity, I will only say, "I love y'all".

Next, I want to thank my treasured team, Nancy Roehrig, the nest to which I return time and time again. She not only listens to my endless prattle, but also consistently volunteers her time to edit my work, always offering up words of encouragement like a mother bird doling out tasty tidbits to her nestling. I would not be the writer I am today without her.

Lauriel Webb-Sawin, my lovely, energetic artist who continually comes to my rescue with fresh and unique ideas every time I call. You are very talented and my cherished friend and Jack Wilson, our Knight in Shining Armor who came to our rescue with his amazing skills in graphic design. Thank you, Jan Marvin for your help with the cover.

Kellye Baldwin, my always funny, always encouraging daughter, thank you for volunteering your time and energy as a second editor for **team pk potts**.

To the folks who are such an important part of me for their consistent support and steadfast love:

Rich Evans, thank you for 'having my back' and being my eternally patient safety net!

Texa Baldwin, Heather and Adam Dowlen and my three heartbeats who bring hope and meaning into my world: Emily Dowlen (my Sunshine), Avery Dowlen (my Moonbeam) and Melody Dowlen (my little Pearl), I will always love y'all more!!!

Love and thanks to all my family in Texas for believing in me and reading my stories.

Thanks to my faithful and dearest friends for prayers and support, Cheryl Davis, Teresa Rush, and Marsha Sommer.

Finally, to my new family in Tennessee, enriching my life in ways I never anticipated: Kathy Barnhill and her mom, Beverly Barnhill, Dorothy and Floyd Raines, Cynthia Harrington, my Aunt Veda Mai Martin Potts, Ann Whitley, Debbie Potts England and her mom, Brenda Potts, and to all the extended family I've yet to know, thank you for embracing this love child with open arms into your family!

To my dad, James Allen Potts, for being my guardian angel from above. I'm looking forward to the reunion.

Always and forever in my heart,

pk potts

A final quote from one of my favorite authors:

~~~~~~

**"After you have suffered great losses
and known much pain,
it is not cowardice to want to live
henceforth with a minimum of suffering.
And one form of heroism,
about which few if any films will be made,
is having the courage to live without bitterness
when bitterness is justified,
having the strength to persevere
even when perseverance
seems unlikely to be rewarded,
having the resolution to find
profound meaning in life
when it seems the most meaningless."**

~~~~~~

Dean Koontz
The City

www.ingramcontent.com/pod-product-compliance
Lightning Source LLC
Chambersburg PA
CBHW020914110726
47900CB00001B/134